RELIC

UNCOMMON ENEMIES: PANTHER FORCE
(BOOK TWO)

FIONA QUINN

RELIC

Panther Force

Uncommon Enemies

By

Fiona Quinn

THE WORLD OF INIQUUS

Ubicumque, Quoties. Quidquid

Iniquus - /i'ni/kwus/ our strength is unequalled, our tactics unfair – we stretch the law to its breaking point. We do whatever is necessary to bring the enemy down.

THE LYNX SERIES

Weakest Lynx

Missing Lynx

Chain Lynx

Cuff Lynx

Gulf Lynx

Hyper Lynx

MARRIAGE LYNX

STRIKE FORCE

In Too DEEP

JACK Be Quick

InstiGATOR

Uncommon Enemies

Wasp

Relic

Deadlock

Thorn

FBI Joint Task Force

Open Secret

Cold Red

Even Odds

Kate Hamilton Mysteries

Mine

Yours

Ours

Cerberus Tactical K9 Team Alpha

Survival Instinct

Protective Instinct

Defender's Instinct

Delta Force Echo

Danger Signs

Danger Zone

Danger Close

This list was created in 2021. For an up-to-date list, please visit FionaQuinnBooks.com

If you prefer to read the Iniquus World in chronological order you will find a full list at the end of this book.

This book is dedicated to
Aiden
In him, I've seen a hero in action.

~ And to all those who fight for the ones they love no matter the battlefield.

1

Sophia
Monday

A remaining sliver of consciousness reminded Sophia that this was a nightmare. She was asleep in her bed in the suburbs of Washington, D.C., waiting for her alarm to release her from the despair of her dream. That dim glow of awareness whispered to her that it was a sweat-drenched sheet wrapped around her legs and not an astronaut's uniform. Her bunched muscles cramped from tension, not oxygen deprivation. And that ringing sound was her phone, not the satellite she chased in her battle to save herself and her two young sons.

On the next ring, Sophia Abadi snaked her hand out from under the covers and pulled the receiver to her ear. She still hadn't settled fully back into her body. Part of her floated in a nebula waiting for the call to be over and the dream to continue. "Yes?" she whispered on an exhale. One eye peeked open to take in the early morning, pearl-gray sky.

"Oh good, you're up!" It was astonishing how chipper her neighbor Penny's voice could sound at—Sophia squinted at her bedside clock—six a.m. Sophia had another fifteen minutes before her day was officially supposed to begin.

Sophia cleared her throat and came up on one elbow. "Is everything okay?" She was exhausted from her efforts to catch the satellite and discover the secret to survival. A lasting web of anxiety tangled around her throat, making her choke on her words. She turned her head away from the receiver to cough.

"Oh sure, everything's fine. Just fine." Penny sounded like she was on her second, maybe third cup of coffee, though the conviviality seemed forced.

Sophia pulled herself around to plant her feet on the ground, steeling herself for whatever Penny had called about at the crack of dawn.

"I simply wanted to make sure that I caught you before you went outside this morning."

Adrenaline snapped Sophia fully awake. She launched herself toward her window, yanked back the drapes, and peered out over the front lawn, scanning for something amiss. "What did you do?" she breathed out in a barely audible whisper.

"Mmm," Penny hummed as Sophia jogged down the stairs. "Me and the girls were playing a little Texas Hold'em and having some margaritas last night."

Sophia threw open the door. Standing in the gentle warmth of a late May morning, nothing seemed wrong.

"We didn't invite you because you're not a stay-at-home mom, and we knew you'd have to work today. School's off for us. Teacher planning day." Penny was stalling.

"What did you do?" Sophia asked again, knowing that the women in her neighborhood had the maturity level of unsupervised middle-schoolers with the key to their parents' liquor cabinet. This deficit was egged on by their ringleader Marla, who had a definite screw loose.

"We played a little prank on you." Penny's voice wavered.

Sophia knew Penny was chewing on a hangnail the way she always did when she said something she wasn't comfortable with. The line was silent as Sophia jogged over the porch, down the brick stairs, and out to her driveway. "Oh, Penny…" Sophia looked down at the outline of a human—like one detectives would chalk around a dead body. This one was spray-painted white. In one hand, a nosegay of pink flowers from her garden wilted; in the other, there was a picture of a hotdog. There was a real bottle of ketchup. The contents had been squirted where the outlined body would have had a heart. "What did you do?" Sophia asked a third time, not quite getting her brain to wrap around what she was seeing.

"Not me. *We*. We were drinking." Penny's laugh seemed artificially bright. "Having a little fun."

"Is that why the police were in the neighborhood last night? I saw them over at the Sheppard's house." The strobe of red-and-blue lights had flashed on her bedroom wall around one that morning. It happened with obnoxious regularity. "Did you ring the Sheppard's doorbell again?"

"Well, Marla did. The Sheppards, of course, called the cops —party poopers. The husband was the one talking to the officer. We were hiding in the bushes at Kay's house, watching the whole thing. Will was beside himself. It was hysterical. I mean, what did he think the officer would do? It's not like we broke the law. There's no law against ringing someone's doorbell." Her voice lilted with a decidedly southern accent.

The front door to her neighbor's house across the way pushed open. Will Sheppard peered about before he moved toward his car, his briefcase swinging with each stride, looking every inch like a middle-management drone. He fumbled his door open then caught sight of her.

Sophia suddenly realized she had run from her house in her sleeping shirt. It hung modestly enough that she couldn't be placed in handcuffs for indecency. But with nothing on underneath, she felt like she was standing there naked. Sophia grabbed the hem in front of her shirt and pulled it lower as she watched Will saunter over in her direction. "Why the flowers?" she asked Penny, wondering how she could retreat to her house without turning. Sophia wasn't in the mood to commiserate with Will, and he was heading down the hill toward her yard.

"After the police left, we thought it would be funny if you found an outline on your drive and wondered if someone had been killed on your property."

"Seriously?" Sophia backed up a step. "You think that scenario is funny? My children are going to see this. Turner's old enough to ask me what this is."

"Oh hush, Sophia, we were having a little fun. Kay can sure whip up a yummy margarita. Whoo, boy! We had a great time. You should have been there." She was giggling, then suddenly stopped, probably realizing that she had said that they had excluded Sophia on purpose. Penny cleared her throat. "It wasn't until after Marla outlined me that I remembered that you asked us not to include you in our little pranks. Don't be ashamed of that, Sophia." Her voice filled with sincerity and kindness. "We all get that you're kind of a geek, and you probably never got to hang with the popular crowd. It's not your fault that you didn't get a chance to develop a good sense of humor. It takes all kinds to make the world go around. Not everyone has to be fun."

Will was moving closer, and Sophia took another step back.

"After I realized our mistake," Penny continued. "We tried to make it friendlier by picking the flowers. Marla had already emptied the ketchup bottle, so we decided to put it on the ground and add a picture of a hot dog. Instead of looking like a mortal wound, now it looks like he spilled ketchup on his shirt." She laughed heartily, then took a deep breath followed by a hum.

Sophia stared at the receiver in her hand, a scowl creasing her face. She meant to count all the way to ten before she spoke, but by the time she said three in her head, she was spitting out, "Get it off my driveway." The numbness of being woken up and finding the strange display was wearing off, quickly replaced with a healthy dose of anger. Sophia took a third step back and looked behind her, realizing how far she was from her front door. "I mean it, Penny. Today. Before I get home." She was using her mommy's voice. The one she thought would get the job done. Sophia held up a hand like a stop sign, hoping Will would stay where he was. "I have to go," she told Penny, punching the raised button on the old-fashioned cordless handset.

"I'm sorry your sleep was disturbed last night." She grabbed the hem of her shirt again. "I saw the police lights."

"They woke you up?" Will asked from the middle of the cul-de-sac.

"Insomnia." Sophia pulled her shirt a little lower.

Will's gaze followed the move. His face flushed red. "Oh dear," he said, working to find another place to focus his eyes, finally coming to rest on her roofline. "Goodbye." He turned abruptly and quick-stepped back to his Volvo.

Sophia stood still until Will was well down the road, then got herself back inside. Upstairs, the gentle chimes that were supposed to rouse her from her dreams in a natural, Zen-like way had reached the point of insistence. She took the stairs two at a time to turn the alarm off before the noise woke her boys. She needed a little extra time getting ready today. She wouldn't be working from home in her usual shorts and t-shirt. Today, she was supposed to do a presentation with her research partner Nadia at Iniquus, the security firm assigned to keep them safe. As Sophia adjusted the water temperature in the shower, she wondered if that security would extend to keeping her safe from crazy neighbors.

She cut the water off again when she heard her phone ringing. This time when she picked it up, she heard five staccato beeps instead of her neighbor's overly enthusiastic voice. She hung up and moved downstairs to her office. She placed her cellphone in front of her, pulled up a map on the computer, opened the code generator on her keychain, and waited.

When the call came in, Sophia read off the alphanumeric code instead of answering with a hello. "938BCK868."

"You have information?"

"I believe I've found what you're looking for."

"Coordinates?"

Sophia listed them off, and the phone clicked, leaving her with dead air.

2
___

SOPHIA
Monday morning

Sophia pulled up to the Willow Tree Learning Center just as the Sesame Street alphabet song hit its crescendo. She slid the car into park and climbed from behind the wheel. She wasn't used to tottering in high heels with pointy toes. With her suit jacket draped across the passenger seat, she felt like a grown-up today. Well, at least the kind of adult who didn't play in sandboxes for a living. In her line of work as an archaeologist, it was rare that she wore anything that required dry-cleaning. At least her pencil skirt was made with Spandex, and she could maneuver the kids out of their car seats with ease.

Somehow, Sophia had made it this far without further morning mishaps, though Chance's eyes looked a little glassy to her as she pulled him into her arms. Sophia pressed a kiss onto his forehead to check for a fever. "You doing okay, sweetie?" she asked as he reached out to play with her earring. He didn't answer, and she was distracted from her concern by Turner. Her soon to be four-year-old had learned to undo his own seatbelt, which was both a blessing and a worry. He clambered past her and his younger brother and was racing for the front door of his school with joyful whoops. Sophia scrambled to catch up with him, grabbing the boys' backpacks and slamming the door shut on her way.

Sophia thought back to the moms in her neighborhood, and for a melancholy moment, imagined how nice it would be to stay at home and mother her kids. Or at least have a choice in the matter. But she had been widowed right after her twenty-fourth birthday. She was all her boys had. In whispered promises, while they slept, Sophia swore she would be their rock. She would do anything and everything she had to do to give them a good life. And today, that meant standing up in front of a bunch of strangers and talking about her work. That thought set Sophia's anxiety skyward. Her fingers shook as she signed the boys in for the day. Her hands were clammy as she rubbed their backs and gave them each a last kiss before leaving. "Learn wonderful things," she called as they skipped off to join their friends.

Exhausted and jittery wasn't a fabulous combination; it made her skin buzz. Sophia prayed her deodorant could hold up to the challenge. She second-guessed her choice of a blue satin blouse as she wobbled back to her car, knowing it would show perspiration badly. She was going to throw the blouse and these darned shoes in the trash as soon as she got home. Sophia checked the time on her cellphone and decided she could stop for a cup of tea for her trek through the morning traffic jam. Luckily, Iniquus wasn't too far from her house, on the Virginia side of the Potomac; she wouldn't have to tangle herself up on the capital city streets.

Sophia turned off the CD of cringe-worthy kiddy songs and

clicked on the radio. As she scanned for something with an upbeat tempo to distract her from her nerves, she stopped at a man announcing that this morning, when Mrs. Murphy, of Harrisonburg, opened the door to let her dachshund in from his romp in the woods, he dragged in a pair of pants with a pelvic girdle still inside. She found other leg bones as she followed his path. Police were investigating. "Huh," Sophia said out loud. "And I thought my morning was going badly. At least that's not me with a stray femur in my yard." She clicked on her blinker and turned right into the parking lot.

Here, only two blocks away from Willow Tree, was her one almost daily indulgence. A little family-run doughnut shop that brewed fragrant cups of chai that always had a way of making her feel loved. The mother, who ran the cash register, would sometimes squeeze Sophia's hand as she handed her the change and say, "It's going to be okay." Sophia had convinced herself that this silver-haired lady was a soothsayer, and she'd read Sophia's fortune in that morning's tea leaves. Sophia just had to hang on until the magical moment when things would be okay. This morning, Sophia was disappointed that it was the daughter who took her money. She didn't get a pre-presentation pep talk.

As Sophia rounded the corner on her way back to the car, she popped the lid off her cup to blow coolness across the surface while she walked. She climbed into her car before she took the first tentative sip of scalding liquid and decided it would have to wait. A burned tongue would make speaking clearly at this morning's presentation that much harder. And this was going to be difficult enough as it was. Sophia glanced in her side mirror to see a rotund man working his way toward the sidewalk. She pulled her door partially shut so he could squeeze on by. As he stepped onto the curb, he lurched sideways, catching himself on her car, shaking it. Chai sloshed across Sophia's lap. Screaming in pain, Sophia grabbed the door handle and leaped from the vehicle. She let the cup fall to the ground and yanked her skirt—sopping wet with blistering hot tea—down to get it away from her skin.

The obese man righted himself and bobbed his way into the shop without a backward glance. With her skirt around her ankles, Sophia leaned over to examine the red streaks running across her thighs. Her blouse just covered her now-damp panties.

A man called out to her, "Are you okay?" as he hustled over.

"This is becoming a theme for today," Sophia mumbled as she reached for the hem of her blouse and pulled it down for modesty's sake.

The man had his focus on her thighs. "Jeez, you're pretty badly burned. Do you need a ride to the hospital? Should I call an ambulance?"

Sophia kicked out of her skirt. She answered with a shake of her head. Her focus was on trying not to cry and add mascara running down her cheeks to her problems. Burns or no burns, she had a speech to give in a few minutes.

"Hang on, I have some cream in my first aid kit."

Sophia picked up her winter-white skirt, now stained chai brown. She turned to take in the puddle on her front seat. The clock on her dash said she was running late for the meeting. Tears glazed her eyes, but she refused to let them fall. She wouldn't cry a single tear. Not a single one. Sophia gritted her teeth as she pulled her gym bag from the back seat and unrolled her yoga pants. At least they were solid black. They'd have to do.

The man was back by her side as Sophia yanked off her shoes to get dressed. He held up a can of lidocaine. "This should help." He held it out for her.

"Yes, thank you." As Sophia sprayed her thighs, she realized that this was truly the stuff of nightmares. While she'd tried to survive against the power of an evil universe last night, she could just as easily have had this surreal dream, standing half-dressed in a parking lot, handing the spray can to a stranger so he could get the back of her legs. Thank goodness there was nothing pervy or seedy about this guy. In her mind, she decided he was a first responder of some kind, and he was out of uniform but still felt compelled to help. She reached down and gingerly yanked her pants into place.

The stranger handed her the can. "I bet you'll need a touchup before the day is through."

She took it gratefully, wondering what the right thing to say in a situation like this was. "You've earned yourself a boxful of good karma." She extended her hand to shake his.

"Perfect. I was running kind of low on it." He grinned and loped off as if seeing a woman disrobe in a parking lot was an everyday occurrence.

Sophia reached for the blankie scrunched in Turner's car seat to use as a barrier between the puddle in the driver's seat and her pants. She put her car in gear and pressed on the gas. Chancing a ticket with her aggressive driving, she fought through traffic to get to Iniquus. She needed to get there on time, looking crisp, calm, and professional. After all, first impressions were impossible to unwind.

3

Monday a.m.

Titus Kane, Panther Force Commander, scowled at the men who had assembled in the meeting room. Sophia and Nadia sat off to the side outside his direct view. Sophia found him thoroughly intimidating. His uniform of gray camouflage battle fatigues and a compression shirt that showed off every bulge and ripple of his muscles, plus the sheer size of him—he felt lethal. Since he oversaw their security team, that should be comforting, Sophia reminded herself. But it wasn't. There was something about this man, beyond his scowl and authoritative tone, that made Sophia feel like he was a hunter, and she might be his next meal. This man was not her friend or protector. From the moment he had scanned her with assessing scrutiny, she knew on a cellular level that she was somehow in danger.

As Commander Kane looked over a note someone had handed him, his men sat at attention. Kane obviously garnered their utmost respect. Sophia's mind scrambled down various pathways to find a reason why her alarm bells were clanging. The only thing she could settle on was that the lidocaine had worn off, and her thighs were screaming.

"Gentlemen." Titus stalked to the front of the Panther Force war room—that was the name stenciled on the door. It seemed an appropriate title. After all, her job was a kind of war, and these were the soldiers who were supposed to help her in her fight. "Panther Force has been assigned a new case. We are tasked with security concerns for The Ancient Artifact and Cultural Preservation Society, or AACP, an International organization with the mandate to discover and protect the world's treasures." He paused as his team scribbled the name onto their notes. "Our assignment will be to develop security teams at various global archaeological sites where the relics are most at risk of being destroyed or plundered." He fisted his hands and planted his knuckles on the table, leaning his weight forward, sweeping his gaze over his teammates, stopping short to exclude Nadia and Sophia. "To that end, in the host countries, we will be using local assets whom we vet and train," he said. "Iniquus will directly provide security for the American scientists who are involved as they travel to the remote areas. While we'll have Iniquus operatives available to fill our ranks on the personal security teams, it will be Panther Force who takes the lead. It's a very interesting case, as you will soon learn." Now he stood and stared straight at the two women.

Nadia reached under the table and squeezed Sophia's thigh. Sophia winced with pain and lifted her friend's hand and rubbed it softly, hoping to give them both a little courage as they wilted under the commander's glare.

"To that end, may I present Dr. Nadia Dajani and Dr. Sophia Abadi, who are here representing their employers to give us a better understanding of what they do and how we can best support their work."

Releasing Nadia's hand, Sophia put on the guise of an Egyptian queen, here to explain the state of affairs to her loyal subjects. It was a ploy she'd used at the university to make it through her presentations. Sophia refused to look in Commander Kane's direction as she moved regally to the front of the room.

"Thank you." Sophia picked up the remote that would start the PowerPoint presentation. She looked to her right. "Could we dim the lights, please?"

An operative in the front row rose and moved toward the wall, exposing his teammate who had been hidden from her original sweep of the room's occupants. Sophia found herself eye to eye with Brian Ackerman. Sophia had thought Brian was a distant memory, someone she'd never see again. He looked back at her with an inscrutable gaze that had Sophia taking a quick step sideways to rebalance herself. Caught off guard, she let her long black hair fall across her face, hiding behind the thick waves as she worked to manage her emotions. She spun back toward the screen. Today was turning out to be a Monday on steroids. She wondered if the universe was pranking her like her neighbors. She didn't find any of this funny.

It's a freaking small world, Sophia thought, brushing her hair out of her eyes, knowing that she already looked like she'd just tumbled out of bed. She reached for a water bottle and swirled a mouthful of cool wetness around her mouth while she checked to make sure the first image was correct. Her heart was beating way too fast. She had already been suffering from an extra helping of anxiety. And now, here was Brian.

She glanced quickly over his way to see if he'd caught her nervous reaction. He had leaned back in his chair and crossed his arms over his chest without the smallest glimmer of discomfort.

Or recognition, for that matter. Huh. Maybe she was mistaken. He could be a doppelganger. Or perhaps, she'd been staring at computer screens so long that she needed glasses. Sophia forced herself to believe that. Mind games were a powerful tool she used to get through life's challenges. She compelled herself to smile at the room of men with their soldier-like demeanors.

"Gentlemen," she began, steeling herself as she drew their attention. She knew this was the hardest part. Once she got talking about her work, her stress would ease. She loved her job and loved that she made a difference to human history. "We'll be working closely together, so please feel free to call me Sophia and my partner Nadia." Sophia's ribs felt tightly corseted, preventing her from taking in enough air. It made her already husky voice sound deeper. Breathless. Sultry. And oh, so out of place in this meeting room full of alpha males. She was glad that the darkened room would help hide her blush. "Our Ph.D. titles sound pretentious, but really what we do for a living is play in the dirt and find wonderful things." She pressed the button to show a picture of her and Nadia at a dig site, covered with filth and sweat, shielding their faces as a camel spat on them.

Low chuckles rumbled across the room

"Not glamorous, but certainly very interesting."

Sophia knew the self-deprecating photo did the trick by the men's smiling responses and relaxing body postures. It plucked them out of their ivory tower and made them accessible. She and Nadia had agreed that this would be the best tactic. They wanted to be among peers—avoiding the sterile relationship they both felt led to their colleague's death in Iraq when his security team had to prioritize who and what they could save. He hadn't been at the top of the list.

Sophia switched to a picture of an astronaut floating in space, which threw her body squarely back into this morning's nightmare. Fear itched over her scalp, but Sophia drew her smile a little wider, a little brighter. "Actually, Nadia and I are Space Archaeologists."

"Has anyone heard about this?" Nadia asked and scanned for affirmation. Getting none, she said, "It's a fairly new area of research. It used to be that a space archaeologist did research-based studies of items made by humans that are now floating around in space. They document those items as part of our human cultural heritage. But in the case of Sophia and I, we use satellite imagery to find possible dig sites of ancient cultures. We also use the data to protect locations we are already aware of. We can see looting happening almost in real-time. We sit in front of computers each day here in Northern Virginia doing our research in the comfort of our climate-controlled office, instead of digging in the Middle Eastern sand under one-hundred-thirty-degree heat." She nodded at Sophia to continue.

Sophia changed the picture to Giza, the Sphinx haloed by a full moon in a velvet-blue sky. "Our first discovery was a pyramid buried under a modern Egyptian city that, over time, was built on top of it." She pressed the button to reveal a lush mountainside. "As well as hidden caves in Slovakia where art from World War II had been hidden by the Nazis. Those finds let us know that we had a formidable tool to protect world antiquities. Right now, because of the global temperature changes, we are at an acute risk of losing many of our yet undiscovered cultural sites to rising sea waters, at the same time as other sites are emerging from beneath the glaciers. There is a sense of immediacy in our need to discover and plot the locations of our shared human heritage."

Sophia switched the picture to a nighttime satellite image of a city, and Nadia gestured toward the screen with widespread arms. Dressed in her geometrically cut fuchsia suit, her long black hair softly curled and draping over her shoulder, Nadia could easily have fit into any Fortune 500 corporate boardroom. All eyes were fixed on her when she moved to the center of the room. Sophia knew her friend was as phobic about public speaking as she was, and while Sophia appreciated any little break from the attention, she wished at least one of them could do this with ease.

"Our world is in crisis," Nadia said. "We believe that our shared human history can help hold us together. It is in humanity's best interest that we do our work at AACP. Thanks to the amazing contributions of corporations and wealthy individuals who agree with that premise, we are now making satellite-related finds a global effort." Nadia sounded like a late-night infomercial. She was rigid, and her words came out as too formal and overly rehearsed. "AACP is about to launch a worldwide initiative to give everyone an opportunity to become space archaeologists." Nadia stopped to smile as if it were written into the script. Then she focused on the back wall over the men's heads. "Imagine, if you will, that this is Google Earth with exponentially more capability. Our teams will process satellite imagery, then we'll upload them to a platform to allow laypeople to help us search."

"I'm Gage," the man sitting in front of Sophia said, leaning forward and pointing at the screen with his pen. "That seems like a very technical process. How is it possible for a layperson, an armchair archaeologist, to do this kind of search?"

Nadia took a step in his direction, obviously glad to be more conversational. "The plan is to give someone a small area to search—only say, twenty meters squared." She turned. "Sophia, can you find an example?"

Sophia flipped through the images until she found what she needed.

Nadia turned to point. "They'll be given the original image

as well as an enhanced image to look at. In comparing the two examples, the patterns should pop out better so that one can see in photo B what wasn't clear in photo A. There will be keys that will help the amateur hone in on what's important. The volunteers can tag the photos with notes on what they think they're seeing. We need fresh eyes on those images. Space archaeologists suffer from eye fatigue from looking through all this data all day. And to be honest, we simply don't have time to search for new sites when we're so involved in saving the ones that we've already identified."

Sophia clicked the button to show a picture of bombed-out Aleppo.

"I'm sorry," Nutsbe said. "Before you move on, it seems to me that the GIS—Global Information System—data is extremely sensitive. If you're crowdsourcing the effort, doesn't it concern you that this might be used by professional treasure hunters? Or others with less altruistic designs?"

Sophia thought the question a good one, astute. It was one of the dangers that had been discussed ad nauseam in their planning meetings. "It's a possibility, but a remote one. The plots that we put up won't have GPS information attached, and our software engineers are working on masking location-defining information. No one should be able to tell where on the globe their plot is located."

Sophia flipped forward in the images to give Nadia an example. "This site is in Peru," Sophia explained. "That's our upcoming trip that Panther Force will be involved with. This site was discovered by a project beta tester. While we're planning an exploration of the area, that person has no idea where it is or what we're doing with the information they provided us." She glanced around to see if there were any more questions. "We're giving you the information on how we're progressing with our site searches as background, but that's not Nadia's forte, nor mine. Our backgrounds are in the antiquities of the Middle East, and our focus is almost solely on Syria."

The image changed to a beautiful mosaic that had recently been unearthed. Sophia stopped and looked at it for a moment. She turned to the men, hoping that they could appreciate the enormity of its significance. The John the Baptist, Roman piece had survived beneath the dirt in pristine condition for over a millennium. "Perhaps you have read, or know through your work, that ISIS is one of the most devastating forces destroying cultural heritage since the Nazis in WWII." Sophia knew these men were being paid to do a job, but from her experience talking to colleagues from all over the world, getting these operatives invested in their project was key to successfully saving the art and maybe even themselves. Sophia hoped she and Nadia had picked the right route to hook their interest and get them invested in AACP's agenda.

"Syria is the seat of human history—of writing and record-keeping, of science and math. ISIS is systematically destroying their ancient architecture." Sophia gestured toward the image. "Artifacts, such as this one from around fifteen hundred years before the Common Era, are at risk. When the pieces aren't being destroyed, they're being sold on the black market. The sales of these antiquities are a major funding source for ISIS. You already know that ISIS is one of the best-financed terrorist organizations in the world." Sophia let her focus move around the room, resting briefly on each man. She wanted to make this point clear. This was not some tutti frutti do-gooder campaign. "Protecting artifacts in Syria cuts off a main ISIS revenue stream and helps to destroy ISIS's ability to proliferate. This is a matter of national security. We are at the forefront of the fight against terror."

Sophia got what she was looking for. The men had a new alertness about them. They had been polite during the beginning of the presentation—maybe even a little bit curious and interested. But now, the mood had shifted.

She and Nadia had been passionate about stopping terror since they went on an ill-fated dig years ago, the very last dig they went on with their fathers. Sophia's thoughts drifted back to the night they'd had to run to the US embassy for help. She caught herself before a full-blown PTSD flashback took hold. She pulled herself back to the present in time to hear Nadia explain, "There are over ten-thousand Mesopotamian tells in the war zone. A 'tell' is a hill created over time as people built and rebuilt on the same site. Tells are filled with important information about how people lived their lives in the past. They are also filled with artifacts that have value on the black market. That black market funds ISIS.

"Right now, there are six sites in Syria that have been designated as UNESCO World Heritage Sites. These include places like Ancient Damascus, Palmyra, Bosra, and Aleppo. Sites that are in the news every day as they're being bombed and destroyed. There are twelve more sites that UNESCO will consider designating in the future, but that largely depends on what can be done right now to save them from pillage and destruction. ISIS hates everything that existed before the Prophet Muhammad. They have already reduced the Arch of Triumph in Palmyra to a pile of rubble. UNESCO labeled it a war crime. Stopping this destruction is another important component in fighting ISIS."

Sophia changed the picture to one of cheering ISIS soldiers. "You see, ISIS is publishing photos like this one to show their disdain for international authority. Their methods are consistent. First, ISIS attacks the people—women, children, the elderly…

men, and even boys are forced into their fighting ranks or face the firing squad. Second, they systematically attack heritage sites both for ideological and propaganda gains. And third, they sell the artifacts using crime families to quickly and easily move the goods from finder to buyer. It is our job," Sophia said, "to document endangered sites in Syria. Nadia and I are connected with Syrian groups who, amid the bombing, are working every day to detail and protect the antiquities."

"Sophia is focused on using GIS to track the looters and to pinpoint possible areas where we could get the good guys on scene before ISIS finds the relics. I'm working on cataloging the items we know about to prevent people from selling them on the black market or prove that the items are stolen if investigators find them in private collections. Bottom line, our goal is to stop the looting, which in turn helps to stop terrorism," Nadia said.

Titus had been standing at the side of the room with his shoulder pressed into the wall. His being out of her direct line of sight had allowed Sophia to put him out of mind. But now, he was asking her a question, and she was having a hard time focusing on his words; she was so affected by his scowl. "Tell me more about the propaganda factor."

After a long moment of standing mute and wide-eyed, Nadia came to her rescue, reaching out to take the remote from Sophia's hand.

Nadia clicked a few frames ahead to a picture of a group of men swarming steps in their black uniforms. "This is the Mosul Museum. This picture was spread far and wide in jihadist chat rooms. It shows that the Western world is powerless to protect relevant sites or artifacts. There was a great deal of gloating over this large-scale cultural destruction. The messages were, look how powerful ISIS is, look how unable anyone else is to stop us. That sense of power is profound when it comes to a group of young men with little education and little in the way of a future outside of the military, the police, or terror organizations."

Regaining her composure, Sophia gestured toward the screen. "And we'd be remiss not to add that this is cultural cleansing. For centuries in this area, there has been a sectarian coexistence. When the terrorists destroy physical structures, they are destroying the texture and rhythm of the communities. This destruction will surely influence how people interact with one another after ISIS is removed. The cultural destruction is laying the groundwork for social upheaval. This will increase regional instability. It follows that saving these sites is imperative to United States security. The world *needs* a stable Middle East."

Nadia moved over to the wall and flipped the switch to bring the lights up. She moved back to stand shoulder to shoulder with Sophia.

Titus joined them at the front of the room. "Thank you, Doctors, this has been enlightening. A good overview of what's at risk, what the ramifications are, and your involvement in mitigating the problem. At this point, I'd like to introduce you to your team liaisons. Their job is to get to know you better, get to know how you work, and assess what security measures need to be in place for you in your travels." He held out an open hand to the man who had turned down the lights at the beginning of their presentation. "Communications and operations will be run by Nutsbe."

A man with closely cropped blond hair stood and nodded at Nadia. He remained standing, his hands folded neatly in front of him.

"Nadia, your liaison will be Thorn."

Another operative pushed to his feet. Like all the men who sat in the room, he looked like he spent long hours outdoors and in the gym. These were the kinds of men who would run marathons across the desert for the fun of it. Thorn had daredevil written all over him.

"And, Sophia, your liaison is Brainiack."

Brian Ackerman stood and faced her. So not a doppelganger. Sophia had only seen that particular shade of electric-blue eyes on one prior occasion. They made this man stand out in a crowd and made him impossible to forget. "Brainiack," Titus had called him. Huh. Sophia stood there, blinking her eyes and chewing on the inside of her cheek, until Nadia leaned over and asked for the thumb drive she was supposed to bring with her.

Sophia patted over her yoga pants before she remembered she had stowed the drive in her skirt. "It's out in my car." She peeked up at Titus, who was sending a considering glance between her and Brian. "I'll run and get it for you," she said, wondering what the commander was thinking in that moment.

"Just hand it over to Nutsbe when you come back. I'm headed in to another meeting. Thank you for your information." Without a handshake or a goodbye, Titus stalked out the door.

Sophia followed Titus out, letting Nadia shut down the laptop and gather her things. Sophia only made it a few paces down the corridor before she heard, "Sophie, hold up."

She squeezed her eyes tight. Brian. *Shit.*

"I'll walk you to your car."

4

Brian reached out and caught Sophia's elbow to direct her down the right-hand corridor, which would take them directly to the garage instead of going through the atrium. Sophia took a tentative step forward, then tilted her face up to catch his gaze, raising a questioning brow as if she didn't trust him to get her to her car safely.

"This way's faster," he said. It was a hell of a coincidence, Sophie showing up and being put under his protection.

She pursed her lips and kept pace with him, though there was an odd little hitch in her step and an occasional wince that made him think she was in pain. He shortened his stride, slowed his gait. It was an uncomfortably silent walk. He should say something to her. Be professional. But instead, he found himself using all his energy to stuff down the anger that rose a little higher in his chest with each step forward. He wanted to confront her, was picking out the right words, when Sophia pulled her keys from her purse and pressed the fob, making the door chirp and the lights flash on a nearby red minivan. He had been heading toward the onyx Mazda Miata sitting two cars down; it seemed more Sophie's style—lush, sophisticated, its lines suggesting class and refinement.

Sophia stopped suddenly, throwing her hands in the air. "Are you freaking kidding me?" She looked skyward. "That's enough for one day, okay?" She seemed to bargain with the heavens.

Brian thought he heard defeat in her voice. She sounded nothing like the polished professional who had his team engrossed in this morning's meeting. He took a step forward and followed her gaze to see that her back tire was flat. Another step showed the front tire sat dangerously low.

Her phone buzzed, and Sophia fished it from her pocketbook. "Dr. Abadi," she said as she unlocked the back of the van and pulled up the hatch to reveal a brand-new tire laying on its side. She raked her fingers into her hair and lay her forehead on the metal body, listening. "Thank you, I'm on my way. Tell Chance that Mommy loves him. I'll be there as soon as I can."

Mommy? Brian looked through the open hatch to the middle row, where he saw two car seats: one facing backward, one facing forward. He checked her left hand to see if there was a ring there and found her only jewelry was a slender gold bracelet with an unusual clasp. "Is your son okay?" he asked as she tossed her phone back in her purse and dropped the bag to the ground.

She was breathing a little too deeply, a little too fast. She reached into the van to lug out the tire.

"Hey, hey, hey." Brian put a hand on her arm to stop her. "That's not going to help. You've bent your wheel. You must've been driving on the flat. Didn't you notice it this morning when you came in?"

Sophia moved to the side of the car and squatted in front of the rear wheel. She closed her eyes, muttered something in Arabic under her breath, then righted herself.

Brian caught her by the arm, spinning her around to look her square in the eye. "It's going to be darned hard to protect you if you're not willing to talk to me." His mounting frustration was on display, but he regretted his tone immediately. What he saw in her eyes was nothing less than desperation and exhaustion. Obviously, this wasn't the time for him to get answers. He dropped his voice, warmed it with concern. "Sophie, let me help. Is your son okay? What do you need?"

She looked at her purse, her tire, the safety seat, and then back to Brian. "I need a Lyft," she said and pulled away from him, moving to the driver's door. "Let me get you that flash drive before I get caught up in this next fiasco."

Brian stooped to retrieve the cellphone from her purse, reaching around the can of lidocaine, which rested on the top of her neatly organized bag. He quickly stood and pocketed the phone as she moved back to him. She was fishing in the pockets of a stained skirt and pulled out a flash drive. Now that he was standing next to her, he realized she was wearing yoga pants with her heels and blue satin blouse. "Seems like you're having a bad day." He gestured toward the skirt.

Sophia locked her jaw.

"Look, we're assigned to work together. We can figure out how best we can do that later. Right now, let's start with a plan for today. All right?" Brian's mind was on hyperdrive, searching for the best way to handle this situation. He knew that the meeting this morning with the two women was only a thin slice of the pie. The FBI was in the Panther Force war room waiting for him to join the team and get briefed on another side of this case.

Sophia stood there looking up at him with her soft doe eyes and those insanely long lashes. He got the feeling that if he made one wrong move, she'd bolt.

He dropped the volume of his voice to sound calm and reassuring. "My car is one row over. I'm going to go get it. We'll move the safety seats, and you'll use my car to get to your son. Okay? I'll have our mechanics come and get your wheel situation straightened out, then I'll bring your van to you." He paused and waited for confirmation.

Sophia seemed to be weighing the situation.

"I understand that you work out of a home office," Brian pressed. "If it's convenient when I get there, you can show me your setup. If not, at least I'll know where to find you."

She turned suddenly to slam the hatch closed. "Desperate times call for desperate measures," she muttered, turning back toward him and brushing dirt from her hands. "Thank you." She made an effort to smile, but the emotion didn't make its way to her eyes. "It would be quickest if I use your vehicle." She canted her head. "You're not afraid I'll disappear again, this time with your car?"

"All of our vehicles are tracked by GPS. You could try to run, but I'd find you."

5

*B*RIAN
Monday a.m.

"You're late," Titus barked.

Brian handed over the flash drive and gave a curt nod. Titus didn't need excuses from him. The point was made.

Panther Force was spread around the war room. The table that had moments earlier held Dr. Dajani's computer now had two chairs facing their team. A man and a woman who reeked of Quantico training filled the seats.

"This morning, we heard from the archaeologists working for the AACP," Titus began. "Iniquus has signed contracts with that organization to guard newly acquired sites outside of war zones and to protect their upper-level employees when they're traveling internationally. Iniquus has also signed a contract with the FBI." He nodded toward the special agents.

"With the AACP's blessing, of course. Our colleagues at the Bureau are interested in the black-market antiquities and the monies that are going to fund ISIS and terrorism. I would like to introduce you to two of the special agents with whom we will be working. This is Alandria Andersson from the arts division, and Steve Finley with terror."

As their names were announced, they stood, nodded, and returned to their seats.

Finley began. "Gentlemen, you've just met two suspects that have been flagged by the FBI for conspiring to fund ISIS terrorism. It's our goal to identify if Dr. Sophia Abadi and/or Dr. Nadia Dajani are in fact culpable, and to what extent they are entwined in the black market sale of Middle Eastern conflict antiquities."

Brian's muscles contracted. Titus turned assessing eyes on him. But Brian had already fought his expression into a mask of stoicism. He'd adjusted his posture to calmly absorb the information.

Andersson took the reins. "During the Iraq war, it came to the Bureau's attention that a United States business, Crafts&More, was possibly involved in acquiring looted artifacts from the region." Andersson's disdain was easily read from the tightness in her facial muscles and the squint of her eyes. "This religious-based company is developing a Museum of the Holy Bible right outside of DC, in Maryland, to be opened next year."

Titus stood in his usual place toward the front of the room with his shoulder against the side wall where he had the vantage point. His face held its natural scowl. "This group is populating its archives with black market pieces?"

"We believe so," Andersson said. "And interestingly, it was Nadia Dajani, Sophia Abadi, and their fathers who brought this to our attention. First, a little background on our marks. These two women come from a long line of prominent archaeologists. Sophia's father was Dr. Amad Abadi, who was born and trained in Turkey, and Nadia's father was Dr. Farid Dajani from the University of Damascus. Both men immigrated to the United States. Both men became United States citizens at a young age, married American women, and had American children. Nadia and Sophia spent their summers in the Middle East from the time they were very young. Both are fluent in Arabic, Farsi, Turkish, and Hebrew. Her last dig with her father, she was still in college. At the time, the two women were pursuing archaeology degrees at their universities. Sophia was getting ready for her senior year of undergrad, and Nadia was beginning her doctoral work. Nadia is four years older than Sophia."

"Are the father's implicated in this case?" Titus asked.

"Sophia's father is incapacitated with dementia, and Nadia's father had a stroke that left him unable to speak clearly or use the left side of his body. We're quite sure they're not involved. But the women have all of their fathers' contacts in that region. It's a close circle of academics that form an extended family."

Titus shifted against the wall, crossing his arms over his chest and staring down his nose at the special agents. "But the last dig is significant."

"Yes, their research group was based out of Israel that summer. At that time, a shipment headed for Tulsa, Oklahoma was seized by US Customs in Memphis. The shipment held two-hundred and fifty tablets inscribed in cuneiform a thousand years ago, when modern-day Iraq was called Assyria. These tablets were headed to a compound owned by Crafts&More. Since that time, Crafts&More has been under investigation for illicitly importing Iraqi cultural heritage to the US for display in their religious-themed museum. We estimate around 40,000 artifacts were purchased by the Gilchrest family, who own the privately run Crafts&More business."

"How do Nadia and Sophia play into this?" Nutsbe asked, his wrinkled brow showing that things weren't adding up for him.

Brian was glad to cut to the chase. Why were they going after Nadia and Sophia?

"Provenance," Andersson said. "Provenance in the art world is the written history of the object. It's the who, what, where, and when of the piece, giving as complete a history as possible. Think of it as a chain of custody. As we understand it, the story is that the two young women—Sophia, then aged twenty, and Nadia, twenty-four—got into a taxi headed for a restaurant. Instead of going where it was instructed, the taxi took them to a warehouse where Sophia and Nadia were held hostage. Their fathers were told to create fake provenances for the tablets that would pass without question through customs, or their daughters would be killed."

"I'm Thorn, Nadia's liaison. I think it's important that we understand what happened that night. Do you have details?"

Finley rubbed a hand across the back of his neck. "Some. The crime was never solved, so the picture is cloudy. Nadia and Sophia were gone for almost seventy-two hours. They said they were blindfolded and tied up throughout that time. The place they were held was filthy, and they were lying in the dirt. They had a bucket to use as a toilet. They were fed once a day and threatened continuously with sexual assault." Finley paused. "It does not appear that that threat was followed through. We can't be sure. The women refused medical exams and left the country. The person who brought the women their food woke them up in the middle of the night and got them out of the building. A motorbike was waiting at the street corner. Their rescuer—a female—got the girls on the back of the bike. The person driving had on a helmet and gloves. Nadia and Sophia couldn't say if it was a man or a woman. The person never spoke to them. They were taken to the US Embassy and left at the gate. The US Embassy contacted local law enforcement, who went to the residence to check on their fathers. As the police breached the door, the captors who were holding the men fled. The families left for Turkey the next day. Between the girls' account of what was overheard, and what the fathers were asked to provide, our embassy contacted U.S. Customs and the FBI."

"The fathers had been told their daughters would be held until the packages successfully passed through US Customs and were delivered to the right people," Andersson explained. "Amad Abadi and Farid Dajani were able to convince the kidnappers that there was no provenance possible that would cover the tablets since it's against international law to remove cultural heritage items from their country of origin. They offered another solution that their captors put into play."

"Wait, the shipment was sent, and the criminals didn't try to silence the families immediately?" Gage, the newest Panther Force member, sounded incredulous. He had been a Marine Raider, a member of the elite Special Forces for the U.S. Marines in the Middle East. He knew as well as the rest of his teammates, all retired from U.S. elite forces, just how violent that area of the world was for everyday citizens, particularly women.

"We're having trouble with that outcome as well. We assume that something else happened, some other threat was made, and that it was at this point that one, or both of the women became criminally involved with the black market."

"The tablets were confiscated by customs, though, right?" Brian asked.

"Right. The fathers explained to the captors that the only way to get antiquities from their country of origin to the United States was to lie about what was being shipped," Andersson said. "Not so long ago, there was a Picasso worth upward of 15 million dollars that a woman, posing as a tourist, brought through customs by saying it was a $37-dollar handicraft. That charade was what the Gilchrest family attempted. They declared that they had ordered replicas of ancient tablets to be manufactured to spec in Israel. They were shipped FedEx and labeled, 'hand-crafted clay tiles.'"

"Which is accurate," Steve Finley put in. "That's exactly what they were. What wasn't honest was the price tag of $3,000, when they're worth millions. The case is still under investigation. The Gilchrests say they don't believe they're antiquities, but instead the tiles they ordered to be made for the museum. Both criminal and civil charges are possible if the decision is made to prosecute. That prosecution is problematic, in that the Gilchrests have a great deal of money and political clout, they've invested in a lot of political campaigns over the years—things are moving along slower than they might under different circumstances."

"What does the punishment look like? Prison time? And are Nadia and Sophia part of that investigation?" Titus asked.

Finley shook his head. "Could go in a bunch of directions. The Gilchrests might have to forfeit the tablets. They might be required to pay a fine. While it's interesting to the FBI to stop the theft of cultural heritage items, it's more interesting to us to stop the funding of terrorism. Nadia and Sophia are not implicated in the tablet case. But the Gilchrests didn't stop with that shipment. We believe that they continue to buy artifacts on the black market and are importing them for their museum, investing huge amounts of money, which in turn goes to fund ISIS. It's not the art theft, per se, that has us interested. We're looking to shut down the black market fundraising. We're focused on the Gilchrest family because they're getting their intel somewhere. We're trying to run down that source. This case extends beyond

Crafts&More. World collectors are probably looking for certain items to place in their archives. It's also probable that there is someone who knows what's on their list and is keeping an eye open, sending that information along to the buyers, so that as soon as a piece is located, they can make a bid."

"Also, that someone has to have enough knowledge that they can spot a fake," Andersson said. "That kind of information would command a premium price. There are very few people with the antiquity expertise and the operational access that is enjoyed by Sophia and Nadia—as a matter of fact, they are positioned to commit this crime better than anyone else in the world. As you find out more about what they do and how they operate, you'll be amazed by their scope of information."

Brian had met Finley in the hallways of Iniquus before. The FBI and Iniquus had a good working relationship. As a private entity, Iniquus contracted with the various alphabets when egos and career-track ambitions got in the way of playing nicely together. And Iniquus could operate in places where the US needed to keep its nose clean for geopolitical reasons. Brian was reasonably sure that was why Iniquus was involved here.

This was the first time Brian was meeting Andersson. Her clothes were tailored to perfection and buttoned up tightly. Her feet were lined up directly under her knees. She held her body rigid, like a soldier at parade rest. There was nothing soft or vulnerable about her. She was tense while Finley was much more at home in the war room. Brian wondered if Andersson would relax a bit with familiarity.

Her demeanor heightened the tension in the room. Panther Force typically liked to keep things low key. A calm mind was a useful mind—a stressed brain made mistakes. Maybe it was Andersson's tightly wound, hyper-controlled composure that set adrenaline flowing through his system, or maybe it was the thought that Sophia might be a terrorist sympathizer. Could his instincts be that far off the mark? Brian squared his shoulders and focused on the information.

"I know the women touched on this earlier," Andersson said. "But here are some more details. We are focused on ISIS funding. ISIS has a variety of ways that it funds itself, including kidnapping for ransom. As we speak, your Rooster Honig is in Iraq working on negotiations to free an American energy consultant captured by ISIS insurgents."

The men nodded their affirmation. There was a shift in the room's atmosphere. A fellow Panther Force member, known by the call sign Honey, hadn't been heard from in over twenty-four hours. He'd missed two of his scheduled check-ins.

"Robbery, extortion, human trafficking, and oil smuggling all help to pay the fighters wages and keep their ammunition well-stocked. We're focused on artifact theft here, which is their biggest revenue producer," Andersson said. "And particularly the way that Americans are helping ISIS, whether it's their direct intention or just short-sightedness. Criminal selfishness."

"How much money are we talking about?" Titus asked.

"We estimate that they're taking in about three million dollars a day in art," Finley responded. "They have about two billion dollars in the bank at any given time."

Gage let out a low whistle.

"These items are thousands of years old. There isn't really a way to value them, is there?" Titus asked.

"Exactly," Andersson said. "The exporters know their clients —who's looking for what, as well as the price they might be willing to pay. Crafts&More, for example, is acquiring items that have a direct connection to biblical scholarship. Those items might bring in a higher price. As ISIS figured out how lucrative the relics were, they've made a business of unearthing them.

There are more and more available, saturating the market and driving down the price, which, in turn, leads to more pillaging to maintain their income flow."

Finley looked Andersson's way, and when she didn't continue, he said, "On the business side, there are three basic ways that paramilitaries get involved in the art trade. As you can imagine, there aren't many ways a man can earn a basic living in Syria. Right now, they view looting as a job, much like fur traders did in early colonial America. They are given coordinates by ISIS, which indicate the specific area that they're allowed to exploit. After the artifacts are removed and sold, they pay a tariff back to ISIS—twenty percent if the looters use their own equipment. Forty percent if they use ISIS equipment."

"Equipment like what?" Brian asked.

"Bulldozers, mostly. Shovels, metal detectors, trucks. The tariff is one way to earn money. The others include running the trafficking networks and offering other services like finding services. This last leg of the business model is where we think Nadia and/or Sophia come in. The trafficking networks often follow the drug routes already in place and are worked by families who are familiar with moving illicit goods to international markets. The finding services are paid to those with specialized knowledge."

"Like the knowledge possessed by Nadia and Sophia," Thorn said.

"Exactly." Finley stood. "Let me give you an example. Because we knew what was going on with Crafts&More, we sent in a special agent to gather firsthand information on the underground world. He made contact with a Syrian living in Turkey who Interpol had identified as being in the artifacts trade. The trader had a picture of a mosaic that had just been unearthed. It was an amazing piece that seemed to tell the biblical story of

John the Baptist. We had our agent on camera receiving a phone call from Gilchrest family representatives who offered $200,000 if the mosaic could be authenticated and authorized—which means they had provenance that would make it okay to have in their collection, signed by a reputable source."

"How did the Gilchrests find out about the piece?" Titus asked.

"Good question. We'd like to know that too. I can tell you that our field office sent photos to an expert—the piece was the real deal. Imagine, our agents are in this rundown apartment in the city, there are two young Syrian men, boys, really, who were hanging onto a Roman mosaic that was at least fifteen hundred years old."

"Did you get ahold of the art?" Titus asked. "What was the next step if you did?"

"The boys dropped the price to $6,000 when they got spooked. We secured the piece to repatriate at a future date. And guess who developed the satellite pictures for AACP that were used to find that art?" Finley asked.

"Sophia Abadi and Nadia Dajani," Thorn answered.

Finley swung his head around to catch Thorn's eye. "Now, guess who was involved in identifying and dating the John the Baptist mosaic that was being offered up by the Syrian boys to our special agents."

"Sophia Abadi and Nadia Dajani."

Finley pointed his finger at Thorn. "Bingo."

6

As soon as she heard an engine pull up to her curb, Sophia jumped up from her desk and ran out the door. She knew she'd eventually need to let Brian into her house; that's where her office was set up. But she needed another day, one with a little less stress, before she felt comfortable doing that. Maybe tomorrow. *Maybe not*, she thought as he opened her car door and unfolded his tall frame.

Sophia was close enough now to see a bemused look on his face. His focus was on his phone. As she approached, he turned it her way. "Who is this?" he asked, laughter in his voice.

Sophia looked at the picture of her neighbor, who lived just around the corner. She was dressed in a flesh-colored bikini and high heels and was posed like a model on the hood of a convertible parked in the middle of her driveway. "That's Marla. I saw her too." Sophia pulled her phone from her pocket and opened her photo album. "I took this when I was heading home from the doctor's office right around eleven."

"That was five hours ago." Brian looked up the road in the direction of Marla's house, though it was hidden behind a copse of pine trees. "That's crazy."

"Pretty much. Welcome to my neighborhood, a treasure trove of unstable individuals. With any luck, you won't meet any of them." Sophia held out her hand for her keys.

Brian looked past her to where a wide black puddle stood out against the weathered grey length of her driveway like a pen that had exploded on a piece of paper. Yellow plastic tape stretched across the drive, keeping people from diving onto the surface until the blacktop sealant cured. Brian squinted as if he were processing why in the world someone would do that. It was hard to fathom even for Sophia, who knew that splotch was covering up the murder victim outline that had been painted there in the wee hours of the morning. She hadn't a clue why Penny and her crew decided that this was "fixing things." It was a problem that could be put off for another day.

Brian pulled his focus back to Sophia, looking for an explanation that she didn't offer. He settled on, "Do you have my keys? I'll help you move the car seats back over to your vehicle."

"They're on your dash," she said, moving toward her van. It was spotless on the outside. She walked around to look at her tires, and two new ones were plump and functional on the right-hand side. She saw through the back window that her tire was still in the back. Sophia popped open the side door. She barely recognized the minivan as hers. There was a box that held her kids' debris, crayons, daycare art, and that light up Bubble Guppies shoe she'd been looking for for the last week. The seats and carpet were free of dirt, spills, and the general schmutz that normally decorated the backseat. It smelled—Sophia stopped mid-thought to inhale the fresh citrus scent that replaced the odor of stale vomit she'd never found a way to remove—so *good*.

Her skirt hung on a hanger, cleaned, and pressed. She searched the front where the chai puddle had saturated the cloth seat. Gone. Sophia wasn't sure that her van had been more pristine, even when she drove it home from the used car lot. Sophia was vaguely disoriented as Brian ambled over with the two car seats dangling in his hands. She stepped out of the way.

"Everything okay?"

"I think you brought me the wrong car." She lay a cool hand on her forehead.

"Iniquus likes to impress our clients. Our automotive team is stellar."

"They cleaned my skirt."

Brian leaned in to reattach Turner's seat. "I think they could tell you were having a bad day. I hope this makes it a little nicer." He sent her a warm smile that stalled her.

Sophia refused to acknowledge a single thought. She hung there in space and time, aggressively seeking a sense of nothingness because the emotions that hovered in the air between them were reckless. She held herself in the void while Brian's expression turned quizzical. She only released herself when he turned to push a knee into Turner's seat and pulled the safety belt taut like he'd done it a thousand times before. Sophia wondered how he knew to do that. *There. That's a safer line of thought.*

"I wish I could have thanked them in person." Sophia picked up Chance's seat, wincing as it hit the burns on her thighs. Before she could do anything more, Brian took it from her and went around to the other side of the car to maneuver it into place.

Sophia stood there, awkwardly with Brian hunched over his task. "I should apologize to you." Her voice was so soft she wasn't sure Brian could hear her. "I left without telling you goodbye. I had my reasons." She rubbed her hands together as if in supplication, thankful he couldn't see her. "I was thinking about your best interests when I decided…" She caught her lower lip in her teeth to stop it from trembling. She wasn't good at confrontations. She deserved his resentment at the very least. She couldn't imagine what he'd thought when he discovered that he was assigned to her security team.

Brian pulled himself from the doorframe, turning slowly. "Sophia, I'd like to apologize to you. I got caught up in the moment when we first met. I thought we were on the same page —that we were experiencing the same things. I was trying to be honest about my feelings. It was too much. I get it. No hard feelings." He extended his hand for a shake. "Let's let bygones be bygones and start fresh."

Sophia had wrapped her arms around herself and was shivering, though it was over eighty degrees in the sunshine. She blew out a breath through pursed lips. She should stop him from taking the blame. And she should tell him the truth—she couldn't keep him safe. And she couldn't bear the thought of destroying yet another life. It was better that she'd walked away. If they had to work together, she hoped he'd stay angry with her, or at least leery. Certainly, he needed to keep his distance.

"Shake my hand, Sophia. Let's pretend this is the first day we're meeting."

Sophia forced herself to slide her hand into his.

"Now, invite me in to see your computer," Brian said, turning and plucking the hanger with her skirt from the hook before he shut the car door.

. . .

Inside, she walked directly to the dining room that she had converted into an office space. It was big enough that she and Nadia could work together without getting in each other's way. One wall was floor-to-ceiling bookshelves with reference texts and file cabinets. She had a wraparound desk, and her computer systems—a series of wide screens—were arranged in a semi-circle, so she could compare visuals with ease.

Brian scanned the room, then turned toward the stairs. "Are your children here?"

"Chance is sleeping upstairs. Turner didn't want to come home. He was having fun with the clay volcano project his teacher had going on. I'll need to go get him in a little bit." Sophia checked her watch. "Would you excuse me for a minute?" She lifted a house phone and dialed a number, moving into the kitchen to speak. "Lana, I'm at home with Chance and have someone here. I was hoping you might be able to get Turner for me."

"I'm so sorry, I can't. Remember my car's at the mechanic? And I'm running out the door. Jeff's boss is in town, and I'm going out to eat with them. I'm waiting for my Lyft."

"Do you need me to watch your kids?"

"I have a babysitter here. I'm sorry, I can't help."

"Not a problem. I can figure this out. I'm thinking positive thoughts for you and Jeff tonight. Do you think he got the promotion?"

"No idea, but I—oh, the car pulled up." Sophia could hear the excitement in Lana's voice. "Keep thinking those good thoughts. I'll catch you up tomorrow. Bye."

Sophia moved back to the office to find Brian examining her digital code creator.

"Security?" he asked.

The device gave her a new pin number every forty-five

seconds. The idea being that as long as no one got hold of the display, they wouldn't be able to hack her files. As Iniquus had pointed out that morning, her data was highly sensitive. Sophia blinked at the device. She had been sure it was in its hiding place that morning. Maybe Nadia had run by on her way in to Iniquus to check on something last minute.

Sophia reached out her hand to take it from him. "Where did you find this?"

"On your desk. You didn't leave it there?"

"As you might have noticed, neither Nadia nor I are comfortable talking in front of groups. We lead introverted lives. One of us must have missed it this morning in our anxiety." Even as she said it, the story sounded off. She'd have to remember to check in with Nadia. "As my security liaison, maybe you can help me find a better way to handle the computer safety issue." She pocketed the coder. "Are you going to teach us some basics in self-defense before we head down to Peru?"

"What were you thinking of?"

"I don't know." She looked at the floor for a moment, then up to catch Brian's gaze. "Maybe some basic ways to get away. Punches and kicks. Maybe you could teach us how to handle a gun."

"Do either of you own a gun?"

"No."

"Have either of you ever shot a gun?"

"No."

"You've been going out on digs for a long time. What was your strategy before?"

"I haven't been on a dig since my undergrad days. My strategy? Scream really loudly. Possibly run." She tipped her head. "Well, run if safety isn't too far away." She sent him a smile. "And it's not uphill."

Brian smiled back. "There. That's the Sophie I met. You have the most beautiful eyes when you're sincerely smiling." The startled look Sophia sent him must have made him realize he'd stepped over the line. He cleared his throat. "You're right. We need to consider your home security. The intelligence you have on your computer is bound to be of interest to lots of different people."

Sophia's brow furrowed. "Like who?"

"Pirates? Treasure hunters? I'll get a better idea as I learn more about your job."

The phone rang, and Sophia snatched it up to keep the sound from waking Chance. "Dr. Abadi," she said.

She heard five staccato beeps followed by a dial tone. Sophia replaced the receiver and grabbed her keys. "Sorry. I need to make a phone call. Will you excuse me for a minute?" Without waiting for an answer, she walked to her kitchen. She slid open the battery compartment on her keychain flashlight to reveal a code creator and waited for her cell to ring.

"65A27C990," Sophia read off in Hebrew.

"Is someone's there with you?" a woman's voice asked.

"Yes, an operative with the security firm AACP hired. He's sitting in my office." She paced over to the fridge and opened the door to let the air cool her face. Milk, butter, and organic juice boxes sat in the otherwise empty fridge.

"Are you sure he can't understand you?"

"I don't know. I'll be careful."

"We followed through on this morning's call. The location didn't pan out the way you expected, though it wasn't futile. We're sending you a courier this evening. It's scheduled for around eight. Will you be home to sign for the package?"

"I will."

"This project is time-sensitive. We need a quick turnaround. Tonight, if possible."

Sophia needed to decompress. To sleep. To catch up on some chores. To take care of Chance. "I'll do my best."

"When I say time-sensitive," the woman's voice lost its friendly tone, becoming cold and threatening in an instant, "I'm not fanning a flame because I like the sound of a whistling tea kettle. You know *personally* what the stakes can be if information isn't obtained in a timely manner."

Sophia reached up and wrapped a hand around her throat. "I'll make sure you have what you need in time."

Sophia stood in the middle of her kitchen, forming a plan. This day was ricocheting out of control.

One step at a time. She'd have to shoo Brian away and get the baby up. Her priority right now was fetching Turner.

She was startled to find Brian in the doorway. "Mommy issues," she said. "I need to get Turner from daycare."

"I can stay here." Brian offered. "Go get Turner and let Chance sleep."

It was a practical solution. But it felt too chummy. Sophia had to keep Brian at arms' length, which meant they could only interact professionally. She looked up the stairs. It *would* be better if Chance could sleep. Her brain refused to help her out of the situation. What could she possibly say that wouldn't sound rude?

"Go get Turner," he repeated. "I'll sit in the office and take a look at your bookcase, so I can feel thoroughly intimidated by your wealth of knowledge." There it was again, that slow smile that wanted to thaw the ice in her veins. With her keys squeezed in her fist, Sophia left before she could defrost.

7

Tuesday a.m.

"Morning." Brian sauntered across the war room, threw himself into a chair, and banged his heels up on the tabletop.

Nutsbe was clicking away at the computer, and without shifting his gaze, called, "You okay, man? You look like your beauty sleep got messed with."

"Trying to settle into this case. It was a hell of a jump from personal protection for two archaeologists to taking down ISIS." He glanced at the door as Thorn made his way in, a travel cup of coffee in his hand.

"Did you start without me?"

"Just got in. What are you printing off, Nutsbe?"

"The translation of Sophia's phone call. She was speaking Hebrew, by the way."

Brian sniffed and cleared his throat. "Yeah, my Arabic and Farsi are tactical—I only know how to say enough to get my job done, but I would hope I could at least pick out the languages in a conversation."

"It didn't sound conversational. She was receiving orders," Nutsbe said. "Let me play it again, so you can listen to the tone from both ends. Thorn, this conversation took place in Sophia's kitchen while Brainiack was in the office. He palmed her phone and loaded the listening software while she was having car problems. He replaced it when she took his car." He glanced at Brian. "Good work." He tapped his computer, and the men leaned forward to listen.

"Short and to the point. So what were they saying?" Thorn asked.

Nutsbe passed them each a sheet of paper, and they looked it over. "Let's play good cop, bad cop."

"All right, I'll start," Thorn said. "She spoke in Hebrew. She was trying to hide the conversation from Brainiack."

"Maybe the other caller doesn't speak English. Or maybe she was talking about sensitive information that even her security team doesn't need to know," Brian countered. "This phone call was preceded by another phone call, in which she didn't say anything that came to the house phone. To me, it seemed to identify that she was at home and signaled her that another call was going to come through—she moved to receive the call in the kitchen. And oddly, she took her keys with her."

Thorn rubbed his thumb against his chin. "What are these numbers and letters she's rattling off?"

"Might be part of the security protocol that she follows with her colleagues." Brian stood and moved to the coffee station at the side of the room. Another cup of coffee might rev his brain cells. "We know that she and Nadia are interfacing with different preservationist groups in the Middle East, especially Syria, that are working to document the antiquities and keep them off the black market."

"Get me a cup too, would ya?" Nutsbe asked. "Sugar, no cream. This call didn't come from Syria—it came from Jordan."

"Still, the scenario could apply." Brian's back was to the guys while he doctored the coffee.

"Except that Nadia usually handles the identification and cataloging, and they called Sophia," Nutsbe said as he reached out to take his cup. "Thanks." He took a sip. "Jesus H. Christ." He grimaced. "This tastes like swill from a cow pasture."

"Probably 'cause it is." Brian took his seat. "We don't know that they were specifically calling Sophia—Nadia works out of that office. The call might have gone to either of them."

"Not true," Thorn said. "The follow-up call went to Sophia's cell."

Brian read the words over again. "How about this? It could have something to do with locations instead of items. And we don't know how cleanly Nadia and Sophia draw the line on their work. There could be overlap like there is here with us."

"I wonder what the courier had—maybe we can trace it," Thorn said.

"When Brian sent the audio, Titus thought it was odd enough that he pushed it to the top of the queue over at the translation desk," Nutsbe said. "He thought that package was an opportunity we didn't want to miss. Since Brian didn't have a chance to get our monitoring equipment installed, Titus sent Gage over to get a license plate."

Brian laced his hands behind his head, slouching into a more comfortable position. "Interesting. I wonder why Titus didn't get back to me with that."

"Dunno, man, but he put his head in earlier and said when you finish up in here, he'd like you to meet with him."

"Wilco. What did Gage find out?"

"The license plates are registered to a company called ReadyMan. The address is a boarded-up house," Nutsbe said.

"Huh," Brian said.

"Yup."

"What happened after the courier left?" Thorn asked.

Nutsbe read from his computer. "Gage had watch. Lights were on until zero-three-twenty-seven. An interesting log note— just after midnight, he saw someone walking around the side yard. He moved in to take a look, but they were gone by the time he worked his way over. Gage checked the windows and doors. It all looked tight. Sophia has alarm system stickers on her windows. There was no siren, so he kept watch until he was sure she was done for the night, and he headed back to the barracks."

"I'll figure out a way to get in her house today and install surveillance." Brian turned to Thorn. "What went on with Nadia?"

"Looks like I got light duty so far," Thorn said. "I synced our phones to install the software while she was packing up from the presentation. She made no calls. She texted her sister Lana and someone named Cathy to plan a girls' night out for Wednesday. There was some back and forth about that. It didn't read like code, and Sophia wasn't part of the exchange. Once Nadia left Iniquus, she had a massage, stopped at a flower shop for a bouquet, then the Godiva store and home. She settled in until dinner when she headed to a restaurant. At that point, I had time to do a search and plant the electronics at her home. Nice place. An end-row townhouse in an upper-middle-class neighborhood. Tastefully decorated—nothing elaborate. No pets. Vegetarian diet. Nothing that points to her living above her means. Yesterday's pampering seems like a one-off."

"Sophia said that they were both introverts and found talking in front of strangers difficult," Brian threw out. "Could be that was her celebration that it was over."

"They coulda fooled me," Thorn said. "The thing I picked up on them most was their passion for what they do, not any underlying anxiety. It seemed a way of life for them rather than a career."

"Yeah…that's what you were picking up on." Nutsbe snickered into his coffee cup.

"They're beautiful women. No denying it," Thorn said. "I saw you sit up and take notice when Sophia started talking about satellite imagery in that bedroom voice of hers. 'That Global Information System data is *extremely sensitive*,'" Thorn mimicked Nutsbe with a chuckle.

"I could do worse. Brains. Beauty. Intrigue."

"Prison-striped pajamas," Thorn countered. "Remember, Finley warned us about that when Andersson was out of hearing. He fell hard for his asset once. Then she chopped off his balls and shoved them down his throat."

"Well-deserved, if you ask me," Nutsbe said. "Finley let his emotions get in the way of his brain cells. He made bad calls. That asset nearly died. She was right to kick him to the curb. And he's right to put us on notice. It's science, but not rocket science. People who are considered beautiful get preferential treatment. They can seduce people to bend to their will. Turn a blind eye. They're held to different ethical and moral standards because humans prefer attractive people. I think it was Freud who said, 'Anatomy is destiny.' Yup. I like danger as much as the next guy, but in this case, I've already decided on a look-don't-touch policy."

"Conveniently, that's also written into our contracts, so no room for confusion," Brian deadpanned.

Thorn shook his head. "Damned shame, though. Nadia sparked my curiosity."

"She's so out of your league, man." Brian tapped the printout. "Getting back to this conversation, what do you think this is —this stuff about turning up the heat and tea kettle whistling? Mean anything to you?"

"It's a threat," Thorn said.

"Someone's keeping her in line? Running her?" Brian asked.

"She could be doing something under duress," Thorn said. "I'm thinking about the fathers when the kidnappers were asking for provenance. Knowledge for someone's safety? I'm brainstorming here. Who might be threatened in Sophia and Nadia's lives?"

"Sophia has two children, Turner and Chance. Where's their father?" Brian asked. "Could he be a key?" Brian had wanted that question answered since he saw the car seats and thought there was a man in the picture. Maybe that explained her behavior last fall. She was already taken. Who was Brian's competition? As that thought came out of nowhere, Brian squashed it back down. Finley was right to warn them. Brian could easily see how Sophia could throw him off his game. *Had* thrown him off his game. She was a moment in time—and that moment had clearly passed. Like he told Sophia, bygones were bygones. He needed to move on.

"I've been putting together some background on Sophia and Nadia. Give me a sec." Nutsbe got up to dim the lights. He punched a button on his computer. "I'm going to skip back to the last dig she was on with her father, the summer the families were kidnapped. I put the knowns on a timeline, or as I've poetically labeled this file," he changed the image to a picture of a hurricane, "Sophia Midah Abadi's Raging Shitstorm."

Crap. Brian kicked his feet up on the table, scooted down in his chair, folded his arms over his chest, and did his best to look professionally detached.

"That summer, according to the FBI files, the Abadi and Dajani families were kidnapped, separated, then reunited in Tel Aviv. Then they headed off to what probably felt like the safer part of their research trip." The image changed to a map, and Nutsbe used a laser to draw a little circle out in the middle of nowhere. "They were working here along the Turkish-Syrian border, near Aleppo. There, Dad Abadi becomes seriously ill with who knows what. He has a fever of one hundred and five. Eventually, he's stabilized and shipped home. That information is in the US Embassy notes from Turkey. The Smithsonian was involved with trying to get the families back stateside when the airlines weren't so keen on doing transport without a diagnosis. After that, Mom Abadi applies for SSDI for her husband. Per the Social Security files, Sophia's father was completely incapacitated with dementia due to the high fever. Mom and Dad Abadi moved to Charleston, South Carolina, where Sophia's mom's family lives. He's out of the picture."

Nutsbe brought up a newspaper photograph of a football field and a man in a jersey with Campbell written across the back. Number twenty-seven. "The next thing on the list is that Sophia got married to Hunter Campbell in February just before graduation."

"That seems like odd timing," Thorn said.

"Right, well, there's a good reason. Sophia gets back from Turkey and heads in for her senior year. She was dating Hunter Campbell, star quarterback." Nutsbe traced a line under the guy's name with his laser pointer. "November of that year, Campbell took a major hit on the field. Brain trauma. He had to drop out of school. Sophia was in her last semester of undergrad when she got married. She graduated summa cum laude. And on June 8, baby Turner makes his debut. He's a full-term baby with no medical issues."

"Why did you stipulate that?" Thorn asked.

"Don't jump ahead in the book. It spoils the plot." Nutsbe put up a picture of the graduation ceremony.

Brian did a quick count on his fingers. "She was pregnant before her boyfriend got hurt. Did he recover?" Brian wanted to get all the cards on the table. Just what was he dealing with here? Wrong damned question. He should be asking what Sophia had been dealing with.

"Wait for it. One step through the turd field at a time. Sophia continues her education with a master's program. She's listed with the university as a teaching assistant, which pays for her tuition and housing. Hunter was awarded SSDI the April before Turner's birth. The brain injury permanently disabled him. Searching the database from her university address, I found phone calls to 9-1-1 for violent outbursts where Sophia is screaming into the phone for help. Campbell was frequently hospitalized for long stretches of time—this is all related to the head injury. And before you ask, Brian—because I can see it sitting there on the tip of your tongue—no, there is no money coming in from a lawsuit. The university cannot be held responsible for their athletes' injuries. The students are just shit out of luck if they get hurt playing for their school." Another photo of a graduation ceremony went up. "Against what I can only imagine are daunting odds, Sophia is awarded her master's degree in May the next year."

"Where's the husband's family?" Thorn asked.

"At that point, they're in the area, and I'm assuming she's getting some help from them because up until that fall, her finances are fairly clean." Nutsbe shot a look at Brian. "Actually, Sophia is living in their house right now."

"With them?" Brian asked.

"Stay with me. We're getting to them in a second. That October, Sophia was working toward her Ph.D. She takes out a personal loan for ten-thousand dollars. That took some digging, but it turns out it was to pay an attorney in Colorado. Her brother's serving a life sentence for killing a guy in a drug-deal-gone-bad gun battle."

"Is there any sign that Sophia could be involved with drugs?" Thorn asked.

"Zero. But that doesn't mean anything. If I were her, I'd be on drugs, that's for damned sure." Nutsbe looked over at Brian. "Seriously, dude, when you sweep her house, I'd look for drug paraphernalia. Given what she's been through, she may be self-medicating. I checked the brother's court documents. He testified that he had been in a motorcycle accident and sustained a back injury. The doctors put him on opioids, but after a while, Abadi was having trouble getting the docs to refill the prescriptions. Abadi was addicted and turned to street drugs to keep himself going. He recognized the problem and was on the waiting list for a bed at a detox. But then a deal he was doing went bad. The dealer accused him of being a cop and pulled a gun on him, yadda yadda yadda. If you're following along, that's kidnapped in July, Dad's brain fries in August, brother's back breaks in October, and boyfriend's head gets busted in November."

"Sophia is ten-thousand dollars in debt, has a baby, a violent husband, no income, no family support, and she does what?" Thorn asked.

"Sticks with her Ph.D." Nutsbe switched to a picture of the AACP logo. "She was hired by AACP. She's been on their research team for years. They paid for her tuition and room provided she do her dissertation on space archaeology, focusing on their work in the Middle East. AACP said that once she had her Ph.D., she'd have a guaranteed job."

"Finally, a flicker of hope," Thorn said.

"Amen to that," Nutsbe agreed.

Brian picked up his now-cold coffee and took a sip. "You still haven't told me if Hunter Campbell could possibly be a key."

Nutsbe scratched his brow. "Well, he's dead. So I'd say no."

Brian stilled, processing that last answer. His respect for Sophia was climbing by the minute. How was she holding herself together through all this crap? "Dead how?"

"Yeah, that's going to take a little more digging. I'm not really understanding the circumstances."

"But there's a death certificate," Brian pressed.

"That's not the interesting thing. There was a 9-1-1 call from Sophia's apartment on December 16^t. It was Hunter's mother saying her son had tried to kill himself. Guess what else happened December 16th?"

Thorn and Brian sent him blank stares.

"Chance Campbell was born. Per the birth certificate, Chance's birth happened an hour before the 9-1-1 call. Sophia goes into the hospital to have a baby, and Hunter is home trying to kill himself. Happy fucking birthday, right? The baby was born at thirty-three weeks and put in the NICU. Lots of hospital bills."

Thorn threw himself back in his chair. "Holy crap, he killed himself."

"No, he didn't. At least not that day. He didn't die until August 11th at the hospital. The same hospital where his dad died fifteen minutes later, by the way. There's something weird in that. All of that is to say, Hunter and Chance Campbell racked up tens of thousands of dollars in medical bills. Sophia is swimming in debt. A few select artifact sales might just put her back on solid financial footing."

"Has she made any large payments? Is there any shift in her financials?" Brian asked.

"Small monthly payments to a collections agency. Also, she's scheduled to be in court the second week in June. That's as far as I got with my research."

"Where's Mama Campbell? Is Sophia living with her? It makes sense if she's swimming in debt." Brian thought about yesterday's issues fetching Turner. Why wouldn't the mother-in-law help?

"Her mother-in-law died on Chance's birthday this year, December 16th. The second anniversary of her son's attempted suicide."

"From what?"

"Myocardial infarction. She was only forty-eight years old—kind of strange. Just seems odd to me. I'll keep digging."

"It's one hell of a story. Sophia's twenty-six now?" Thorn asked.

"Yes, twenty-six. Nadia is thirty."

"What do you have on Nadia?" Brian asked.

"She was quick and easy. After her Ph.D., she started working right away with AACP. She bought her house two years ago. She bought her car at the beginning of the year. She pays off her credit cards monthly. She likes to travel for long weekends to New York, Miami, Chicago. She has a 401k. She's made conservative investments. Her financials all add up. Her mother and father live in upstate New York. Her sister, Lana, lives around the corner from both Nadia and Sophia. Lana is a stay-at-home mother to three young boys. Nadia's squeaky clean. I can't see how anyone would have leverage over her or her life."

"Lana Dajani. We didn't hear that name from the FBI."

"Lana Taylor is her married name. I talked to Nadia about her sister," Thorn said. "Lana is a homebody. She never wanted to go on digs with her father. She stayed back in the United States with their mother. She has a bachelor's in English Literature. Her life revolves around her family and reading. There's nothing in that direction."

Brian examined the pen he was holding. "It seems kind of cut and dry. Sophia is a woman in crisis. But let's not get tunnel vision. Evidence lies. Clues, like statistics, can be manipulated to show what we want them to show. If Sophia's culpable of terrorist activities, I'll be the first one to slap those cuffs on her wrists. But until we have a crystal-clear picture of who, what, where, and why, let's stay away from assumptive thinking. The FBI believes that something happened when the women were kidnapped. Why would that something affect one of the women and not both? Why would this be going on for nearly five years? And is it possible that there's an unsub somewhere who hasn't shown up yet?"

8

As her minivan thumped over the bump at the top of her drive, and Sophia steered her way down the steep hill, Brian came into view. He was sitting on her stoop, his long legs stretched comfortably out in front of him, resting back on his elbows. Sophia thought for sure he'd have given up and left by now.

She threw the gear into park and slowly pulled her keys from the ignition, stalling her walk of shame. She wore blue night shorts covered in leaping sheep. Her t-shirt read "Sweet dreams, I love ewe" and wasn't made of a thick enough material to mask the fact that she'd left the house without a bra, or any underwear, for that matter. Her hair was mussed, her face sweaty. She was covered in grime. Her thighs still had the bright red marks of yesterday's burns.

As she moved up the sidewalk, a grin spread across Brian's face. "This is going to be a good story."

"No, it's not." She rattled through her keys until she found the one for her front door and climbed past Brian to unlock it. "I apologize for being late."

"That's all right." He followed her through the door, not offering to come back another time the way she wished he would. "I had some things I needed to think through. It was a good opportunity."

Sophia moved from her office to the Florida room door and over to her stack of tires. "Before I get sidetracked, I need to put one of these in my car." *Please go home, Brian.* She reached up to maneuver the top tire off the stack.

Brian reached over and helped her out. "You had another flat?"

"Don't sound so incredulous. I'm the queen of flat tires." She gestured toward her pile. "The guy at the tire store felt so bad for me, he sold me a dozen at cost, so I could have them on hand." She reached over to roll the tire out, but Brian held it in place. She shifted her gaze to his face, where she thought she'd find amusement at the ridiculousness of her problem. Instead, she saw animosity. She didn't know what to make of that. "I'll admit, though, that I played the 'single mom with two little kids' card. I asked for a good customer discount."

He turned toward the stack. "After this, there are only seven left."

"Like I said, I'm the queen of flat tires." She tried again to pry the tire away from him. He held it fast.

"Have you always been?" he asked.

Sophia stood upright and combed her fingers through her hair. "No, not always, just since I moved here last June, right after the car accident."

He settled the tire against his leg and reached for her arm, turning it over. Sophia worked hard not to snatch it back.

He ran a finger over the long scars that ran down her inner arm. "Where did you get them?"

The gentleness and concern made her breath catch. Sent her already tenuous equilibrium spinning. She turned away from him to step into the office, forcing him to let go of her. "My mother-in-law was driving when we got t-boned."

Brian hefted the tire over his arm and rested it on his shoulder as he made his way toward her car. "And that's why you're late today? You were on the side of the road, in your pajamas, changing your tire?"

"In a church parking lot. But yes." Sophia hustled after him, pressing the key fob to make the hatch open.

"Do you always go out like that?" Brian had put the tire in place and was closing the back when his eye focused across the street.

Sophia followed his gaze to the upper window, where one of the Sheppards was staring at them. Sophia turned and headed toward the house. Yesterday, she was in her nightshirt, today, sheep shorts. She wondered what the Sheppards thought of her.

Brian kept pace. "I want to talk to you about these tires. You being out like this on the side of the road is a safety hazard. I've been tasked with your security."

"When I'm on a dig." Sophia shut the door behind them and crossed her arms over her chest for modesty's sake.

"I've been tasked with your security." Brian's blue eyes crackled with electricity. "Yesterday, the guys at Iniquus's garage said there were construction bolts in the front and back tires."

"I assumed. I don't know how I find them. I've tried different tires, different routes, different times of day for driving. I seem to magnetize construction materials to my car."

"Only your car. Not Nadia's, for example."

"No, she's never had a flat tire in her life."

"You weren't having flat tire issues when you lived at student housing. Then you moved here…"

"After the accident, I moved in to help my mother-in-law out. That month I had my first flat. Then once a month, like clockwork, I could cross 'fix a flat' off my to-do list. In the last few months, it's just become obnoxious. *Beyond* obnoxious."

Brian considered her for a long moment. "You look tired."

The concern in his voice caught at her mask and tried to pry it loose. Sophia scraped her teeth over her lip.

"Is Chance okay? Is that why you're in your pajamas?"

"Chance is doing better. The antibiotics are working, thank you." Sophia tried to use a professional voice to build a wall between them. "I was up late working on a project. I got to bed after three, but then my house alarm went off an hour later, so it took some time to calm down. This morning I slept through my wake-up chimes. Lana, Nadia's sister, is keeping my kids for me today. I thought I'd run them over and slip back in the house to shower and change and leave a note for you to let yourself in." She offered up a rueful smile. "So much for plans and good intentions."

Brian's muscles tightened, and his eyes grew keen. "Did the police come to check your property last night?"

"Oh no, the alarm isn't attached to a service anymore. I ran up too high a bill with the police department." She looked at the keypad on her wall. "And I'm not going to turn it on again. It wakes the boys up, and then they're in a terrible mood the next day."

"Wait. Hold up. Go back a step. Why are the police charging you?"

"When you have a false alarm, they come and check it for free. The second time, if nothing's wrong, the police charge you fifty dollars. The third time it's one-hundred dollars and so on. I was out of town this past January, and by the time I got home, I owed the police three-thousand-six-hundred and fifty dollars. Every night at 11:10 on the dot, someone or something rattled my office door."

"Some*thing*?" Brian's brow furrowed. "It stopped?" He moved toward the back of the house. "Which door was it?"

"That door there." Sophia stood to follow him but remembered what she was wearing and kept her distance. "I let my alarm service go. I sometimes engage the system just to alert myself if someone is to try to get in. Maybe scare them away."

He moved into the room and leaned his back against the wall. "Why did you have it on last night?"

"I got spooked. It felt like someone was out there watching my house, so I turned the alarm on in the hopes it would make me feel less vulnerable. I paid the price." She moved toward the stairs. "If you'll excuse me, it's about time I got some clothes on."

The quick shower did its job; she was human again. Sophia walked down the stairs just as Brian shut her front door. The look of sheer bewilderment he wore as he turned to face her was priceless. Sophia found herself grinning at him. "Who was that?" she asked.

"Marla?" Brian scrubbed a hand over his closely cropped brown hair. "Does she own clothes beside the flesh-colored bikini?"

"Yeah, she usually only wears that one to garden at eight in the morning and around five in the afternoon. In between, she's usually dressed for the gym."

"So, she's in the garden as people leave for work and come home."

"Yup, leaning over, fanny in the air, weeding her little heart out."

"That's insane."

"I'd have to agree with you on that one." Sophia made her way down the rest of the stairs. "She must have caught sight of you coming and going and wanted to check you out for herself. She wouldn't have kept the bikini on for my sake. She collects male admirers as a hobby. What did she say she wanted?"

"She said she came over for a little sugar. I told her you were out."

"That's how she phrased it? 'I came over for a little sugar'?" Sophia raised her hand. "Wait. Don't answer that. Instead, tell me what's on your agenda. Why did you need to come by this morning?"

"Since the AAPC computer systems are here, and they contain sensitive information, I need to go over your house from a security point of view. Your alarm system story has me concerned. While you were getting ready, I checked out your Florida room. There's a stack of outdoor automatic lighting fixtures in there. I'd like to get those put in place." He turned his tablet to show a gallery of pictures—one from each side of her house, with sketches of light placement and trajectories. "You have enough to cover your property three-sixty, and a couple extra that I could put in the trees nearest to your house."

"Because people are climbing my trees?"

"Someone small could get near enough to your windows to see in. I'm not suggesting that's ever happened. I was just trying to find a way to incorporate all the lights you bought."

Sophia reached for the tablet and looked things over like she knew what this all meant. She smiled and handed it back.

"Thanks. I'm going to make myself a cup of tea and get to work. Do you need anything?" The phone on her desk rang, and Sophia felt the blood drain from her face. Her breath caught. Brian's gaze was hard on hers. By the fourth ring, she had the receiver in her hand. There were five staccato beeps, then a dial tone. She picked up her keys and said, "Would you excuse me?" She didn't even look Brian's way as she jogged up the stairs to her bedroom.

9

Wednesday a.m.

Brian clanked the barbell back into place and sat up to take a swig from his jug of water. Titus moved his way and thumped him on the back. "I got hung up yesterday, so I missed you," he said, sitting on the bench across from Brian. "We were working on locating Honey."

"Any news?" Brian mopped the sweat from his forehead and leaned in so they could keep their conversation private. Rooster Honig, whose call sign was "Honey," was in Iraq working solo, which was generally against Iniquus policy. He'd been on loan to Strike Force operatives when a distress call had come in. One of their clients had an energy executive kidnapped while on a business trip. Honey was one of Iniquus's best negotiators and spoke fluent Arabic. He took off with a friendly, heading from Jalalabad to Kirkuk. Dagger was supposed to hook up with him—a two-man team, low and lean. But Dagger never made contact. The Panther Force operatives all had their go-bags sitting by their front doors, ready to jump into action if the situation didn't clear up.

"All personnel accounted for. The kidnapping victim is still in the wind, but Honey's opened up a line of communication."

Brian nodded. Their work was full of twists and turns. Danger. Violence. Adrenaline. It was where he belonged. His mind and body were built for this job. He felt lucky that as he transitioned from FAST—the Marine Fleet Anti-terrorism Security Team—to a civilian job stateside, he could continue to serve America and put his specialized training to use. Having been deployed to that region, Brian knew just how bad things could get if Honey went incommunicado.

Titus glanced around the room before he said, "I noticed during Monday's meeting that you and Dr. Abadi know each other. You didn't bring that to my attention when I made the assignments."

"I wasn't aware at that time that she and I *were* acquainted. I never knew her last name. She introduced herself to me as Sophie."

"When was this?"

"Her birthday, November of last year. We met at the bar in the hotel where I was staying during the New York mission. We talked into the wee hours of the morning. That's the end of it."

"Did that *talk* include having sex?"

"Yes, sir."

"She was distressed when she saw you."

"She was embarrassed. When I woke up the next morning, she was gone without a goodbye. Like I said, I didn't know her last name. Had no clue she was an archaeologist. I haven't seen or spoken with her since."

Titus gave him a hard stare. "Is it in the best interests of the case that I reassign that duty?"

Brian kept his posture neutral, his expression indifferent. "If that would make you more comfortable. I don't have a problem with it one way or another." But he did. The idea of someone else being in Sophia's home, in her life, protecting her when it should be him, didn't sit well.

Titus stood. "Let's leave things as-is for now. Let me know if any concerns come up."

Brian moved toward the locker room to shower before his powwow in the war room. Protecting Sophia was only part of his job. Figuring out if she was a terrorist was the other. It was going to be one hell of a challenge. How could he both protect *and* try to expose Sophia at the same time? If the situation called for it, could he take her down? A picture of her lying on his bed, her long, black hair draped over the side as they laughed together the night of her birthday, had him closing his eyes. It was the most amazing thing he'd ever experienced. If pressed to describe the sensation, he'd call it a religious awakening. It was a revelation that he could feel that perfectly connected to a person—a stranger, no less. In his mind, he'd thought it was the first night of a life of nights together. He couldn't imagine ever being without her. Then he woke up and reached out for her, only to discover she was gone.

Even with all of Iniquus's resources at his fingertips, he'd never been able to find her. When he saw her walk into that morning meeting, all those feelings rushed back to the surface. He had to come to grips with the idea that he'd fallen hard for someone who could very well be a terrorist sympathizer. Could he take her down? At his core, there was no question. To save his brothers and sisters in arms, to protect America, damned straight he could. He slammed his locker shut and headed to the Panther Force war room.

"I've been compiling information for you." Nutsbe popped open his laptop and set it in front of Brian and Thorn. "The good news is that everyone's surveillance is functioning. Brian, we may need to move to night vision on your outdoor cameras if things keep up the way they did last night."

"She had visitors?" Thorn asked.

"I think she had a poltergeist," Nutsbe said. "I'm going to fast-forward this section of tape. This happened over a three-hour span of time, but I've compressed it into two minutes."

The light from the right-hand side of the house blinked on. The vantage point was from the eaves, where Brian had placed the light the day before. They had a momentary view of Sophia's minivan and her mailbox. As soon as the light went off, it lit up again. It turned off, and the next view was of the sidewalk and front stairs. That light flashed on, then off, then on again.

"What's the timer on these lights?" Thorn leaned over to ask.

"Fifteen minutes," Brian replied as that light went off and the next one in line blinked on. "Nutsbe, does each light flash twice?"

Brian knew that he'd put six lights in place. Lighting up each section twice would take an hour and a half.

"Twice on the first round, twice on the second round. It looks like a dog running up to an invisible fence, testing the boundaries before he'd get zapped."

"That's exactly what it looks like. Calculated." Brian's stomach muscles tightened. "I'll get Titus to sign off on a camera upgrade. She has an alarm system in place, but she isn't using it." Brian explained to his team about the daily door rattles and the police bill.

"That's damned odd," Nutsbe said.

"Ya think?"

"Was Nadia okay last night? Any unwanted visitors?" Thorn asked.

"Nadia went to Lana's house for dinner. Then she went home and read until ten when she went to sleep. Nadia likes to walk around her house in a slinky little teddy." Nutsbe touched his cursor to pull up the image. "There's my bonus for all the hours I had to sit and watch lights flashing on and off at Sophia's place."

"Shut that off, Nutsbe," Brian growled.

Nutsbe sighed and flipped to an audio file. "Fine. Moving on then."

The first thing they heard was a nine-digit alphanumeric code, in English this time. Brian leaned over and tapped the key to pause the recording. "First mystery solved. You'll notice that code was different than the first time she got a call. On Monday, I found a PIN generating device on her desk."

"On her desk where anyone could get to it? How is that secure?" Nutsbe asked.

"Exactly," Brian said. "She seemed genuinely surprised to find it in my hand. She said there was a place that she and Nadia hid it and guessed that one of them, in getting ready to do their public speaking gig in front of Panther Force, must have forgotten to return it to its usual spot."

"Was it out yesterday when you were there checking on security details?" Thorn asked.

"No, and I was looking for it. But returning to the phone call, it's odd to me that both times she took one of those calls, she picked up her keys and left the room. At first, I thought maybe there was something on the keychain she didn't want me to see. I had her keys Monday when the mechanics were fixing her car. We made duplicates of all of them. House key, car key, four storage keys. Her keychain is a flashlight."

"Storage keys?"

"They belong to PODS that line the back of the property. I opened them and am guessing it's her in-laws' personal effects, furniture, clothes, photo albums, kitchenware. Someone could start a whole new life with the stuff packed up out back."

"Why is she keeping it, do you think?" Nutsbe asked.

"Don't know." Brian shrugged. "It's costing her money. I was hoping you could do some digging, Nutsbe. I'm kind of stuck on the dad and son dying in the same hospital, minutes apart. And then the mother, what—a year plus later? As for the PODS, maybe there's other family involved. Maybe she needs to hang on to that stuff for some reason. I think the more we know about the stressors in Sophia's and Nadia's lives, the better we can find their pressure points. We know they both have the means and opportunity; the missing piece is the motivation."

"So, how do her keys tie into the phone calls?"

"Her flashlight runs on a button battery. The battery tube holds a randomized digital PIN creator, a tiny version of the one that Nadia and Sophia use for their AACP computer."

Thorn twitched his lips to the side, staring past Brian, thinking. "That doesn't have to be nefarious. She could be clarifying her identity to the people who are functioning in ISIS-held areas if they need assurance that they're talking to the right person. We do the same with our fake pre-school website with the animal and color of the day."

"See what you think after you hear the conversation." Nutsbe reached out to start the audio file again.

"We need those contacts we talked about." It was the same female voice from the first call.

"I'm working on it," Sophia whispered. *"Things are delicate right now. I have to be extra careful about who I reach out to and how. I'll figure it out. I need a little more time."* There was a warble in Sophia's voice that made Brian think that the person Sophia was speaking to scared her—made her feel threatened somehow.

"The information you sent us was helpful. We took a major piece off the board."

The unsub's information was met with silence. The mystery voice continued, *"Have you heard the news out of Palmyra?"*

A long pause, then Sophia whispered, *"No."*

"You'll want to watch Al Jazeera."

The line went dead.

"Do you know what the caller was referring to?"

"Possibly. Andersson sent me a file last night with an email that said *concerning news out of Palmyra*," Nutsbe read. "Our partners at Interpol sent us word that Sadiq Bikar was killed in Palmyra yesterday."

Thorn tossed his pen in the air and watched it rotate twice before it landed neatly back in his hand. "Why is this Bikar guy interesting to us?"

"Here are the FBI bullet points—Bikar, aged eighty-two, was a world leader in the preservation of relics, architecture, and antiquities in Palmyra. He taught ancient studies at Stanford University. After retirement, Bikar became the Head of Palmyra Antiquities and Preservation for the UNESCO World Heritage Center." Nutsbe moved the cursor down the page, his eyes shifting rapidly left and right. "Okay—here's the gist. Palmyra's city dates to two-thousand-years BC, when it acted as a waypoint for caravans crossing the desert. Before ISIS took over the area,

Palmyra was filled with ancient pieces that quickly disappeared from their museums. Some are assumed to be hidden by concerned citizens, but most are assumed to be in the hands of those running the black markets. Four pieces found in the Gilchrest collection were flagged by the FBI as having a high probability of being stolen from the museum collection. That's why they sent this to our attention."

Brian's phone buzzed, and he looked down at the readout. "Sophia's on the move again. At zero-eight-hundred, she took the boys to daycare." He swiped the screen. "Yeah, she's leaving Willow Tree. She said she and Nadia are working in her home office today."

Thorn's phone vibrated. He pulled up the same app to track his target. "Nadia's heading toward Sophia's house," Thorn said and slipped his phone back in the thigh pocket on his BDUs.

"Continuing on," Nutsbe said. "Finley got word from the Syrian Human Rights Observation Alliance that Bikar was beheaded in the public square. His body was tied to a post. His head was placed between his feet. Their informant said that ISIS interrogated Bikar, trying to find the location of hidden museum artifacts and two chests of gold rumored to be buried in the city. They also wanted the names and locations of all the academics throughout the world who were helping to protect Syrian treasures and causing hiccups in their trade routes. The human rights asset didn't know if any of that information was revealed or not. He's worried that those directly involved with stopping the black market have been compromised, specifically those working with AACP."

"Why does the asset think Bikar talked?"

"Bikar's three sons disappeared around the same time that Bikar was taken hostage. His wife was killed in their home. It could be that ISIS was torturing the sons to drag information from the father."

Brian turned to Thorn. "Nadia and Sophia may have been compromised. This puts them in even greater danger."

"Finley agrees," Nutsbe said. "We need to up our efforts making sure the women are protected while we're looking for any way they might have been connected to the event. Sadiq Bikar was supposedly in hiding with Interpol protection. Reading between the lines, they lost operatives in this event."

Brian tapped his middle finger on the desk while he processed that information. "Until we have a better handle on things, I think it's a good idea to move the women to status orange. That way, we can be more aggressive in the actions we take. I'd rather be proactive here."

The men sat in silence, considering the situation.

"One other thing you both should know. ISIS sent a video to Al Jazeera that showed ISIS militants demanding that Bikar pledge his loyalty to their organization. He refused. They beat him to a bloody pulp before they tied him to the post. They revived him to give him one last opportunity to sign on as a member. He spat at the man and was promptly beheaded."

"The caller told Sophia to watch Al Jazeera," Thorn said.

The fine hairs on the back of Brian's neck prickled. What the hell was going on here? In his gut, Brian thought Sophia was doing her job saving the world's antiquities and trying to stop ISIS, but even he couldn't deny that this looked bad. "Was that before or after Bikar was killed? What time did this happen?"

The beheading was at twelve-hundred hours Syrian time. That's zero-five-hundred hours here in DC. Two hours before-hand, at zero-three-ten hours, Sophia Abadi made a phone call to Jordan on her landline. Sophia said nothing, but on the Jordan side, there were five beeps. Sophia then received a call back from a different Jordanian number on her cell. She read an alphanumeric string and said in Arabic, 'I've assessed your information, and I concur. I'd proceed as planned.' There was no reply on the Jordan end. The line was cut directly after. I tried to trace it, but the exchange was so short, all I got was the city of Amman. With four million people in that city, it doesn't narrow things by much."

Thorn scanned down the communications printout. "This makes sense," he said. "Dr. Bikar could be the 'major piece off the board' the caller refers to. He was working to protect the antiquities and might have been preventing the black marketers getting their hands on the better-quality artifacts".

"Or these two things could have nothing to do with each other." Brian scrubbed a hand over his face to give himself a moment to process. It looked like evidence was piling up against Sophia. What had she gotten herself mixed up in?

His phone buzzed in his pocket. He dragged it out to check the screen. Sophia Abadi. He tapped the speakerphone and lay it on the table. "Brainiack here."

"Brian, did I catch you in the middle of something? It's Sophia."

"You're all right. What can I do for you?"

Nutsbe turned his computer screen toward them to show Sophia's car moving down the highway in their direction.

"I'm up the street. If you have a minute—" There was a sudden bang—the squeal of tires. Horns blasting. Sophia screamed. Silence.

Brian was on his feet, adrenaline pumping through his system. "Sophia?" he called into the phone. "Sophia, tell me what's happening."

Nutsbe's fingers flew over the keyboard. He yanked his phone out. "Lynx, Panther Force needs urgent assistance. You're the closest operative to a client in immediate distress. I'm sending coordinates to your phone. It's a Chrysler Town & Country, red. It might have been in an accident. It might have been attacked. Approach with caution."

Brian was running out the door with his keys in his hands when he heard, "Brainiack is backup. ETA five minutes."

10

SOPHIA

Wednesday

Sophia couldn't feel her body. Her ability to process came down to blurred vision, dappled by the flicker of her eyelashes, and the whooshing sound of cars flying by close enough to suck the paint off her van. She reached for those words. Her van. They made strange hooks that pierced through the bubble that held her suspended. Sophia knew she was going to die. She waited for it. She wasn't breathing. She wasn't sure her heart beat. She swallowed, though. The saliva gathered in her mouth and slipped down her throat in a thick glob, sticking in the center, holding there, then finishing the slow slide. That was all the saliva she had had in her mouth, and now her gums were dry. Her tongue too big.

A rapping sounded to the side of her. A *chuck-a-chuck* sounded as someone tried to open her door. "Sophia? Dr. Abadi?" A female voice hollered down an echoing tunnel.

Sophia's eyelids slid over her eyes then flicked up, mechanically. She wished death would do its job and get it over with.

The *pop-pop* came at her back door, her hatch, then to her right. "Sophia. Sophia, are you all right? Open the door."

Sophia's brain demanded oxygen. She wanted to move, but she was paralyzed. Her head faced forward. Her hands clenched tightly around the steering wheel.

"Sophia!" The woman's voice was replaced with a man's. There was a metal scraping sound and a loud pop to her left. Wind blew her hair across her face, the strands weaving themselves into her lashes.

"What's she doing? What's wrong?" the man asked.

A horn honked. Debris blew into Sophia's eyes. When she blinked, she could feel the grit under her lids.

"My name is Lynx. I'm going to help you." It was an angel's voice filled with golden light.

Warm skin touched Sophia's lips and nostrils, then fingers pressed into her neck.

"Can you tell me your name?"

Sophia's thoughts walked through the mist, looking for the answer.

"Do you know where you are?"

A hand brushed over her face, sweeping her hair to the side. A bright light flashed twice in one eye then twice in the other.

"What's happening?" the man asked.

"It looks like she's having a seizure. Was that listed on her medical intake paperwork?"

"We haven't gotten to that point," the man shouted over the ambient noise of Washington gridlock traveling at high speed. "Let me get in touch with her partner, Nadia."

Sophia felt warmth radiating into her body, and she knew it

came from the angel. Bubbles of hope effervesced across her chest.

"It's safe. You're safe." The angel's voice was pink and blue with streaks of tangerine like a sunset sky. "Brian and I are here with you. You're having a seizure. You've had them before. You know that this will be over soon. You'll be fine."

There was a prickling sensation on the backs of Sophia's thighs as they pressed into her seat. Her muscles slackened as the attack faded, and exhaustion took its place.

"Lynx, this location is too dangerous." The wind caught the man's voice and blew it around like a balloon. "Do you think we need an ambulance?"

"What does Nadia say?" The angel had morphed into human form. Sophia could see the woman's long blonde hair.

Too tired to hold her head up anymore, Sophia collapsed forward until her forehead rested on the steering wheel. The woman moved her hands from Sophia's chest to her back. Her touch was prayerful. Powerful.

Sophia could hear Nadia talking over the speakerphone. "NEAD. Non-epileptic attack disorder. She hasn't had an episode in over a year."

"Does she need to go to the hospital?" That was Brian's voice.

"No to the hospital. They don't have any way to help her. But if you could get her to her home, I'm already there."

"We can do that," Brian said. There was a pause before he asked, "Lynx, NEAD?"

"It's a chronic seizure disorder caused by psychological distress. It often stems from severe trauma. The seizures look like epilepsy, sometimes manifesting as tonic-clonic seizures where people fall and lose control of their muscles. Others have absence seizures like Sophia just did."

The van shuddered as a truck whizzed by, its horn held down.

Brian slid his hand across her stomach to release her safety belt. "Sophia, here, put your arm around my shoulder. I'm going to lift you up."

"Stop hovering, Brian, you're making me nervous." Sophia lay on the couch. She curled deeper into the blanket Nadia had brought down for her. "I promise I'm not going to spontaneously combust."

Brian moved to a chair and sat down. "One of the things I need to work on with you is a health history. We have medics go over the information when we're headed out of the country, and they pack medical kits to match the requirements of known possibilities in case there's an emergency when we're far from a health center. We also have satellite comms that put us in touch with an Iniquus doctor. I've been talked through everything from an emergency appendectomy to breech birth. Twins, no less," he said with a grin. "Both girls, one's named Brianna. The other is Charlotte." He put his hand on his chest. "My middle name's Charles."

Sophia gave him a weak smile.

"When you're up to it, I'd like to work on your profile with you, so we've got that covered." He glanced over to where Nadia moved around the kitchen. "Thorn will be doing the same with you, Nadia. Titus said we'll probably be heading to Peru in another few weeks."

"Is that what that woman does? Lynx? Is she a medic? How did she know my name when she stopped?"

Brian's eyes shifted from concerned to impassive, like a curtain closing. "I was on the phone with you when your tire blew. We weren't sure what was going on. It very well could have been gunfire from the sound of things. Iniquus traced your call and found the nearest operative. That was Lynx. She happens to have an EMT background, so that was a piece of good luck."

Nadia bustled in with a fragrant cup of chai. Sophia accepted it gratefully.

Outside, an engine powered down the drive. Brian went to get the door. He came back with her keys. "Who's your neighbor across the way? The one who looks out the upstairs window every time I come over."

Sophia reached for her keys, glad to have them back in her possession and away from the curious eyes of Iniquus operatives. "Will Sheppard or his wife, Janice. Ignore them. They're paranoid, but for good reason."

"Why is that?"

"Because," Nadia said, "this neighborhood is filled to the brim with looney tunes." She squinted at Sophia. "You need to move."

Sophia pulled the pillow from behind her head and buried her face in it, muffling her reply. "If it weren't for nine-tenths rules, I'd be out of here in a heartbeat." Sophia moved to hug the pillow, looking up to find a line creased between Brian's brows.

His eyes had brightened with what she had come to call his 'duty focus.' "That didn't answer my question."

"In the case of the Sheppards, the women in the neighborhood think it's a hoot to get liquored up and run up to their house and ring the bell or throw rocks at their windows to wake them up."

"Why do they do that?"

"That's not all they do," Nadia said. "They have neighborhood parties once a month—they grill at the end of the cul-de-sac, everyone brings a dish. Nice, right? Not really. They get drunk, send their kids home, and then do things like take off their shirts and bras and streak half-naked to the stop sign and back. Why? Because they're crazy."

"How often do they get drunk?"

"Whenever the kids don't have school," Nadia answered.

"Every time?"

"*So*...someone brought my van back?" Sophia could feel anxiety catching hold of her breath. She needed to change the subject fast.

Brian tipped his head to study her for a long moment. "Yes, they did, and we had all your tires replaced with run-flats," he finally said.

Sophia pulled her shoulders up to her ears. "What is that?"

"The other day when you got the flats, I thought we had the problem solved. The tires Iniquus put on the right-hand side of your car were self-sealing. If you drove over a nail and then pulled it out, the tire would fill the hole. Unfortunately, they work best when the puncture is small and in the middle of the tread. Your puncture was another piece of construction debris."

Sophia turned her scowl toward the window.

"There are some things you should know. A run-flat is basically a tire with sidewalls reinforced to support the weight of your vehicle even if they go flat. That means you can drive on a flat tire, and I want you to. You are *not* to stop and change it. Just keep driving home or to Iniquus or some other place where you feel safe. Then call me or the Iniquus hotline."

Sophia swung her head toward him.

"I programmed the number into your phone as number one on quick dial. When you call, they'll know who you are and where you are. You need to tell them the circumstances, so they know whom to dispatch. Today, Lynx was only a short distance from you and was able to get to you in less than three minutes while I made my way to you. There is always a Panther Force operative on duty. You always have support. Okay?"

When had he programmed her phone? Sophia wondered. She didn't like what Brian was telling her. Sure, it should put her at ease that a group of hot-shot retired Special Forces guys was at her beck and call. There was a time back in high school when that genre of book was her preferred reading. But living vicariously through the words written on a page and living them in real life… They created completely different body responses. Knowing that it might be necessary to push that button on her phone to save herself or her kids… Sophia's eye caught on the photo of her boys and held.

Brian waited until she turned her attention back to him. "You can still have a blowout with these tires, though. It's not a foolproof solution. How about you make it a habit to check your tires for anything foreign before you get in the car to drive?"

"I can do that," Sophia said.

"Sophia, this is important. You've been parking your car at the bottom of your drive under the crepe myrtle. You need to park at the top of the hill next to your mailbox. I know it's a hassle, with the kids and all. But the person who's sabotaging your tires is using that tree to hide behind."

"Someone is doing this *on purpose*?"

"Sophia, come on, be serious. This is life-threatening."

Sophia thought she caught a hint of exasperation in Brian's tone.

"I told her the same thing, but she thinks she's just jinxed. And the 'bad luck,'" Nadia made air quotes with her fingers, "is her paying for her sins."

Nadia's comment felt like the betrayal of a sacred trust. Sophia couldn't believe she had said that aloud.

Brian leaned forward and waited until Sophia was looking him directly in the eye. She couldn't hold the intensity of his gaze, so she lowered her lashes to shield herself.

"What sins, Sophia?" he asked gently. "What have you done?"

Sophia rubbed her palms up and down her thighs and focused back on the picture of her boys.

Brian must have realized she had zero intentions of answering him because he moved the conversation along. "You drive with your kids in the car. Today, when the tire blew, you almost had an accident. Yes, you got to the side of the road and out of harm's way, but it scared you so badly you had a seizure. What if your boys had been with you then? What if you were on the side of the highway, and you were unable to protect them?"

Sophia's whole body began trembling. Nadia moved over to her side, reaching her arms protectively around Sophia. Sophia buried her head against her friend's shoulder. Her mind flashed back to the accident last June that would later take her mother-in-law's life. The boys had been cut and bruised but hadn't needed hospitalization, thank God. She now wore the long silver scars where her arm was pieced back together. The thought of another accident was terrifying—the shrieking brakes, the splintering glass, being thrown around the cab despite her seat belt. Sophia pulled herself away from Nadia and caught Brian's gaze. She nodded. "I can do that, park at the end of the drive. Make it a habit to check my tires."

"Here's the thing that I want you to keep your eyes out for. If someone is doing something to you and you take that something away, they don't just stop. They're going to look for another way to get to you. If you experience anything new, anything that seems off, you call me. Immediately."

Sophia reached for her bracelet, sliding her finger into the gold ring that was part of the clasp.

"Now, you were calling me when your tire blew. What did you need?"

Sophia cleared her throat. "The neighbors were all pissed at me this morning. I bought high-powered lights, thinking they would make me safer, but I was up all night with them, flashing on and off. Will Sheppard across the street was livid—even Marla around the corner, where you'd think the trees would have protected her from the light show."

Nadia squirmed forward on the seat cushion. "You didn't sleep again. You're going on three nights now." It was a stern, sisterly rebuke. "No wonder you're having seizures on the side of the road. You know better. Your doctor told you, point-blank."

"When's the last time you had a good night's sleep?" Brian asked softly.

Sophia clasped her hands in her lap like a penitent. "I was on the last dig with my father, oh so many years ago." She tried to laugh it off.

"Nadia told me that you've been diagnosed with PTSD and NEAD, and I know that sleep issues can go hand-in-hand with those diagnoses—but right now, I'm talking about you being kept up by external forces. The lights going off. The alarm…"

"She has sleep medication, but she refuses to take it because she's afraid the boys will need her."

"Sophia? How long?"

"I can't think of a time I got to sleep all the way through the night since I moved here a year ago. Something seems to happen most every night. Some of it I can explain away. Some things make no sense at all."

"Give me a for instance."

"I don't know—I can't think of anything beyond lights and

alarms at the moment. If I remember, I'll tell you. In the mean-time, if you'd help me shift the sensors on the lights to make a pet corridor, it will stop the light show. I must have had some raccoons in my yard or something. I need my neighbors to calm down."

"You think that was an animal doing that?"

"Do you have another explanation?"

11

The Panther Force door cracked open, and Lynx leaned in. "I had a few minutes, so I wanted to poke my head in and see how Sophia is doing."

"We were about to go over today's events," Brian said. "Do you have a few minutes? It would be great if you could give us your input."

Lynx stood out in the war room like a red balloon in a black-and-white photo. Her job with their fellow Iniquus team, Strike Force, included an array of hats she wore. From what Brian had seen, her main duty was to shock the system. The Iniquus environment was constructed of rigid lines and industrial chrome. The operatives and support staff wore shades of black and gray. The men in their compression shirts were able-bodied and hard, while Lynx went out of her way to look soft and pliable. Lynx wore reds and pinks in decidedly female styles. Brian had seen her work time and time again. The person who was being inter-rogated would be steeled against most of their tactics, then Lynx would walk in, sit down, and smile. She'd chat with the person, and soon there would be a font of information being shared.

Lynx was as capable in mind and body as any of the force operatives—she was the Iniquus wolf dressed in sheep's cloth-ing. And she got away with it because she was, in fact, genuinely kind.

While they waited for Thorn to show up, Brian took a minute to lay out the basics of what they knew about Sophia and why they thought she might be the one they needed to target in the case.

Nutsbe moved to pour yet another of the ubiquitous cups of coffee that fueled Iniquus. "Anyone?"

"Yes, please. Cream and sugar," Lynx said. When Nutsbe turned his back, she leaned over to talk under her breath. "This can't be easy," she reached for Brian's hands. "I saw how you looked at her. I know how affected you were by her seizure. You had a relationship with her in the past?"

Brian reached for an impassive response. Gripped it. Forced it into place.

"Brian, we were in the middle of a crisis, and you responded naturally. This isn't censure. I'm checking in on you, that's all."

Brian tried to brush it off. He liked that Lynx was tuned in when she was developing a case. Having her skills turned on him felt intrusive. "Sophia and I met one night months ago. It was a fun evening. She's a lovely woman. Yeah, I'll admit finding out she was the subject of an FBI investigation rocked me. I thought my instincts about people were pretty solid."

"I always trust my instincts." Lynx's voice was pure convic-tion. "That first impression is everything. Things can happen thirty seconds later that work to change your mind, but that first visceral emotion, that first understanding, that's the one that will bear itself out, even if someone plays a charade for years." Lynx paused. "From what I saw when the curtain was pulled back, that must have been one hell of a first impression."

Brian swallowed. Yeah, seeing Sophia walk into the hotel bar had pretty much rocked his world. His first impression was that she was *his*. His first thought was, "Well, it's about time." He hadn't stopped to examine that thought at the moment. It felt like he'd been waiting for her to show up, and boom, there she was. Easy. Natural. A done deal.

Nutsbe put a mug with a trigger handle in front of Lynx that read, "Keep Calm and Squeeze Gently." He winked at her.

"You could try," Lynx said.

Nutsbe laughed as he took his seat. "No thanks, I like the fact that my spine's intact."

They turned as Thorn made his way into the room. "Sorry. I stopped by forensics on my way here, and the tech got chatty. What have we got going on? This whole tire deal is from bizarro land." Thorn tossed a file onto the table and took a seat in their circle.

"I have a theory," Lynx said.

Nutsbe took a gulp from his mug. "I thought you might."

"Gaslighting."

Brian leaned forward. "I'm listening."

"Let's start with the PTSD first. It's significant. Sophia and Nadia were kidnapped, gone for days. Sophia developed PTSD, where Nadia did not. I'm wondering if there's any more information about the women's experiences in the FBI file, how they were treated if they were kept together. Not to say that all people come out of a traumatic experience in the same way, but I'm wondering if, as the younger of the two, or for some other reason not readily obvious, Sophia was singled out to get information from her or possibly to be turned." Lynx pinched at her bottom lip, her attention turned inward. "I would guess that Nadia recovered from the experience because she was given the opportunity to. Sophia went from the kidnapping to her father's debilitating health crisis, to her brother's motorcycle accident, to an unplanned pregnancy, to her boyfriend's head injury, to the marriage, to violence at home, to a new baby. She was overwhelmed in a very short time, and those crisis events seemed to present themselves on some kind of horrible continuum. Sure, her system went haywire this morning. Who's wouldn't?"

"Do you think she could be guilty?" Brian measured his tone carefully.

"From what little I've seen and read in her file, all the ingredients for the stew are in the pot. Possible? Absolutely. She's a woman in crisis, and where that crisis would cause her to react one way as an individual—as a mother of two small children, the only family they have, she would have to feel desperate. Is her guilt probable? I just don't know. I wouldn't think so—but people with their necks under the guillotine will do improbable things to extricate themselves."

Brian flashed back to the garage when he'd offered his car for Sophia to use to pick up Chance. She'd said, "Desperate times mean desperate measures," like it was her mantra.

"I'm surprised the woman can walk and talk, let alone be so high-functioning. As you're working through this case, your team needs to be aware of how fragile she is." Lynx pulled out a printed list and laid it where the men could get eyes on. "When I got back to Iniquus this morning, Nutsbe let me peek at the intake file he's compiling. I was looking for stressors to apply to the Holmes and Rahe stress scale. That's a scale put together after they studied about five thousand medical files, trying to pinpoint a correlation between illness and life events. They developed a chart with forty-three stressors—some could be read as positive, like a new job or a pregnancy. Others are obviously devastating, like the death of a spouse. The forty-three stressors were each given a numeric weight. The death of a close family member, for example, is worth sixty-three points. It turned out that if a patient scored over three-hundred on their table in a year's time, it was predictive of a serious illness."

Brian scanned down the list while he listened. Change in financial status, thirty-eight points, housing issues, thirty, troubles with in-laws, twenty-nine, end of school, twenty-six, change of living conditions, twenty-five, change in residence, twenty, change in sleeping habits, sixteen… Five-fifty-five plus. He put his finger on the total. "What happens when you get to five-fifty-five plus?"

"She has a much higher number than that. I was getting depressed, just tabulating it. First, you should know that that number happened over the last five years. I didn't try to break it down to individual years because stress is accumulative. Also, PTSD and NEAD seizures have their own physical and mental impact. What I wanted you to see here is that your client, who is also the subject of your investigation, is walking a tightrope. She could lose her balance and fall at any time."

Brian's physical reaction to that statement surprised the hell out of him. It was as if he grew and expanded, his nostrils flared, and he wanted to race forward, smashing and destroying anything and everything that put Sophia and her boys in harm's way. He squashed those feelings down when Lynx turned her perceptive gaze on him. He needed to stay in this game, and the truth about his feelings for Sophia could easily get him sidelined. "You used the word gaslighting before."

"I'm curious about her series of flat tires. It is certainly a weird way to try to kill someone but think about the impact.

Right off the top, there's the cost of replacements, the inconvenience. Dig deeper, and there's the sense that whenever you drive, there's the additional threat of losing control of your car, your safety, the safety of the children, the chance that you'll hurt others and incur more significant costs. June of last year, the family was in a car accident."

"It totaled the car," Nutsbe said. "The mother-in-law, Jane Campbell, sustained injuries that led to her death six months later. Sophia incurred hospital bills for herself and the boys." Nutsbe rubbed his thumb across his chin. "The thought of a car accident would have a specific and significant impact on her since she survived one."

"It also led to her moving to the high-stress neighborhood." Thorn tapped the file he'd brought in. "Forensics concludes that the metal found in Sophia's tires on Monday and those found today are from the same source. They sent an investigator to follow the route that Sophia took from the time the mechanics put the GPS tracker on her car. The team couldn't find anything that would pose a threat. There's no construction on that route. Forensics was able to lift fingerprints from all three pieces, and they are all the same. There are no matching prints in the database."

"So she's been targeted," Nutsbe said.

"But why?" Lynx opened the file and scanned through the information. "Gaslighting happens when someone uses psychological means to make you question your sanity. It's not the perfect definition for this particular circumstance. What the tires are doing—along with her lights going off and on for three hours straight—is keeping Sophia in a chronic state of fight or flight. Adrenaline, cortisol—it's like living in a war zone, but no bombs are dropping, so she keeps trying to convince herself everything's fine...normal. It isn't. This creates cognitive dissonance

—her internal and external cues are in conflict, which in turn lights up her limbic system, makes her body respond as if her life were on the line."

"I had a hard time convincing her that someone was popping her tires on purpose. She said she was jinxed," Brian said.

"Exactly my point, her brain can't process with clarity and dispassion. Flat tires being bad luck she can handle, flat tires being caused by someone who might have the power to hurt her or her children? Crazy-making."

They all sat silently, processing the information.

Lynx picked up a pen and drew a dollar sign on the corner of her paper. "Nutsbe said Sophia ran up an almost four-thousand-dollar bill with the police department when someone rattled her door at *exactly* the same time each night."

"You'd think after a few nights, the duty cop would catch a clue and set himself up to see who it was," Thorn said.

"Why? They knew they were making easy money for the department," Nutsbe scoffed.

"That's damned cynical." Thorn pointed at Lynx. "But to your point, a single young mother, home alone, not counting all the other stressors that put her over the five-hundred mark, thinking your home might not be secure, that you can't afford to have the alarm connected to the police, feeling vulnerable? If I were Sophia, I'd want to get myself out of that situation, STAT."

"I would guess that the only thing holding her back from moving to a safer place is money. And again, as a single mom of two kids under four years old, that's got to play into her every choice," Thorn said.

"She's in survival mode." Brian was staring at the floor between his feet. He needed to find a way to get things calmer in Sophia's life. Give her a chance to think and make better decisions. Maybe they could turn her into an asset and keep her out of jail. That was *if* she *was* guilty. Even though the narrative continued to build against her, even if this psychological war she was fighting did give her motive, Brian couldn't believe that Sophia would do anything that supported terror. "Would Sophia really help to fund ISIS? They're bombing cities and killing little kids like hers every day. Would she help Assad do that? It seemed antithetical to her life's mission."

"*If* she's culpable, and that's a big if, I'd imagine she's in it for self-preservation. I'm not getting a good read on her—her body language, her facial expressions, her macro and micro tells. To be honest, her limbic system is lit up so bright, it's hard to get a good assessment."

"Nadia said Sophia hadn't had a seizure in over a year. That must mean that her mental and physical systems were faltering this morning," Brian said.

"If I'd been riding that shitstorm for as long as she has, I'd do whatever it took to get myself out of that mess. I can't say that the idea of some quick money wouldn't be too enticing to let pass by," Nutsbe offered as if that scenario was a done deal.

"I'm thinking about my teammate Jack and his fiancée Suz right now," Lynx said. "In February, they got caught up in an Eastern European terror plot when a senator was the victim of a tiger kidnapping, where a family is kidnapped and one of the parents, for example, is forced to take some horrible action to save their children. Whereas people might have the fortitude to allow themselves to be hurt or killed rather than go against their moral compass, it's quite another thing when your loved ones are the ones who would suffer the repercussions. Do you remember when that London delivery driver whose van was filled with explosives rammed into a police department because the kidnappers had his family? The driver ran before the bomb detonated, only to find out his family had been murdered as soon as the task was accomplished. My point here being, this everyday-Joe was willing to kill and maim dozens of people because the kidnappers had the speakerphone on when they broke his son's knees. Those screams, knowing his daughter was next—all reason went out the window." Lynx raised her brows and tilted her head.

"They'd need some kind of pressure, something that gave them leverage over her," Brian said.

Lynx nodded. As she thought, her lips pursed, and she wiggled her mouth from side to side. "This could be the convergence of multiple stressors in some kind of perfect storm. It could be that someone's running Sophia and knows exactly what they're doing, keeping the heat turned up to the boiling point. It could also be that the looks are deceiving, and Sophia has nothing at all to do with the sale of antiquities to fund terror." She stood. "It's an interesting puzzle. I hope you'll keep me in the loop." Looking around at the men, she said, "I'm going to tell you right now, though, Sophia's in danger. Her seizure was a major warning sign." She turned to focus on Brian. "I'd watch for any sudden shifts in behavior. She could be at risk of hurting herself, and maybe even the boys."

Brian's brow drew tight. "Wait. Are you saying she might be suicidal?"

Lynx laid a hand on his arm, and Brian felt warmth spreading out, radiating toward his shoulder; it had an instant calming effect. "I'm not a psychologist. It might be a good idea to run this by our psych department. I'm just saying that she has a known diagnosis. One of the risks of PTSD is suicide. And if someone you know commits suicide, like her husband attempted, the chances go up multifold. Do what you can to take her stress level down. Try to make her feel she has a better level of security. Something has to give, or you're at risk of losing a major player in this case."

"You're serious." Brian's scalp prickled, sending a line of cold down his spine.

"Oh, absolutely." She lifted her eyebrows for emphasis. "I'm sorry, I have to head out now. I'm expected in a meeting." She stood. "Good luck. Let me know if there's anything I can do to help." She turned and walked out.

"Huh," Nutsbe grunted, his eye fixed on the door as it swung closed. He turned his attention back to his teammates. "Have you ever known Lynx to be wrong?"

Brian ran his tongue over his teeth. "Nope."

"Here's a question," Thorn said. "Let's assume for a minute, Sophia is culpable—that someone has some kind of control over her and is exploiting her personal situation—do you think we could turn her? I mean, it seems to me that Sophia is a small fish. Beyond making her an example and trying to scare private buyers, why would the FBI be investing this much money in taking down an archaeologist? Are they going after AACP, do you think? My opinion is that we don't have the whole picture."

"We need to keep our eyes open. Lynx is right, though. I think one way or another we have to shake some of the monkeys off Sophia's back," Brian said, glad that it was Thorn who had brought up making Sophia an asset. "Thorn, can you call Nadia and take her and Sophia out to dinner? I want to get some more equipment in place—especially an infrared alarm on Sophia's perimeter that will signal me whenever someone moves onto the property. I need to get the thermal cameras in place outside. It won't take me long, but I need Sophia off property. I can join you later at the restaurant."

"I'd need an excuse."

"We got word from AACP that the Peru expedition is set for some time in mid-July," Nutsbe said. "Tell them you want to gather some basic information about what they've got going on down there."

"All right." Thorn pulled his phone from his thigh pocket and flicked through his contacts. "Maybe we can also talk to Sophia about alternative housing choices. Maybe suggest she spend a few nights at a hotel."

"Yep. But if we can't convince her to do that, I'm going to stay the night at her place, at least for tonight."

"Sounds like a plan," Nutsbe said. "But what if she says no?"

12

Wednesday p.m.

"Four, please," Thorn told the hostess. "We have someone joining us later."

The group trailed their way to a booth toward the back of the restaurant. Sophia was glad to be out of her house and to have a chance to unwind a bit. Lana, a sister of the heart if not biology, had taken the boys for a few days. Actually, Nadia and Lana had ganged up on her, refusing to let her keep her boys overnight until they thought she'd rested enough not to be at risk of another seizure. Sophia didn't like the idea of her sons being away from her, but pragmatism won out. She needed to take medication and sleep. Nadia was right; two or three nights of deep sleep might restore her. The seizures were too dangerous. They'd sometimes trigger with a thought, a smell, a movement, and they left her babies completely unsupervised. What if she were cooking and she started a fire, or they were in the bath alone?

Nadia turned and blocked her way. "Let's go somewhere else," she whispered, catching Sophia's arms.

"Why? We like it here." Sophia looked over Nadia's shoulder and saw Marla at a table with a group of women she didn't recognize. A pitcher of margaritas sat almost empty in the middle of the table. Sophia leaned in to whisper in Nadia's ear. "My therapist said to do nothing that gives her power, ignore her as much as humanly possible, and be neutral. Sociopaths feed off those who show any weakness to make themselves feel powerful. So, we move to our table. We sit down. We ignore her completely, or we embolden her."

"Is everything okay?" Thorn put his hand on Sophia's back and leaned in.

"Peachy." Nadia smiled and turned back to the hostess, who gestured them toward their seats. Luckily, they were a comfortable distance from Marla and her entourage.

Thorn gestured for Nadia to slide in, and he took the outside seat, facing the restaurant. Sophia slipped in on the other side, happy that she was out of Marla's view. The hostess mentioned the day's specials and moved away.

"All right, now can you tell me what's up?"

"Sophia's neighbor, Marla the sociopath, is here. You should be ready for something nuts to happen."

Thorn shifted his gaze to Sophia as he took Nadia's words seriously. "She's been diagnosed? She's a known sociopath?"

"I have no idea," Sophia said under her breath. "I described her actions to my therapist, and he diagnosed her in absentia in order to give me some coping strategies."

Thorn raised his menu, but Sophia could tell he was using it as a tactic to observe Marla's table. "This is the chick who sits on her car in her bikini for hours on end?"

"Yup. Insane." Nadia put her menu down. "I'm getting the usual. When is Brian getting here?"

"Probably by the time our food arrives." He glanced at the time readout on his phone. "I'll order for him." A spitball landed on Thorn's menu. He stared down at it. "Really?"

Sophia reached out and laid her hand on Thorn's. "We're going to ignore her completely. Let's talk about Peru. Did you see the report that came in? The mystery was solved. How cool is that?"

Thorn looked at Nadia

"Puquios. Heard of them?"

"No, sorry. Is that what you're getting to eat?

"Ha, you must be hungry." Nadia looked through her lashes at Thorn, running her fingers through her hair.

Was she flirting? Sophia wondered with amusement. Well, Nadia always had a thing for bad boys. Thorn missed the flirtation, though. He had been scanning the menu. Sophia tucked that little scene away to tease her about later.

"Puquios are enormous holes dug into the earth. The mystery of why they existed was an important question that was recently solved from space. Tada!" Nadia stopped to indulge in a self-satisfied smile. "There's a region in Peru called Nazca that is famous for something called the Nazca lines. Ancient people developed these enormous carvings in the landscape. They've found ceremonial burial areas and signs of a complex society. The thing that perplexed archaeologists was how the ancient people were able to not only survive but to flourish. We can tell from research that droughts in the area could last for years. It turns out that those big holes in the ground created a complex hydraulic system that pulled water from underground aquifers, turning the inhospitable region into one where their society could thrive."

"Satellite imagery to the rescue," Sophia said. "The information helped archaeologists and anthropologists see how the Puquios were distributed across the Nazca region. How they were situated compared to the various settlements."

"Is that where we're headed?" Thorn put the menu down and signaled the waitress.

"It's a bit farther from where we're setting our study, but I'm planning a quick side trip to see the Puquios in person." Sophia leaned back as the server came to take their order and collect the menus. When Sophia ordered a glass of wine with her meal, Nadia leaned in to whisper that she shouldn't mix her sleeping pill with alcohol. And alcohol on its own would disturb her sleep. Sophia turned to the waitress. "Make that a water instead, please." Though a glass of wine might stop her nerves from buzzing. Marla, in such close proximity, set off her danger sirens. She wished the ladies' night out table would finish up and leave.

Nadia opened the cloth covering the basket of steaming rolls the server had left to tide them over, passing them around before she helped herself. "We have a colleague, Alejandro, who grew up in both America and Peru. When he was a little boy, his grandparents would tell him about the Spanish conquistadors looking for gold. The Spaniards wanted to go into the Amazon to find their fortunes, but the locals warned them that there were man-eating snakes, wildcats that stalked their prey and pounced without warning, and rivers that could cook a man with their boiling waters. Of course, these were just bedtime stories for him like *Little Red Riding Hood* or *Winnie the Pooh*."

"Until they weren't," Sophia said.

Another spitball hit the table, and before Thorn responded, Sophia said, "Look at me. Smile. Give a little laugh. She has no power at this table."

Thorn did as she asked, and Sophia relaxed a little. The last thing she needed was for GI Joe to go over and flex his muscles. "Alejandro was with his in-laws having dinner when he told his nephews the story about the conquistadors. His wife's aunt says, 'I've been there, it's absolutely beautiful.'"

"Where? The boiling river?" Thorn leaned in.

"Yes, it's so hot that if an animal falls in, it cooks right there. The locals use the river like an automatic hot water dispenser. They cook their food. They do their laundry. They bathe. It's an incredible resource for them."

"You'd think it would be a huge tourist destination. Why haven't I heard of it?"

"The locals don't want the intrusion of the modern world," Nadia explained. "They recall the stories of the destruction and illnesses that outsiders brought to the South American peoples. They're content to be quiet about it."

"Alejandro respects their decision. The AACP does as well. We're going into the area very quietly, with the blessing of the village shaman—small footprint. Our archaeological inquiry will be under the radar, so to speak. We absolutely do not want to be disruptive to the native peoples. But we *do* want to get some answers to greater questions, like those discovered at the Puquios."

"Wait, I thought you were Middle Eastern specialists," Thorn said, sitting back to let the server distribute their drinks.

"In a way, that's true. But we're not the ones who will be doing the excavation. We're simply going in to lay grid lines and drill core samples to see if what was found with satellite technology can be verified. You remember my telling you about the beta searchers—the novices we had trying out our system we hope to open to the interested—" Nadia turned toward Thorn. "What did your colleague call it?"

"Armchair archeologists," Sophia responded before taking a sip of her water.

"That's right." Nadia stuck her hand in the air with a little wave. "Here comes Brian. Anyway, several of the beta testers pointed out this particular area as interesting. Sophia and I agree. It'll be good to get out of our desk chairs and into a jungle. Clear our heads."

Brian arrived and, with a nod, slipped into the bench seat next to Sophia. The seat was narrower than it looked, and Sophia found herself hip to hip, thigh to thigh against the sheer size of Brian Ackerman.

"I ordered you a steak." Thorn pushed Brian's glass of water over to him.

"Thanks. What did I miss?"

Another spitball landed on the table with a splat. Thorn and Brian stared at it. "Really?" Brian asked.

"Since we've been here." Thorn quirked a derisive brow. "We've been following Sophia's advice from her therapist and not giving the sociopath the satisfaction of a response."

Brian turned bright blue eyes and a warm smile her way. "How are you doing?"

Sophia wished the booths in this restaurant were a little bigger, that there was more space between them. She wished he didn't smell like lemon soap. It reminded her of her days back before she went on the dig that turned her life to hell.

"Sophia!" Marla yelled. "Sophia!"

"Holy hell, she's coming this way." Nadia shifted in her seat, planting her elbows on the table and hiding her face behind her curtain of long black hair.

Brian reached for Sophia and pulled her into a kiss.

"Sophia's busy at the moment." Laughter bubbled up with Thorn's words. "Can I take a message?"

After a moment, Nadia whispered, "She's gone now."

Brian released her. He blinked several times like he'd been thrown off-kilter. That's exactly how Sophia felt. "Sorry," he muttered. "It was all I could think of, spur of the moment."

The blush painting over Sophia's face burned her cheeks. She turned and drank down her glass of water. Brian touching her and kissing her *wasn't* okay. She had torn herself away from him the night they met in order to protect him. Every step he got closer to her, the more endangered he became. She needed to get him away from her, out of her life. But even if he wasn't assigned to her directly, he'd still be on the team. Short of quitting her job, Sophia couldn't think of a way out of this predicament. She reached up and twisted her gold bracelet around and around her wrist.

"That woman is not normal." Thorn unwrapped his cutlery from his napkin.

"That's an understatement," Nadia said, following suit.

Brian's, "Are you all right?" was interrupted when the server arrived with their plates.

No, Sophia thought, I'm not all right at all.

13
_____

BRIAN
   Wednesday p.m.

Brian excused himself from the table when his phone pinged. Someone had passed through the infrared sensor he had just established around Sophia's house. Outside, under the buzz of the flickering parking lot light, he opened his phone app to see Nadia's sister, Lana, climbing out of her van and going into the house. She moved into the far corner of the living room, standing beside the curio cabinet, texting. Then she went into the den to pick up what Sophia had told him was Chance's "wubby"—a beloved and well-chewed stuffed rabbit. He waited until Lana had pulled out of the drive before he headed back toward the restaurant. As he sauntered up the sidewalk, Thorn and the women pushed through the restaurant door, walking through the gentle warmth of the night toward Sophia's van. Brian cut across the lot, timing it, so he arrived as they did and joined the huddle of goodbyes.

"Sophia, Nadia told me you were planning on taking a sleeping pill tonight that's pretty potent." Brian pushed his hands into his pockets and rocked back on his heels. "It's dangerous to sleep at your place alone. If there were an emergency—a fire, or what have you, you wouldn't be able to respond. Nadia has plans tonight with some friends that include drinking, so she'll probably end up staying at one of their apartments. Do you have someone else you could call to stay the night with you?" Brian held his breath, hoping that he'd left it until too short a notice to get anyone else to come over.

Sophia shook her head. "I don't have anyone to call, and anyway, I wouldn't dream of imposing on one of my friends. I don't need babysitting. I'm a grown woman, for heaven's sake. The boys are safe with Lana. That's my only worry."

"I'm going to stay with you then. I'll crash on the couch." Brian used a specific tone of voice to deliver that information. He'd learned this trick when he was in Iraq, needed compliance, and had a limited vocabulary to make it happen.

Sophia gave another little shake of her head, looking confused.

Thankfully, Nadia got involved. "Oh, Brian, would you?" She put her hand on his arm. "That would make me feel a thousand times better." She pressed her fist to her heart. "I've been torn about this all day. I have a friend going through a breakup, and she needs me, but then so does Sophia."

"I don't need a babysitter," Sophia said again.

Both Brian and Nadia pretended not to have heard her.

"Are the boys coming back in the morning?" Brian asked.

"No, Sophia has to catch up on her sleep, the doctor suggested five uninterrupted nights, so Lana is keeping Sophia's kids until Monday to give her the time she needs. But we'll all be together on Saturday when the community pool is having its potluck. Do you think you could stay with her through the week-end?" She turned to Sophia when Sophia pinched her arm. "Ouch!"

"Nadia! You've not my mother, arranging a sleepover. I'm not a baby, and I'm *Standing. Right. Here.*" Sophia's dark-chocolate eyes were vivid with anger.

"I'm sorry, Sophia," Brian said. "I don't want you to feel disrespected, but I've been doing this kind of work for a long time. I've been around when people have been through hell. I know, for a fact, they can make bad decisions while under extreme stress. Choices that put them and others at risk. Crazy things like not being able to sleep for days and deciding to go for a drive—that's what killed a man I was tasked with protecting. I bear the weight of that death to this day. I'm just glad he didn't hurt someone else that night." They were toe-to-toe, looking into each other's eyes. Brian desperately wanted to touch her, wanted to run his hands down her arms, gather her close, so her cheek rested against his heart, wanted to kiss her hair, and take her home. He blocked those feelings, knowing that stupid-as-hell kiss in the restaurant, while effective in getting Marla to move on, might have been a fatal error. If she reported it, Brian would be off the case. Period. Maybe even out of a job. "I want you to rest. I want you to know you're safe while you sleep. My hitting the rack on your couch doesn't inconvenience me—it's part of my job."

"It's not you who would be inconvenienced," Sophia muttered so softly, Brian almost missed her words.

"My teammate dropped me off earlier. I'll drive your van home." He held out his hand for her keys.

"Don't you need a bag or something?" Sophia was obviously grasping at straws.

"Nope, I left one at your house earlier." He waved his hand for her keys, which she reluctantly handed over to him.

Sophia looked thoroughly deflated as she turned to kiss Nadia on the cheek and then moved toward the van's passenger seat.

Brian felt victorious.

The restaurant was only five miles from Sophia's house. Sophia had scrunched herself over toward the door as if to create more space between them. Brian had his eye on the rearview mirror. A car had pulled up on his tail so close that it looked like they were sitting in the backseat. He pushed the gas down, and the person behind him held tight. Brian wouldn't be surprised if they were touching bumpers. A passing car lit up the other driver's face as they passed. Marla. Son of a bitch.

"Sophia, do you have trouble with Marla riding your bumper?"

"All the time." Her forehead was resting on the window. She seemed unaware that they were being followed. "I can't slow down when she does that. One false move and it would be a car accident. She scares me. I don't know what she's capable of— how far she'd push things. My therapist says there's no way to tell in advance. That doesn't help my anxiety."

"I'm sure it doesn't."

"I've talked to the police about it, and they just shrug their shoulders. They think she needs to cause me harm before they can do anything." Sophia sat up and turned around to see Marla behind them. "It's uncanny how she always seems to find me."

Brian whipped the car to the right and slammed on the brakes, reaching out his hand to steady Sophia. Marla flew on by. Brian yanked the wheel to the left and got right on Marla's bumper as he followed her all the way home. "*This*, Sophia, is against the law. It endangers you and your kids."

Sophia was gripping at the door handle. "Then why are you doing it?"

"Giving her a taste of her own medicine." Brian stopped at the top of Sophia's drive, where he wanted Sophia to park from now on. "Wait here."

Marla had turned in the cul-de-sac and parked in front of the Sheppards' house, jumped from her car, and was racing toward the van with her fists up like she was ready to rumble. It would have been laughable, except this woman thought she was coming to pummel Sophia. Brian stepped out of the van and put his hands on his hips. He had the woman by eight inches, a good sixty pounds of muscle, and the fierce hand-to-hand combat training of his Marine anti-terrorism unit. Marla came to a screeching halt, and her mouth hung open with shock. She looked toward the van, but Brian moved into her line of sight so she wouldn't see Sophia. He didn't say a word. He didn't have to; his body radiated hostility. Marla turned on her heels and beat a fast retreat. He watched her until she was all the way home.

Brian walked around the back of the van, stowing his combat energy. Sophia needed calm. By the time he opened the passenger door for her, he was fully back to his impassive guise. "This is where you park."

"Got it," she said. A few steps later, she stopped him with a hand on his arm. "Is this a good idea?" she asked.

"I wouldn't be here if I didn't think so."

"I need to make sure that we're clear on this, especially after you kissed me."

Brian wasn't about to mention that she'd kissed him back.

"I'm not interested in having a relationship with you outside of my capacity with AACP and the need to have security in place. That I'm even considering letting you into my house to spend the night is against my better judgment. I only agree to this," Sophia shook her finger at him, "because Nadia needs to be with her friend. And I don't want her to feel conflicted or guilty because of me." She moved her hands to her hips and squinted her eyes. "This isn't your job. Your job is to secure us while we're on our expedition. Why are you here, exactly?"

"So Nadia doesn't feel guilty." Brian sent her his most winning grin.

Sophia let out a huff, spun on her heels, climbed the stairs, and stuck her key into the lock. "This is so damned awkward."

"That's not my intention," he said sincerely.

She walked in and flicked on the lights. "I know it's not." She turned, and the look in her eyes tore at him. "I owe you an apology. I'm having trouble being around you because I feel guilty. I left you without an explanation or a goodbye. Please trust me when I say I was trying to keep you safe. I hope you can forgive me. It was a wonderful night. An amazing birthday. And it's also over. Done."

Brian was caught on the fact that she said she'd left to protect him. It was an odd turn of phrase— "trying to keep you safe." It was hard to listen to the regret that he heard up until she said an "amazing birthday," then her tone turned to stone-cold finality. "Apology accepted," Brian said without a shade of emotion. "I'm glad we've come to an understanding, so we can move forward. Right now, that looks like a pillow and blanket for the couch, please."

Sophia huffed out the breath she'd held while he spoke. She glanced up the stairs, then looked to her curio cabinet and seemed to focus on a crystal goblet for an over-long time. She turned her beautiful eyes on him, soft and sad. "I have a guest room. Upstairs. End of the hall. Linens are in the bathroom, next door on the right."

They both spun around as the front door crashed open.

"What the hell are you two doing in my house?" a man bellowed, holding his walking stick like a bat. His face was livid red.

Brian swung his foot in front of Sophia, creating a barricade with his body. But Sophia pushed around him.

"Mr. Rochester. My name is Sophia Abadi. I live in this house now. You live next door with your son, Joe."

"Joe?"

"Your son, Joe. Let's walk over, and you can talk to Joe."

"But this is my house."

"You're right, Mr. Rochester. This is your house. But Joe is playing next door. We need to go get him. It's past his bedtime, don't you think? Come on, I'll walk with you to get Joe."

The man spun to face Brian. "I'm not leaving this hoodlum in my house!"

"Of course not, Mr. Rochester, he's coming with us. He wants to say hi to your son. Joe's waiting for you." Sophia gingerly took the old man's arm and started him across the grass between the two houses.

They were halfway across the open space when they moved in front of a pine tree, a white bucket filled with engine parts sat beside the open hood of the Buick. Rochester sauntered up and unzipped his pants. Sophia waited patiently as the man pulled out his dick and took a piss. Whoever owned that car was going to be in for one hell of a surprise. Rochester stuffed himself into his shorts, then undid his belt and button so he could get his shirt tucked neatly in place. Brian kept his distance, hoping he was forgotten. The last thing he needed was to have this man try to fistfight him.

Sophia smiled. "This way, Mr. Rochester, let's go collect Joe." She rang the bell and delivered Mr. Rochester to his family.

———

"You handled that well," Brian said as they headed back to her place.

"My dad has dementia. I've had a little experience."

They climbed the stairs, and Brian stopped himself from putting his hand on the small of her back to guide her in. As a matter of fact, he was consciously keeping a fair amount of distance between the two of them, hoping it would make Sophia feel more comfortable.

"My heart goes out to families who are trying to care for their loved ones. I wish I could take some of the burdens off my mom. But my being near her would just increase the problems. Better that I stay away." Resignation filled her voice. Her shoulders drooped. That unexpected visitor seemed to take the last of her strength.

Still, Brian needed to know. "Does that often happen, Mr. Rochester coming in your house?"

"Yes, well, he lived here when it was built. When he was first diagnosed, his son moved in next door to be close to his father, but as the disease incapacitated him, they moved him in with them. My in-laws bought this house from Mr. Rochester. In his confusion, this is where he thinks he belongs. He lived here for over forty years. I understand the situation. I just have to do a good job of keeping the doors locked."

"Sophia," Brian said softly. "Take your pill and go to bed. Sleep."

Sophia nodded and dragged herself to her room.

14

"Nutsbe, can you do a search on Marla Richards in connection with the AACP case?" Brian asked. The three teammates assigned to the case had gathered ten minutes early to put their cards on the table before their FBI counterparts showed up for a meeting.

"Got anything else?"

"An address." Brian pulled out his phone and texted the information to Nutsbe. "Looks like Sophia Abadi has a stalker."

"Seriously?"

"Marla's actions are serious enough that Sophia's taken it to her therapist," Thorn said. "The therapist is advising Sophia to treat the woman as a sociopathic threat."

"That's fucked up—but how does Richards tie into the AACP?"

"Interesting coincidence." Brian crossed his ankle over his

knee and scrunched lower in his seat. "Sophia gave me a time-line of the car accident that we already have in her file, followed by the move, immediately followed by her tires blowing. Within a week of Sophia moving, the empty house at the entrance of her neighborhood was rented. A week after that, Marla Richards was on scene with her sights set on Sophia."

"Sophia made that correlation?"

"Sophia's so far down the rabbit hole, she's just swatting at the next crisis. She can't see a broader picture—heck, I'm not even sure there *is* a broader picture. It would be good to have background on the woman in case she was shipped in to gaslight Sophia."

"But not Nadia?" Nutsbe asked, his fingers tapping across his keyboard.

"Nadia isn't a good candidate for gaslighting—her stress history is clean," Thorn said. "Her dad had a stroke five years ago. Other than that, it's the normal everyday shit of modern life."

"No love interest?"

"Nothing significant, and it doesn't look like she's looking." Thorn rotated his pen through his fingers at a hypnotizing speed. "To talk to her, she seems generally satisfied with how things are going. She gets her baby fix when she's with Lana and Sophia's kids. When she gets tired of them, she leaves. She has a handful of close friends. She dates on occasion. When she's not working, she goes to the gym. She reads." He looked up. "What's this meeting with the FBI about? Anyone have a heads up?"

"Nada," Nutsbe said. "Okay, so this is interesting. The house Marla is in is owned by Pierre Richards, a plastics engineer from Toronto, Canada. He's here on a work visa. He's single, with no children, according to his papers. The visa was issued right before the car accident. Anything seem odd about that accident?"

"I looked over the reports," Brian said. "Guy had a heart attack, caught them broadside. He died at the scene with no insurance and no assets. So the Pierre Richards visa lists no dependents? I've seen two kids at that house, young, maybe three and five years old."

"I have nothing in the database on a Marla Richards at that address. Not even a driver's license in the state of Virginia. Have you seen the husband around, Brainiack?"

"Nope."

"Okay, this looks like it bears further investigation. I'm on it."

Titus arrived and held the door wide. Andersson strode purposefully across the room, followed by Finley. The Panther Force operatives rose respectfully while the special agents took their seats.

Once everyone had gathered in a loose circle, Titus said, "Gentlemen, you've had a couple of days now with our suspects. Are you starting to get a clearer picture of the players?"

Brian knew if they shared the data they had collected so far, the spotlight would shine on Sophia. It was a trap. Once an investigation honed in on a player, the brain worked to see all evidence as a link and an affirmation. Sure, if he had to pick one of the two, Sophia had all the branding for a perp walk. Maybe Nadia seemed *too* clean. Maybe she hid behind the fact that if authorities were looking at the partners, she would look wholesome, while Sophia looked vulnerable to recruitment pressure.

While Brian didn't reject the concept of Nadia using Sophia as a scapegoat, it seemed farfetched. Lana and Nadia both supported and, he believed, loved Sophia. There was a palpable sisterly bond. "We'd like to get a better understanding of this investigation. It would help us to understand the net you're casting, so we can identify any possible links to move the case forward." Brian dodged and wove away from the tackle, trying to pass the ball in a different direction.

Andersson caught Finley's attention. "I'll take the art side." She cleared her throat and smoothed her hand over her trousers to remove a non-existent wrinkle. "Private collectors here in America, such as the Gilchrest family, are one aspect of the illicit market that we've discussed. We're also seeing conflict antiquities show up in auction houses. Once the pieces move from terrorists to shipping to private homes, it's hard to find the pieces again. However, they often resurface when, for example, Christie's publicly displays a piece for auction."

"That seems like a hell of a gamble to put trafficked goods up for auction," Thorn said.

"It could take a business down if the seller hasn't sufficiently laundered the piece. However, from the FBI's point of view, it's all but impossible to prove in a court of law that the artifact was freshly dug up. The more recently the piece was unearthed, the safer it is. There's no prior history, probably not even a record that it exists, certainly no way that we can prove that it was acquired illegally."

"Are there industry standards to prevent the auction houses from selling black market goods? Guidelines? Why would they take such a risk?" Nutsbe moved from his computer station to sit in the circle with the others.

"We talked about how lucrative it is for ISIS to steal and sell artifacts," Andersson said. "But in the Western arts market, there is a far higher profit to be made from the sale and resale of illicit antiquities. Let me give you Cambodia as an example. When the government fought against the Khmer Rouge, thousands of art pieces were stolen. According to research, in a seven-year span, from 1998 to 2005, Sotheby's sold more than three hundred of those pieces. AACP and other international art and museum organizations developed what they call red lists to address this issue. The first was for Cambodia, but they've also developed lists for Egypt, Peru, Afghanistan, and a handful of other countries since then. An emergency list was created several years ago for Syria. The AACP was a powerful force behind that list, and that list is one of the things that Nadia and Sophia are charged with maintaining. You could see how their positions would give them a unique opportunity to manipulate what can be sold and what is listed as hot, and therefore not saleable—or displayable, for that matter. From the art side of the investigation, we don't want these items in the mainstream, turning high profits and encouraging the continuing tide of illegal artifacts pouring into the country."

"My focus is on terror," Finley said. "Stopping ISIS from getting its three-mil-a-day bankroll would go far in shutting them down. Traffickers are entrepreneurs. They know that to stay in business, they must A) maintain a supply chain of looted artifacts and B) have a buyer who doesn't give a flying flip about the piece's origin. The traffickers also know that they have to stay ahead of the law. They shift their routes and methods, continually evolving their tactics to avoid detection.

"Bribery, fake documentation, finding different carrier systems, are all ways to get the artifacts out of the conflict area and into the US. And what makes it an even harder task to shut down the illicit sales is that the smugglers know that the punishments are basically a slap on the wrist at the end of the day. In our last meeting, we told you that the Gilchrests are looking at a fine and the confiscation of the contested items. That's it.

"And that's why we're not trying to prove art theft. It's not worth spending our limited resources. Since the Syrian pieces have a direct link to funding ISIS, we're going for terror charges. Big headlines. Long prison sentences. We want to frighten anyone and everyone that we can pinpoint as having anything to do with the sale of these artifacts. Going back to the business model, we don't see any way to shut down the supply side of the relationship. We have to go after the buyers, and those who are complicit in getting the items into the hands of the buyers."

"Okay, and so how do you read that directive in terms of Nadia and Sophia? Do you want them in a jail cell? Headlines reading: *Eminent Archaeologists Jailed for Aiding ISIS*? Or do you need them to supply information?" Titus asked.

"Both. Either. We got Iniquus involved because we simply don't have the manpower to determine their roles. Right now, we only know they have unique qualifications, unique access. What's our end goal here? Well, we're waiting to see what roles Nadia and Sophia are playing in these crimes."

"If any," Thorn said before Brian could get his mouth open.

Brian wondered if Thorn was as doubtful about this fishing expedition as he was.

Finley shot a speculative look Thorn's way. "You think they're innocent?"

"They're passionate about their jobs. Both Sophia and Nadia light up when they talk about what they do. Are there questions? Sure. Do I think this bears further investigation? Absolutely. But I haven't come to any conclusions yet."

"Our next step might help to make things clearer. We've set up a sting," Andersson said.

Okay, good, Brian thought, leaning forward and resting his forearms on his knees. Thorn struck the same pose.

Brian had found the space between being a protector and an investigator an uncomfortable squeeze. It wasn't an impossible task—when he was in Iraq, he always knew that the people he depended on had no real loyalties to him and his team. People in crisis blew with the prevailing winds. If he was expedient in keeping them alive today, they might just as easily find the Taliban helped them survive the next day. He learned to be wary. Distrustful. To question. To arm himself with a healthy dose of skepticism. And to walk that tightrope. In the Middle East, losing your balance was life or death. And if he was honest with himself and listened to that little voice he'd been pushing down, he'd admit that this task seemed equally perilous—though it was his heart, not his life, that was in danger.

"We've recruited an AACP contact in Syria. We gave them two pieces that would appeal in particular to the Gilchrest family."

"Where did you get these pieces?" Nutsbe asked.

"They were identified and acquired by our assets," Andersson said. "Tracking units have been put on the pieces."

"Surely the traffickers aren't that stupid. They'd do a sweep looking for that kind of thing. They're bound to know they're on your radar."

Andersson tipped her head toward Nutsbe. "He's right. We've tried and failed to follow the routes by planting simple trackers on pieces. However, it's not a fruitless effort even if the trackers are found. It forces the black marketers to change their trade routes. From our experience, though, we have a good chance of going undetected this time. It's only on rare occasions that anyone checks. And we're using a new technology that thwarts the basic tools for finding the GPS signal. We're banking on the traffickers being rather low tech if they do a sweep."

"How does this lead back to Nadia and Sophia?" Brian asked.

"Sunday night, information was sent separately to Nadia and Sophia about a unique piece that we've assigned to each woman —a marble slab for Sophia and a mosaic for Nadia—that would appeal specifically to the Gilchrest family. Immediately after the original message, the women were contacted and told that the information was sent to them by mistake and was being handled through other channels. Disregard. These pieces were designed to be too good to pass up. Now we wait and see which piece is taken."

"Or both," Thorn said.

Brian shrugged. "Or neither."

"We'll have to keep tight tabs on their communications," Nutsbe said. "We can do that if they're talking at either of their houses or on any of their phones. But I see lots of holes in this plan. For example, Sophia could share information with Nadia, Nadia's people could act, and Sophia would look culpable or vice versa. Or they could be sending information over the computer."

Finley edged forward, concern creasing his forehead. "Aren't you watching their computers?"

Thorn scratched his fingers along his brow. "The problem is, on their AACP computer system, they use a code developer, so every forty-five seconds or so, a new code is produced, and that's the only code that can access their computers. No amount of hacking software can break-in. If we could get to those computers while they're working—"

"A scenario that hasn't presented itself in the short time we've been on the case," Brian interjected.

Nutsbe gave him a nod. "If we can get access, then we could plant spyware. The only other option we have right now is to put a keystroke capturing device on the computers, but since their computers don't have a tower system, it would catch their attention. They'd know for sure someone was gaining access to their system and point the finger at Iniquus—"

"And we're in the women's lives by invitation at this point.

Imagine how swift that kick would come, giving us the boot out the door," Thorn said.

Brian was glad to sit back and have Thorn and Nutsbe poke holes in the plan. He was mindful that if he protested too vigorously, his loyalties might be called into question, especially since Lynx had picked up on the emotional complexity of his situation. Of course, he knew his loyalties *weren't* in question. Duty first. Period. "On Sophia's end, I have external cameras set up. She has four monitors up. Three making a U-shape, one set apart that looks like the place Nadia typically works. The lighting and angles make capturing a clear picture of any of the screens difficult.

"On Nadia's end, I have spyware on the laptop she used at their presentation. It looks like a bunch of PowerPoint presentations and nothing more. There's a complete search history in place. It's mostly Google searches that pertain to people in their field, hotels, conferences, airlines. She uses her phone for her day-to-day stuff—email, social media, web searches."

Finley looked like he'd licked a lemon. "I highly suggest you find a way to get that software loaded onto the AACP computers then." He pointed from Brian to Thorn. "And remember, this sting is already in play."

15
_____

The four of them sat in front of the computers as Sophia manipulated the images, changing the coloration and the depth of saturation until she was satisfied.

Brian and Thorn each had a thumb drive ready, all they needed was two minutes alone with a computer window open, and they'd get the spyware in place. So far, they'd been unsuccessful at clearing the room.

The women were sharply focused. Anxious. The atmosphere in the office felt like the war room when a case was at a tipping point. Something made this feel like a mission. A low-level hum of danger vibrated the air. They weren't talking. They pointed things out to each other and nodded. Their fingers flew, and they typed in Arabic. Brian was sure that both women wished their security would clear out. He wished he knew what was happening.

Brian had been in the room when Sophia had booted up the computer. He'd hoped to see where she hid the PIN generator. Then he'd simply come in when she was asleep that night and do what needed to be done. She had faced the left-hand screen, mumbled under her breath, and typed rapidly. Brian had given Nutsbe a heads up. Nutsbe, in turn, had gone over that video, again and again, trying to figure out how she was getting the number. They had been in the room well beyond the forty-five seconds that a number was active—but he saw nothing that even remotely resembled the PIN generator. If Brian didn't get the flash drive in at some point today, he'd come back and give the room a hard shake. She had to have it somewhere on her desk. Maybe there was something under the lip of the desk, and she dropped the device into her lap.

The Florida room door rattled, and a man's voice called out, "Joe, come let me in."

"Sounds like Mr. Rochester," Brian said, tipping his head to ask if he should open the door.

Sophia pushed her chair back, her gaze lingering on the screen, obviously frustrated to be pulled away from her task. "I've got it." She pushed through the door and pulled it solidly closed behind her. "Mr. Rochester, you're looking for Joe? I saw him earlier, playing next door. Let's go get him home. It's almost time for dinner."

"That boy's supposed to be grounded. Why the heck isn't he in his room? Who are you? Why are you in my house?"

"I'm the babysitter. Let's go find out why Joe's being naughty and bring him home." Her voice faded as they left the house. Brian slid the curtain back and watched as Sophia guided the elderly gentleman back across the yard.

Thorn got up and moved toward the arch that separated the kitchen from the office. "Nadia, do you think Sophia would mind if I made some coffee? I'm headed for an afternoon slump."

Nadia glanced away from her screen. "She doesn't drink coffee, no stimulants to up her anxiety levels."

"Tea? Does she drink tea?"

Nadia quickly typed something, then, with poorly veiled exasperation, moved to the kitchen to help Thorn. Brian slid his thumb drive into Sophia's computer and watched the light blaze red; this thing was about as subtle as Rudolph's nose. Nadia moved back into the office almost as soon as he pulled his hand away.

Brian swung around and planted his hips on the desktop, blocking its view. "Nadia, Sophia had a good night last night. The house was quiet. She said she was groggy this morning from the meds but otherwise felt all right. You know her as well as anyone. What do you think we should do to continue this progress?"

"Honestly? I think she needs to get the hell out of dodge. This neighborhood is full of freaks. Old men rattling her door at all hours of the day and night. Bikini-clad nut jobs following her through the grocery store, hissing at her."

Brian blinked. What? "*Hissing*?"

"Hissing. It got to the point where Sophia eats only freeze-dried foods and foods she can have mailed or carried out to her car with curbside delivery."

"You're talking about Marla?" he asked, hoping to god he'd get a chance to pull out the thumb drive before Sophia got back. "Why do you think she's stalking Sophia?"

"Marla? Of course, Marla. And why? I'd just be guessing, but I read a book called *The Sociopath Who Lived Next Door*, and the conclusion I came to is that a sociopath has to have a target. Others see how that target is treated and will do anything not to have that level of crazy pointed toward them. Having a victim allows a sociopath to exercise control over a whole group.

"When Marla moved in, Sophia had just been in the car crash that injured her mother-in-law. Sophia moved here to take care of her. Jane Campbell was in terrible shape and was completely dependent on Sophia. The accident was just another horrible event in a long list of horrible events that Sophia's gone through. She reeks of vulnerability. I think Marla picked Sophia because she's an easy mark." Nadia paused and considered him. "I have to thank you for telling Sophia that she's being stalked by that mad cow. Sophia turns a deaf ear to anything I say to her on the subject. As a matter of fact—"

Sophia opened the door to the Florida room. Her face was white, and her eyes were wide. "I don't know what to do," she gasped out. "Mr. Rochester got violent. I asked if I should call the police, and Joe yelled for me to just get out and go home." She looked at Brian. "Do you think I should call the police? When Hunter got like that…" She shook her head. "I don't know what to do," she told the floorboards.

Thorn had been listening from his spot, leaning against the kitchen counter. He righted himself. "I'll go see if he needs help. Is one of the doors open?"

"Yes, I left the front door unlocked so the police could get in. But Joe said not to call. The expense can be enormous if he's taken to the hospital. It's a lot to weigh. But Mr. Rochester was punching Joe." She watched Thorn jog out her front door. "This is terrible," she gasped. She exhaled forcibly—a shallow breath in, a deeper breath out. One handheld to her forehead, the other clenched to her stomach. Her eyes were wild with anxiety.

"Sophia, sit down," Nadia said, pulling a chair around. "Thorn's got this. Mr. Rochester is an old man—he's weak. Joe can protect himself. Mr. Rochester's not an athlete like Hunter was. He's not strong like Hunter was. This isn't you and Hunter, Sophia," Nadia said, raising her voice, becoming stern. "This is *not* Hunter. You and the kids are safe."

Sophia collapsed into the chair with her head in her hands. Her glistening black waves formed a barrier to their scrutiny.

Brian wanted to crouch by her side, to get her a drink of water, to find something warm to wrap around her shivering frame, but his body was hiding the damned thumb drive.

Sophia looked up. "Brian, can you go see if Thorn needs help? Please? Adrenaline and anger can make people incredibly strong."

Before Brian could answer, Lana opened the front door, holding the hands of two young boys. "Hey, ho!"

Sophia immediately pulled herself together and scurried over. "Is everything okay?" She picked up the younger of the two. The boy was like a doll, with his mother's huge ebony eyes and pink cheeks; his black hair a mop of curls. He tucked his head under Sophia's chin.

"My kids are in the car." Lana glanced over her shoulder out the door to where her minivan was parked in front of the mailbox. "The boys wanted mama, so I thought I'd bring them by for a quick hug. We're heading out for ice cream."

"With sprinkles," Turner stipulated. Two dimpled cheeks showcased a happy grin. He held out a piece of orange construction paper to his mom.

Sophia squatted, balancing Chance on her hip. Opening the three-year-old's masterpiece with one hand, she took a moment to appreciate Turner's picture. "Oh, sweetie, look how beautiful. I love all the colors. Can you tell me about this?"

Focusing over her shoulder, Brian could see random lines and scribbles decorating the page.

Turner pointed earnestly at his work. "We're reading a book."

"I love when we read books together." She kissed his hair. "And I love having this picture to remind me of snuggling up with you and Chance." Sophia pushed to standing, obviously practiced at juggling the children. "This goes on the fridge, so we can all enjoy it."

Lana turned to her sister. "I thought you were working from home today. I didn't expect to find you here." She peered into the office. "And Brian." She gave him a finger wave.

Thorn came in the back door. "Rochester's good. They're watching football."

"And Thorn too? There's a whole crowd holding down the fort today."

Brian detected something nervous about Lana. She seemed overly bright. Maybe she, like Nadia and Sophia, didn't like to be around big groups, but honestly, with only four of them there, that didn't make much sense.

"Are you sleepy, baby?" Sophia asked her youngest son, tipping his head back so she could peer at him, then plant a kiss on his cheek. "He's looking better. He smells like garlic and olive oil. I could eat him up." She nuzzled at his neck until he chuckled and squirmed.

"Yeah, he was pulling at that ear, so I tried a home remedy. Seems to be working." Lana moved forward to reach for Chance. Lana and Nadia were obviously sisters, but where Nadia was tall and athletic, her sister was a shorter, rounder, softer version. Their personalities differed along the same lines. Nadia was cosmopolitan and wore the polish of someone who sipped cocktails in sophisticated circles. Lana seemed like someone who preferred the comfort and intimacy of her home.

"Let me hold him while Turner and I go hang his picture."
Sophia took Turner's hand and moved toward the kitchen.

"The boys missed you last night," Lana called after her.
"They need some mama time. I told them that you'd read two
books and sing one song over the Internet before they go to
sleep."

Brian took advantage of the shift in attention to pull out the
flash drive that had thankfully turned green. Mission accomplished.

Thorn had gone back to the Iniquus compound to have the
Arabic notes that Sophia and Nadia had been sending all day
translated and to see if anything tied to the FBI sting came up in
their work. Right now, the computer was off. The electricity had
been flickering. Brian had his phone out and was watching an
enormous storm inching toward them on the radar. High winds
were causing power outages to the west.

He, Nadia, and Sophia had initially planned to go out to grab a
bite to eat but had decided to order a pizza. Sophia didn't want to
miss FaceTime with her children. She'd headed up the stairs to
read them their books when Brian heard a car in the drive. He
fished out his wallet and pulled out a couple of bills, moving
toward the door. It burst open, and Lana stumbled into the room.
Her eye caught on Brian, and she froze. "Hey there," she finally
said, turning and leaning her body into the door to get it to shut.
"Can you believe this weather? Whew!" She pushed the hair out of
her face and sent Brian a smile. "I thought you all went out to eat."

The doorbell rang. "Too lazy. We ordered a pizza instead."
Brian shifted around Lana to take the pizzas and pay the guy.

Lana moved over to the corner of the room. "I'm just going to send a quick text to the hubs and let him know how bad things are getting." She raised her voice. "Hey, Nadia," she said without looking up from her task.

"Tell him it looks like you might be sheltering in place." Nadia took the pizzas from Brian and set them on the kitchen counter, pulled out some plates, and they dug in after Nadia said Sophia had told them to go ahead without her.

The wind shook the house and bent the trees. Sophia made a brief appearance, her eyes rimmed in red. Mascara streaks painted her cheeks where she'd wiped away tears. "Hey, Lana. Did you need something?"

"The boys wanted to play with their puppy pals, so I thought I'd stop by while I ran to the store for more bananas. It's hard to keep them in stock when there's a troop of monkeys swinging through my house. Are you all done talking to the kids?"

"The cable went down. I had to call the boys on the phone to finish the book and tell them good night." She tried to force her frown into a smile.

"Are you okay? Come and eat something." Brian lifted the box but forced himself to stay put and ignore how badly he wanted to pull her into his arms and comfort her.

She shook her head as she reached into the cupboard for a mug. "What I want is to take a long hot bath, but looks like the lightning is here." She pulled a jug of milk from the fridge. "I'm going to make some hot milk while we still have electricity." She tapped the button, and her microwave whirred. When it beeped completion, she opened the door. "I'm going to take my sleeping pills and go to bed. Today seemed to wring it out of me."

Lana smiled encouragement her way. "Saturday we'll spend all day at the pool. We'll relax. It'll be good."

Sophia's attempted smile fooled no one.

Rain continued to hammer down. The trees scraped their branches back and forth over the windowpanes, making high-pitched otherworldly shrieks that unnerved the women. The lights wavered and dimmed. The storm sat right on top of them. The women certainly couldn't go home in this deluge, with no visibility and no streetlights or signals. Nadia had gone up to change the sheets on the guestroom bed where Lana and Nadia would sleep. Brian planned to sleep on the couch in the den.

Brian went to check the doors. The security lights and cameras didn't have a backup battery. He'd have to work on that.

With the flashlight on his phone, Brian slipped up the stairs and into Sophia's room. He checked her breathing and pulse. She didn't move. He picked up the bottle of sleeping pills sitting on her bedside table and counted them into his hand. Something about her mood earlier had been flat. Despondent. The vitality that he usually saw in her eyes when she spoke about her work had faded. And it worried him. Lynx's warning that Sophia was at risk of suicide was at the forefront of his mind.

He thought back to the hugs she gave to her kids. She was obviously a gentle and loving mother, but she'd had the same energy and look as women he'd seen in war zones. He vividly remembered talking with his translator one day. The female officer was assigned to his FAST unit to talk with women and do the female pat-downs. He had wanted to understand the melancholy look in the mothers' eyes as they sent their children off to get water at the well or to sell the bread the women had made that morning. They'd put their hands on their children's heads and held their gaze for a long moment before shooing them off.

"These mothers see no tomorrow, no future for their children. They're waiting for the next bomb to drop—the next strafe of gunfire. One way or another, this is a land of bad outcomes.

There's no expectation for a better tomorrow. How else should these women behave? What else could they feel but despair?"

Brian had no idea. He was from America, where tomorrow held promise, options, and opportunities. But the look in Sophia's eyes told him that she was just like those women in the war zone. He examined Sophia, curled into a ball, her brow furrowed, the blanket held in a fist beneath her chin, as though the act of sleeping took immense physical concentration and effort. He wanted to reach out and stroke his hand over her hair. To comfort her. To tell her he was going to protect her. But that was a lie. He was the one tasked with taking her down. Brian replaced the pills, tightened the child-proof cap, and moved the vial away from her reach, hiding it from sight behind her lamp.

He jogged down the stairs to find Lana texting in her usual spot. She glanced up when he held the flashlight on her. "The children are sleeping right through this, hubby says. How? I have no idea. It's probably because he's piled them all in bed with him and the dogs." Her voice was tight.

"This is eerie," Nadia said, carrying a candle into the room and moving over to stand near Lana. "I can't remember ever being so unnerved by a storm."

Lightning reached out and touched the top of a nearby pine, exploding it in a fireworks display of golden sparks in the neighbor's yard. Lana slapped a hand over her mouth to buffer her shriek. Thunder clapped immediately—long and low, rumbling across the sky and shaking the house on its foundation. The crystal on the curio shelf clattered. Spinning, Lana reached out reflexively as a goblet slipped from the shelf. It slid through her fingers and hit the floor hard, shattering.

Nadia, the candle still in her hand, moaned as she crouched. "No!" She exhaled. "No. No. No." She lifted the stem. It was the largest piece still intact. Lana hovered over the shards, her hands on her head, her eyes wide. Brian waited for some explanation about what upset them so much.

Nadia let the crystal shard fall and came upright. The sisters stood, still as statues, staring into each other's eyes. Cold brushed over Brian as the fine hairs on his arms stood up. A howl of wind made Lana jump closer to her sister.

"What just happened?" Brian asked.

16

*B*RIAN

Thursday Night

Lana was fixated on the starburst of crystal on the wooden floor. "When she finds out it's broken, it's going to be bad," she whispered.

"This was special to Sophia?" Brian tried again to get details.

Nadia sent Lana a questioning look, and Lana responded with the smallest of nods. Brian knew they had decided to break a bond and share a confidence. He steeled himself for what was coming.

"Sophia's great-great-grandmother Adeline brought that goblet with her from Limerick when she immigrated to America. It has been passed down through the generations. It dates back to the early 1800s. *Dated* back." Nadia cleared her throat. "When Adeline got married, they gave a wedding toast with that glass, then her grandmother, then her mother, and eventually Sophia did the same. In their family tradition, taking a sip of wine on your wedding day from that goblet connected the new bride to the wisdom of the women who had come before." Nadia used the hushed tones of a storyteller as if they were around a campfire deep in the woods.

"Sophia had just moved into this house, her mother-in-law Jane hadn't been released from the hospital yet after the car accident. Sophia was out of her mind. She had been crying for days. She had been through so much for so long, and now she had to make decisions for a woman she barely knew. So Lana suggested we ask her grandmothers." Nadia's voice faltered, and she looked away, bending her head.

Brian took the candle from her hands and set it at their feet. It left eerie shadows on their faces. He shifted the jar to the side with the toe of his boot. He didn't need to add to the atmosphere. The women were already shivering. Their nerves were pulled so tight.

"I had no idea." Lana shook her head. "I was half-joking."

"We fashioned a kind of Ouija board. I filled out slips of paper with the alphabet, the numbers zero to nine, a card for yes, and a card for no. Sophia turned the goblet upside down, and we all sat around the table and rested our fingers on the base."

Lana's shivers became trembles. Brian knew that what happened next was the stuff of nightmares and horror stories. A chant had begun in his brain behind the melody of his other thoughts. *Our Father who art in Heaven, hallowed be thy name...* As the prayer cycled forward, he felt as if each phrase was building the next layer of a wall that would separate and protect him from whatever it was that was frightening these women. "What happened?" he urged.

"As soon as we put our fingers on the goblet, the room started to hum. I expected that we'd be waiting... I thought it would… I had no idea what I was doing. But it happened incredibly fast. The room filled with electricity."

"Static," Lana said. "Our hair floated out to the sides like we'd rubbed our heads with a balloon. Our clothes zapped us as we shifted. Nadia asked, 'who's here?' and the goblet immediately spelled out Jet."

"Who's Jet?" Brian asked.

"We didn't know," Nadia said. "I mean, we figured it out in context. Sophia told us later that she called Hunter Jet as a pet name, a private joke. Hunter, her husband, had these beautiful black eyes. All the girls fell in love with him because of his eyes."

"Sophia," Lana said. "She looked like she was in a trance. She asked Hunter if he was okay. The goblet slid to yes."

"Hunter tried to commit suicide when he found out that Sophia was in premature labor. She was alone in the hospital giving birth to Chance. Christopher John Campbell was the name they had chosen for him. Sophia changed the name to Chance when she filled out the papers. She never talked about why—but it's easy to guess. They gave her husband and son the same chance of survival that day. Ten percent." Nadia paused for a long moment. "The second question Sophia asked was if Hunter's dad was with him and the goblet slid over to yes. Then she asked if he was in Heaven, and the goblet went back to the side that had the no."

"Was there a reason why Sophia asked about his father?"

Nadia shifted her weight. "Hunter was in a coma, braindead after his overdose, but his parents couldn't bring themselves to remove him from life support. Sophia was dealing with life and death decisions for her new baby, and she felt very strongly that Hunter's parents should have whatever control she could give them over their son's life. At first, they decided to keep Hunter on life support while they looked for alternative treatments. But there's nothing that brings someone back from being braindead. In late spring of that same year, Hunter's dad was diagnosed with advanced heart disease. His only chance at survival was a heart transplant."

A low note slipped between Lana's lips.

Nadia reached out and pulled Lana to her side. "Jane begged her husband to take their son's heart. If he didn't, she was sure to lose both of them. If he did, then she could keep them both alive in some way. So that was the plan. They'd try to save both the father and some part of the son with the operation. They had started the surgery to remove Hunter's heart and were prepping his father—Matthew was his name—for surgery. But Matthew had a massive heart attack and died. Sophia had already said goodbye to Hunter, but now she was mourning her father-in-law. And Jane, to be perfectly honest, went crazy. She had to be institutionalized for a time. Sophia had to make the funeral arrangements for her husband and father-in-law all by herself."

Nadia released a jagged breath. "There we were, using the goblet to talk with the dead. Sophia asked, 'Where are you?' The goblet spelled out, 'Waiting for mom. Let her come.' Now, all of us were barely touching the goblet. Sophia couldn't possibly move the glass on her own. Lana and I didn't know that the doctor talked to Sophia about palliative care versus aggressive choices in treating Jane. We had no idea that Jane might die."

"Holy crap," he said under his breath. Brian tried to imagine the women sitting around the table, having this otherworldly experience.

Nadia pursed her lips, waiting for the thunder to finish rolling across the sky. "It gets worse. The next thing it spelled out was, 'I love you. I'm so sorry.' I thought that now that we had answers, we'd stop. Sophia needed to know what to do, and now she knew. But Sophia—I have never seen a human look like that. She was white to the point of being...translucent. Her lips were colorless."

"Terrifying," Lana said. "It was as if I could see right through her like she had become vapor. I wanted to magnetize her particles back into a solid whole, but I couldn't pick my fingers up off the glass. I was stuck. Powerless. It felt like Hunter had gone, and something evil had slipped through a door he had left open."

"It was as if I was on a spinning ride where you're held in place by centrifugal force, and the bottom drops out," Nadia explained. "Lana's right. I couldn't get my fingers off that goblet. I knew that I'd only be allowed to let go when whatever it was that came in the room was satisfied."

Brian began to wonder if this was a performance. If the sisters' story was something they heard or saw or came up with... If that were true, they were damned good actors. "What happened next?"

Nadia bit at her lips. It seemed to Brian that she was having trouble forming the next words. "It spelled out 'Your fault.' Sophia's body vibrated. Her whole body shook. But her hands were steady on the goblet. I was getting angry at Hunter. I didn't realize that he'd switched. I was thinking, how dare he blame Sophia when his depression and suicide were caused by a head injury? I yelled at the goblet to stop."

"The goblet spelled, 'My grave,'" Lana whispered, then whipped her head around to look across the ceiling and into the corners. "Sophia was shaking so hard the rim of the glass bounced on the table, then it spelled, 'You desecrated my grave.'"

Brian shook his head. This was so farfetched that they had to be pulling his leg.

"Sophia screamed the highest pitched scream—held it inhumanly long. The dishes were rattling in the cupboards. I'm going to be disgustingly honest here." Nadia turned to look him in the eye. "I peed myself. I was so terrified."

Brian thought she'd burst out laughing and let him in on the joke, but she didn't.

"When the scream ended, Sophia collapsed. The static electricity left."

The quiet that followed was one Brian experienced after a bomb blast when everyone in the area was in shock. Unsure, unclear, unable. He stood quietly until one, and then the other sister seemed to come back to themselves. In his mind, Brian heard the prayer that had continued this whole time, say one last time, *Lead us not into temptation, but deliver us from evil*, followed by an *amen*. The weird feeling of being watched or eavesdropped on vanished.

"Lana, what are we going to do about the goblet?" Nadia whispered. "She'll lose her mind. She's already terrified for the boys."

"I'm not following. Why is she worried for the boys?" Brian asked, wondering if he was going to find yet another stressor that might make Sophia desperate.

Lana caught Nadia's eye and held it with as close to fierce conviction as he had ever seen on her face. "I think we've told too much of Sophia's story already. That's really her burden to share if she wants to." Lana turned pleading eyes on Brian. "Please don't tell her we told you about the Ouija game," she whispered. "I don't know that she'd forgive us." She grabbed his arm. "It was an intensely private moment—a unique and dreadful experience. There aren't words to explain the profound horror that we felt. We've *never* talked about it. Sophia refuses to let us. She says she doesn't want to give it any more power than it already has."

Nadia explained, "Sophia believes that words, thoughts, and deeds all have energetic properties."

"What does that mean? You said the entity spelled out, 'You desecrated my grave.' Desecrated seems like a long word for a ghost to spell out."

"You're probably joking," Nadia said. "I can't imagine that anyone in their right mind would believe a word my sister or I just said. But it's crazy what's happened to Sophia. Did she ever tell you we were kidnapped? Held tied up for days with bags over our heads?"

Brian stalled. He couldn't answer that truthfully. He wasn't supposed to know that. It was interesting that Nadia's mind was on being kidnapped. There must be a correlation. "Is that when bad things started to happen? Desecrating a grave—does this have something to do with an archaeological dig?"

"A dig? No. That kidnapping and every single other horrible thing that's transpired over the last five years are because of what happened beforehand. And all Sophia wants to do now is turn back time, go back, and fix her mistake."

Brian reached down to pick up the candle.

When he stood, Sophia, dressed in a thin white nightgown, slipped into their circle, skirting around the broken goblet.

"I was having a nightmare." She crouched down to lift the stem, just like Nadia had, and put it back in the pile. She stood up and looked from Nadia to Lana. "I thought it was the storm." She shifted her hair out of her face, letting her gaze rest on the picture of her boys. "Bad things are coming."

17

Sophia
Friday a.m.

The phone rang on her desk, pulling Sophia's attention from the newest images that had uploaded overnight while the storm had raged. She waited until all five beeps sounded, then placed the receiver back in its cradle. She opened the case on her keychain flashlight and waited for her cell phone to ring. Typically, the delay was less than a minute. Today though, Sophia finished half the chai tea Brian had brought her this morning when he ran out for coffee. Sophia didn't have any coffee in the house, and Brian claimed it was his main food group. She had directed him over to the little shop near Willow Tree. Right now, Brian was outside hanging from the eaves, dealing with some storm damage. Sophia was simply too tired to say no to his offer.

She was in her office alone. Nadia had gone home to shower and change, and Lana had gone back to her house to relieve her husband of kid duty. The tumble of boys was five deep when she and Lana mixed their broods. Good thing they piled together like puppies, no one making familial distinction when they were together.

When the buzz came from the cellphone in her hand, it startled her. Sophia brought the phone to her ear and read out the alphanumeric code that told her contact that it was safe to speak.

"You have information?"

"I think I've found exactly what we've been looking for," Sophia said. "There's a tablet that needs a new home that some would consider museum quality."

"Some? You can give this piece a clean bill of health for shipping?"

Sophia swallowed hard. "I can."

"Thank you. Forward the pertinent data through the normal channels. We'll handle it from here."

"Okay. Moving forward with the other project." Sophia picked up a book from her desk and turned to put it back on the shelf. "I can't make an assessment from the picture you sent."

"You'll see Jael on Monday. He'll be traveling with the diplomatic corps through customs. You can figure it out then."

"Oh, good." Sophia paced over to the window and looked out at her leaf-strewn lawn. The flowers had been pounded into the ground by the relentless fury of the storm, but she could see that they were already pulling their faces up in search of sunlight. "Be aware that the location of our last conversation is no longer secure. I'm picking up unusual activity."

"I'll make sure that information gets to the right ear."

The line went dead.

If all went well, this was the deal they'd been looking for. Then this chapter of her life would be over. Wouldn't that feel like victory? Sophia's mind traveled to last night's fiasco with the crystal goblet. Success was probably too much to hope for.

She looked at the boys' picture hanging on her wall. "I'm trying to do what's best," she told their smiling faces.

Brian knocked three times in a tattoo he had created so he could go in and out without startling her. He had a box on his shoulder. Sophia was glad she'd made it through her call before he burst in.

"Special delivery," he said as the roar of the mail truck moved up the hill.

Sophia clapped her hands as she hustled over to take the box. A smile lit her face.

"You look like a kid on Christmas morning." Brian grinned. "What's in here?"

She ran her finger over the tape sealing the box. "It's pretty awesome. Got a knife? I'll show you."

Sophia dug through the protective Styrofoam and pulled out the black object wedged inside. "This," she announced like a new mother presenting her first child, "is a specialized 3-D digital camera with an integrated computer system to perform measurements, and map planes, developed with the help of archaeologists. Nadia and I are testing it out." She held it up to her eye and focused on different objects around the room. She stalled on Brian's face. "Imagine an FBI computer system that has pictures of people all over the United States, all over the world."

Brian leaned forward in his chair to accept the camera she held out for him.

"Their computers can quickly search through their data-banks to find people whose physical attributes match those of their unknown subject, thereby giving them a name and prob-ably a file of information about that person, right?" Sophia's smile faded when she saw an odd little something in Brian's eyes.

There and gone again as he held his typically impassive expression.

"This camera is meant to gather data for a similar database. Only this one would be for artifacts. As you well know, our goal at AACP is to protect antiquities and keep them in their country of origin. With so many pieces flowing through the black markets and into private collections, how do we prove that the piece was taken illegally? We've had a hard time with that. From our discussions and talking with people involved in CSI, we came up with the idea of equipping our teams in hot areas with these cameras. They're cheap. Thirty-four dollars each. That was the main criterion—or we simply couldn't get them widely distributed. Our volunteers will collect information and send it back to us."

Brian was looking over the camera he held, turning it this way and that. "Sophia, did I ever tell you why I was assigned to your team?"

"No, you didn't." Sophia curled onto the couch and pulled the throw blanket over her feet.

He leaned forward until his forearms rested on his knees, letting the camera dangle from his hands. He was eye to eye with her. There was a quality to him of earnestness. Solemnity, even. "I was in Bagdad in April 2003." He stalled for a moment, then nodded his head, as if he'd made up his mind. "We went in fast and hard with our sights set on toppling Saddam Hussein. We were in the center of Bagdad in the blink of an eye. My platoon was in Sadr City and crossed over the Tigris. My squad was sent to the National Museum of Iraq. There were reports of looters, and we were supposed to clear them out. Which we did. The museum workers were there, old men with canes, young men with sticks. They had been trying, without much success, to protect the artifacts. They begged us to leave people in place there. To park some tanks in the yard. But we were on the move. We couldn't stay put." He drew his thumb down his jawline. "To be perfectly honest, we knew all along that the museum was at risk."

Sophia was staring at her knotted hands. She was trying to absorb the story without jumping to conclusions. She had sat by her television and screamed at the military to get themselves in there and protect the museum. Brian had been there. She had unknowingly sent waves of hostility toward him at that time. But Brian was a Marine following orders, not a decision-maker.

"A lot of Western media jumped on our backs for not safe-guarding those artifacts. But there wasn't a lot of sensitivity about *objects* when people's lives were on the line. Save a vase or save a girl? It was a no-brainer for me."

Sophia listened quietly. It sounded like a confession. Maybe he was hoping for absolution from his sins. Maybe his eighteen-year-old self, fresh out of boot camp, needed the archaeologist in her ivory tower to understand what it had been like on the ground. In 2003, when she was livid and indignant over the loot-ing, who had she been but a pimply teen who liked to play in the dirt? What had she done in her life that would in any way compare to the sacrifices of those who fought in the war?

"That first day, we went in and chased a bunch of looters out. We knew they'd be back as soon as we left. We probably were there all of thirty minutes. The Iraqi military was gathering up women and children and forcing them to be human shields to protect their arms caches and other points of concern, like water and electricity."

Sophia reached for the ring on her bracelet and twisted it with her finger. She understood what Brian was telling her. Certainly, her work with the AACP taught her about the genuine dangers and the very real pain of the Syrian people. That they risked themselves to save history—that was something she was willing to do from the comfort of a DC office. She was sure that she wouldn't spit directly in the face of ISIS, knowing that her head would be removed by the blade of a sword, then placed between her feet to rot in the desert sun. She wasn't that kind of a hero.

"They said that about fifteen thousand pieces—ritual vessels, amulets, ivory, and more than five thousand cylinder seals were dispersed across the countryside. I've always wondered if there was some way I could have done more." He glanced up at her, then handed her back the camera.

"I think everyone understands that lives are the priority. Always."

"We reported what we saw. Our reports made it through the chain of command. A guy, Colonel Bogawrath was his name—went to the US Central Command and got a 'Monuments' team together."

"Wait. Like the Monuments Men of World War II? Antiquities experts heading into the fray to save what art they could?"

"Well, they were fourteen men with investigative experience. They weren't really from the museum and preservation crowd." Brian chuckled. "That would be a stretch."

"You were one of them?"

"I was assigned as part of their support and security team. I helped establish a perimeter at the museum, and I helped them take an inventory of missing items. We sent the descriptions to everyone we could think of—border agents, Interpol, archaeologists. I remember Nadia's father's name and your father's name because they were still trying to function in Syria. They'd answer questions for us. Well, for the colonel, not me. I was just some dumb grunt fresh off an Idaho farm for the first time in my life. I'd never been to an art museum before. It was my first taste of culture that didn't revolve around football and potlucks at church. It was mind-blowing."

Idaho. Sophia hadn't considered where Brian was raised. His body, the way he moved, every aspect of this man projected "rough and ready." He had impeccable manners. An intelligent, educated mind, and palpable goodness about him. Maybe that's what he carried away from his Idaho upbringing—deep roots that gave him stability.

"I honestly can't imagine what jumping from rural America to a Middle Eastern desert was like for you—my life was always a smorgasbord of languages, new places, beautiful and very old things. And of course, camel spit." She smiled. "I'm sure your parents gave you a great many gifts—it seems to me you're pretty comfortable in your own skin. That you have an internal compass pointing toward what's right and wrong. That, in my experience, comes from being well-loved in your growing years. And by that, I mean you could experience hardship, knowing the ground you stood on was solid."

"Yeah. My family, we were hard-working from dawn to dusk. Good times came and bad times followed, but our family was always solid." He sat quietly for a long moment. Then looked her in the eye. "Interesting that it shows."

Sophia pulled her legs up and wrapped her arms around them, laying her head on her knees. "What happened next with your fourteen museum men?"

"We started finding things. Sometimes people brought them back. There was this one, the Sacred Vase of Wark—sounds like something in a sci-fi B-movie. They said it was from over three-thousand BC."

"BCE."

"What?"

"BCE—before the common era. It's the way scientists are saying it now. They've replaced the before Christ."

"Is it still AD?"

"No—it's CE now. Common era."

"Huh. Well, one day, this little old granny came with a plate of cookies. A couple of us were trying them. We thanked her and handed her back the plate. She gave us what we thought was a garbage bag. We almost threw it in the trash. But my buddy Ben opened it up, and there was a pot. One of the museum's oldest pieces. From 6000 BCE." He raised his eyebrows and let them drop, emphasizing that he'd used the term correctly.

Sophia sent him a smile as a reward.

"We found stuff in car trunks and buried in vegetable gardens. Sometimes we'd lock up to hit the racks and come back to find pieces had been put on the shelves overnight. We couldn't figure out how they were getting in. As we kept looking and investigating, we figured out that hundreds of the best pieces we thought had been gone since the Gulf War had been hidden for safekeeping in the Central Bank. I got to carry Nimrud's jewels back to the museum in a box on my lap with my AK resting on top."

"Wow." In Sophia's mind, she was making all kinds of inappropriate jokes about family jewels but managed to stay straight-faced to say, "That's incredible."

"Before I got transferred, we thought we got about half of the pieces back. I'm damned proud of helping with that. And I'm equally proud to try to protect the antiquities from Syria. This isn't just an assignment to me. My hearts in it, for sure." Brian's eyes flickered with something poignant as he looked at her.

Sophia thought she saw a flash of deep pain and wondered at it. She almost asked what he was thinking, but Brian had obviously stuffed those emotions away, so she moved their conversation along. "I remember vividly my outrage that people had stolen the Iraqi museum pieces. I loved the museum as a kid. My dad would take me. He worked for the Smithsonian during my childhood, along with Nadia's father. Can you imagine what a loss it would be if the Smithsonian was destroyed? That's why I wanted to do this work when the opportunity came up. I wanted to protect our world heritage."

"You don't talk much about your family. Why is that?"

"What's to say? Dad planned to be a professor of antiquities in his retirement. He got sick in Turkey, and the fever cooked his brain. He has functioned very much like an Alzheimer's patient ever since. Mom is busy trying to keep him home and not put him in a nursing facility. He doesn't recognize me anymore. My brother—he's living out west with his own problems. I'm pretty invisible to them all." Her gaze rested on the portrait of her boys. *Why the heck did I say that? I sound pathetic.* She blinked her eyes hard and waited until she could form a smile again before she looked back at Brian.

His eyes were on her. His gaze too intense to hold. "You're not invisible to me, Sophie. I see you."

Sophia looked past his shoulder and out the window for respite. This conversation was headed into dangerous territory. "You have siblings?" she asked, forcing herself to look his way.

"I'm the seventh son of a seventh son." He grinned broadly. "But there are ten kids in my family, all told."

Sophia shook her head. "You're teasing me."

"I would never do that. It's the God's honest truth."

Still dangerous territory. They had a professional relationship. Period. They shouldn't be talking about personal stuff. "About the cameras."

Brian's look told her he thought she was a chicken, and he was right.

"It won't surprise you to learn that we have a loose-knit group of academics fighting back against the antique thefts. Many of them I knew as a child and young teen. I haven't been to the Middle East since the summer before my senior year. One of my tasks is to find key sites and get the information to my team to document what's there and what's possibly already missing. They also have another huge task. They need to hide artifacts that are at risk of being looted."

"How do they hide them?"

"One way is to dig a big hole, put in a storage container—like an old truck, or something—and bury it. Then they file the GPS coordinates with me—well, the AACP. The braver ones, usually older men who look like grandfathers, will pose as antique dealers, trying to lure looters to them so they can photograph what they have."

"That's dangerous work."

"Too dangerous right now. Too difficult as well. The looting, since ISIS made it systematic, is happening at such a pace that our people can't possibly keep up. And the death toll is massive. More than three hundred thousand people have been killed there since my last trip. Our team hasn't gone unscathed. We're losing people every day. And Aleppo. I loved Aleppo. I loved the people." She swiped at a tear that broke through her barriers.

"I can't watch the news anymore. I can't bear what's happening. Just the other day, Sadiq Bikar was beheaded for trying to save antiquities." Sophia blinked furiously, trying for control. "He was my father's mentor." She finally got the words out, then cleared her throat. She looked at the camera. "It is so damned easy for me to sit here in my living room and order cameras. To send an email that has a coordinate. To make suggestions from the distant safety of a satellite image. But every time I do anything, ask anything, people on the other end risk their lives."

Brian turned his head as a car parked in front of her house. "Nadia's here."

Good timing, Sophia thought, needing a minute to clear her head before she said something that could put everything at risk. The next few days were crucial.

18

When Sophia returned with a tea tray and cookies, Nadia lifted the second prototype from the box. "This one's only twenty-seven dollars?" she asked. She looked through the lens. "Oh, I see the difference. I think we need the planer identification. This one isn't going to give us the level of detail they'll need in court." She worked to re-wrap it. "The Institute of Digital Archaeology and Preservation came up with some grant money, so I don't think we're going to have to compromise."

"I'm not willing to put people at risk for data that's not strong enough to protect the artifacts." Sophia set the tray down and poured a cup of tea to pass to her partner.

"Sophia was telling me why you're going to disseminate these. They seem like a pretty amazing forensics tool. I'd like to get the specs on these and get that information to Iniquus. We have 3-D cameras to help us process crime scenes, but this camera's ability to demark planer distinctions isn't something I've come across."

"And it's a good price," Nadia said.

"There is that," Brian agreed. He wanted to get the women chatting about their objectives, to see what was on their minds, and what they were working on now. Maybe, just maybe, one of them would mention the artifact from the FBI sting. "What are the projected uses?"

"Our goal is to get five thousand cameras to Syria by the end of the year," Sophia said, then looked up at him. "Tea?"

Brian held up a hand to indicate no.

Sophia passed a cup to Nadia. "The cameras have memory cards that can be brought to America for Nadia and me to work with. We'll curate the images and make them searchable. The teams will have rechargeable batteries, and we're sending solar panels for them."

"Five thousand cameras take up a lot of space. When you get them into Syria, along with all their paraphernalia, how do you get them distributed? And how do you get folks trained in their use?"

"That's a challenge." Sophia took a nibble of the cookie and put it back on her saucer. "We're giving them to our network—people working on the ground, and asking them to do their best. It's a fluid situation, and we don't have a lot of information. Every time we receive a communication, it means someone is putting themselves and their families at risk of being tortured and killed. We can suggest sticking one in their glove compartment, driving it out to a village. But that might be lethal. We'll let those in the know do what they can. You understand what I'm saying. You were talking earlier about decision making in Bagdad. Lives over art. Always."

Nadia sent Sophia a look asking for an explanation. When

she didn't get one, Nadia turned back to Brian. "We hope that the distributors can teach their contacts what to do. For example, there are a lot of ancient structures that are being demolished. If the rubble is left in place, and we had 3-D images pre-destruction, then historical restoration experts may be able to—after the conflict cools—go in and put the monuments and edifices back together. That's a big if. A lot of big ifs. But right now, it's all we have."

"Whoever designed the cameras did a good job," Brian said. "They don't look like anything special. It'll make things a bit safer for your colleagues."

"Nadia, how big is the grant? What are they expecting in return for their money?"

"Two point three million, and they want ten thousand images this year."

"What? How are we going to get anything else done?"

"I haven't a clue. But we can talk about it with Jael. He's coming in on Monday."

"Oh, is he now?" Sophia winked at Nadia, and Nadia blushed fiercely in response. Sophia turned to Brian. "Nadia's first crush is still squeezing her heart. Poor thing." Sophia's voice had the teasing lilt of a sister. She turned back to Nadia. "Do you want to see what he sent this morning?"

"Yes." Nadia set her mug on the floor, gathered the tray, and walked it back to the kitchen. "Hey," she called out. "What's this thing?" Nadia came back with a sharp piece of metal in her hand.

"Brian told me to walk around my car before I drove. That was wedged under my back tire. If I backed up, I would have been out changing the darned thing again."

"When did you drive this morning?" Brian asked.

"I didn't." Sophia didn't understand why he sounded so accusatory. She could drive her darned car without Brian Ackerman's permission. "I was checking out the property to see what needed clearing up. I looked at the tires because—I don't know, I just looked at the tires. I thought you wanted me to."

Brian picked up a piece of paper from her printer and held it out under the metal spike. "May I have that please, Nadia?"

Nadia dropped it onto the paper. Brian folded it up and went to take it to his car.

As he was slipping out the door, he heard Nadia say, "He's going to find out who's doing this. I know he is. This is a good thing. He's protecting you. You're safe."

He held the door for a moment to hear the rest but shut it quietly when Nadia said, "Come on now, show me what Jael sent."

The three of them were huddled around the desk in a tight circle. Nadia was calling out GPS coordinates, and Sophia was mapping. As the information populated the map, they saw clusters emerge. On another screen, Sophia had the same map overlaying a satellite image she had been investigating.

"What are these numbers you're inputting here?" Brian pointed at the red pin she'd just placed.

"I'm indicating significance."

"What makes them more or less significant?"

"Nadia and I have a scale that's more feel than fact. We judge rarity, age, size, scale, beauty. The kinds of metrics that would be taken into consideration at auction houses and on the black market. Of course, it's mostly a stab in the dark. With the images we've been getting from a normal digital camera, we have to hope that, for example, someone thought to include a marker—a coin, for example—that can help us understand the size."

"If you're guessing, why do you do it? Give them a significance number, I mean."

"Sometimes, our allies have to choose which areas to protect. They look to us for guidance. This system gives us a hierarchy. If we have a thousand examples of item x, but y is precious, unique, and amazing, then that's where we should put our effort."

"Who asked you to do that?"

"No one," Sophia said a little too quickly, like a child who had been caught with her hand in the cookie jar.

Someone most assuredly had asked for this data, Brian thought.

"I agree with Sophia," Nadia said. "If the Pentagon were to call and ask if there were areas that they shouldn't bomb, and we only had a few minutes to get them the coordinates, then we can scan this map and make a good assessment based on a mathematical formula."

"Academically flawed as it may be," Sophia said.

"We can only do what we can do."

Brian felt the buzz of danger running from the back of his neck over his scalp. "Who has access to this data?"

"Sophia and I, you, and we can show it to Thorn if you'd like. Since you're part of the team that's supposed to keep everything secure, you should know what we're trying to protect."

"No one else knows about this?"

Nadia put up another photo. "You seem a little intense, Brian. What are you thinking?"

Brian pointed at the new image. "Can you zoom in on that?"

Sophia adjusted the screen, letting her software fix the pixilation, making the image of the hand holding a small statue stand out.

"Can you go left? I want to see that guy's tattoo."

Sophia worked to change the focus. "You have a thing for tattoos?"

"Stop there. Get closer. Do you know this guy?"

"Yeah, sure. Nadia and I have known him since we were little kids. That's Jael."

"I know someone with that exact same tattoo. Where's this guy from?"

"Dual citizen, US, and Israel. His dad worked with our dads on digs. Jael and I played in the sand together." Sophia sent a wicked grin toward Nadia. "Of course, the games Jael and I played were nothing like the games he played with Nadia."

"Shut up."

"Why is he involved in collection work?" Brian pulled his phone from his pocket, pretending to check a text. He took a surreptitious picture of the screen.

"He was educated in America and joined his father in the non-school parts of the year, like Nadia, and I did with our fathers. He's very knowledgeable about antiquities, though he has no formal education. When he turned eighteen, he joined the military in Israel, it was required. And he went into the Special Forces. We thought he had died in an attack on a military convoy, but he turned up later, which was a great miracle."

"I imagine it felt that way," Brian agreed. "And why is he working with you now?"

"The Israeli government is afraid that Hezbollah and Hamas are getting a good-sized cut of the ISIS money because ISIS is shipping artifacts along the drug routes. He's doing what we're doing. Trying to preserve and protect. Trying to stop the sales and profits."

"Does he have access to your information? These maps, for example. Do you share them with him or anyone else in your network?"

Nadia sent him a worried look. "Well, yes, on occasion."

"Are you ladies going to be working on this more today?" he asked.

"All day. We have a lot of data to get through," Sophia said.

"If you don't mind, I'm going to leave for a few hours." He stood. "I have some paperwork and meetings. I'll be back tonight."

"That's okay. You don't have to," Sophia said. "I've had two good night's sleep now, and I only plan to take half a pill tonight. That lets me get to sleep and stay asleep, but in an emergency, I can handle myself."

Brian stalled. *Shit.* "It's not an inconvenience. I don't mind at all."

"Thank you. But it's Friday night. I'm sure there's someone who's expecting you to take her out for a good time. Sitting on my couch, counting dust bunnies is well above the call of duty."

Brian stood, mind racing, trying to find some way to talk himself back into Sophia's guest bedroom. He turned pleading eyes on Nadia, the voice of reason who had gotten him in the door in the first place.

"Tomorrow, we'll be over bright and early," Nadia said. "Three women, five kids, and a pool potluck. It'll be good to relax. We should probably talk Monday morning, though, and get a game plan together. I have more information about Peru. And Jael is flying in. You may want to be around for that."

Brian didn't miss the startled look, Sophia shot Nadia's way.

19

Friday p.m.

"Ready for some shit?" Brian asked.

"Bound to be connected with Sophia," Nutsbe said.

The three of them were gathered around Nutsbe's computer. Thorn was flipping through papers that were shooting into the printer tray.

"Sophia *and* Nadia." He scrolled through his phone to pull up the picture of the tattoo.

Thorn and Nutsbe came to immediate attention.

"No way," Nutsbe said.

There on the man's left arm, exactly where the face of a watch would be found, was a geometric design based on the Sephirot from the divine tradition of the Kabbalah. It was the emblem used by an esoteric group dating back to the Crusades and the Knights Templar.

"I thought we got the whole group. Did the feds release anyone?" Nutsbe's fingers flew over his keyboard.

"This is Sophia and Nadia's childhood friend. A dual citizen —American-Israeli. He's on their team to help save Syrian artifacts. He seems to be in a leadership role. The women communicate with him frequently, and they share their data with him regularly," Brian explained. "His name is Jael Cohen. They thought he died in an explosion, but then, ta-da! He showed back up on the scene. Sound familiar?"

Just this past December, their fellow Panther Force brother, Gage Harrison, killed two men with this same tattoo when they broke into his fiancée's apartment and tried to kidnap her. As they dug their way through the case, Panther Force captured or killed twelve men, all told. Every single one of them had that tattoo. All were listed as KIA in the Middle East, only to show up a decade later, happy and healthy and living in America. Panther Force thought they'd rounded up all of them. The Panthers called them Rex Deus after the ancient group swore that they would return to the Holy Land and find the treasures safeguarded there. The Rex Deus band of brothers hadn't given up a single detail about their group.

"Jael Cohen," Nutsbe muttered under his breath. "He's listed with Israeli military as KIA in Israel. It doesn't look like they know he's risen from the ashes. I don't see any information about him being dead in American databases. Date of birth... American social security... He's traveling on an American passport between Turkey and the US on a fairly regular basis. Lists business travel... Hmm. Let me put this through the database and see if we can't get his face associated with his tattoo." He clicked another key. "This'll take a minute."

"We can get eyes on him ourselves. Apparently, he's coming to Washington on Monday," Brian said.

"We need to let Gage know we've got a new Rex Deus on American soil. It would be nice if we could drag this guy's ass into a room and ask him a few questions about their organization." Nutsbe typed as he spoke. "I'm sending Special Agent Prescott an email. I'll cc Gage and Titus—they may want to get a protection detail on Dr. Kealoha while Cohen is here."

"This guy feels like he's on a different task. I don't think he cares much about Dr. Kealoha and micro-robotics. Do you think Rex Deus might be Israel's Iniquus?"

"Hell, no. Can you see us doing anything like what they've been up to? I'm betting that Israel put together a black ops unit. They staged a catastrophe that took their special forces off-grid, and now they're being deployed in ways that can't be sanctioned by the state. And I think that Israel is probably none too happy that we've already got hold of a dozen of their special boys."

"Interesting twist. Right now, we've got nothing on the guy beyond his training, his tattoo, and his long-term friendship with Nadia and Sophia," Thorn said.

"Nadia's relationship with him goes beyond friendship—well, it did at one time. Seems like she'd like it to now as well," Brian added.

Nutsbe gave a thoughtful nod. "The plot thickens."

"What else have we got?" Thorn asked. "All these pages Nutsbe's printed out from the women's correspondence are what we'd expect to find. Checking up on people. Checking in. Warning folks to stay away from certain areas. Nothing we could take to court."

"Speaking of court, I found out why Sophia's got a date in front of the judge in ten days. She's trying to make a case for her children inheriting Grandma's estate."

"Who's making a claim?"

"Betty Campbell. Matthew Campbell's daughter."

"Matthew's daughter, not Jane's?" Thorn asked.

"Right, this was an out of wedlock baby, born to a different mother well before Matthew and Jane married and had Hunter. Matthew and Jane had a typical will. If Jane died, Matthew got everything; if Matthew died, then Jane got everything. If they died at the same time, their offspring would split everything. Betty wasn't mentioned by name, only Hunter."

Thorn cocked his head to the side. "Sophia doesn't want to split the estate with Betty?"

"Matthew died first, leaving everything to Jane. Betty is not kin to Jane. Jane's son is dead. Following the will, all of Jane's possessions should go to Hunter's offspring."

"Huh." Thorn scratched his hand over his chin. "Do we know anything about Betty? Was she close to her dad? Not that it matters much."

"Betty has a rap sheet of petty crimes, mostly drunk and disorderly. She obtained her GED while in jail. There's nothing in the database for the last six years. The lawyer who's representing her is the kind who takes a major cut of the cake if you win and walks away with nothing if you lose. We all know that that makes them kind of rabid in the courtroom."

"Betty doesn't have a case, though, does she?" Brian said, thinking back to the reason Sophia told Nadia she wouldn't leave the neighborhood. *If it weren't for the 9/10ths rule, I'd be out of here in a heartbeat.* She must be entrenched in that toxic atmosphere to preserve her children's inheritance. He pulled out his phone and dialed. "Sophia, Brian, here." He tapped the button for the speakerphone and laid it on Nutsbe's desk.

"Hey," she said, then her voice became muffled. "Try that area there on the left-hand side of the screen." Her voice came back louder. "How can I help you?"

"One of the things we always do is run background on folks

we're watching over. We're looking at security risks, and I just came across the name Betty Campbell with regards to you."

His pause was met with silence.

"It says you two are headed to court. I'm just wondering if you feel threatened by the woman in any way. Is she a risk to your work that we need to spend time on?"

"Betty's my deceased husband's half-sister. Why would you think she might be a risk to my work?"

"The court documents say she wants to inherit your mother-in-law's estate. I'd imagine it's sizeable."

"It's not like the Campbell's were millionaires." Sophia's voice trailed off. "Betty wouldn't be taking anything from me. I'm not in line to inherit." Her voice cracked. Nutsbe turned the monitor so Brian could see that Sophia had wrapped a hand around her throat, her eyes wide with fear. "Do you think she might do something to hurt my sons?" she whispered.

Brian immediately understood his mistake and wished he'd taken a less direct route. Asked Nadia. Done more digging on his own. "There's no reason to think that. None. But I can tell I've made you nervous. I'm sorry. I'll give it a thorough look, I promise—but I'm sure there's nothing there. Can you tell me about her? How do you two get along?"

"Betty was Matthew's estranged daughter. Jane's stepdaughter. I've never met her."

"She never went to the funerals? Not even her dad's funeral?"

"No. I don't think she had any contact with the family at all. I'm not even sure how she found out Jane died. She filed court papers that same week, though."

"Do you know if she ever asked her dad for money as an adult?"

"I heard stories about her as a rebellious teenager. She ran away from her mom's house, played with drugs, was in and out of juvie. I can't recall hearing anything about her as an adult. Matthew was in high school when Betty was born. He was way too young to parent."

"Do you have a photo of her?"

"No. I went through all of Matthew and Jane's things when I put them in storage. There's not a single picture of her as a child or as an adult."

"Interesting."

Sophia had moved over to the arch separating the office from the kitchen and lay her head against the wooden molding. "Really? That's your take on things?"

"Wrong word. I meant I'm interested in how and why she feels entitled to your mother-in-law's inheritance."

"Because Jane's money came from her husband, Betty's father. And because I'm under a perpetual shitstorm, and there's no practical reason to expect a change in the forecast." Sophia paused, then whispered, "Brian, you promise you'll let me know if my kids are in danger?"

Brian kept his tone light and unconcerned, hoping that would ease the stress he'd just put on Sophia's shoulders. And here he was supposed to be pulling monkeys off her back, not adding to her distress. "I highly doubt there's anything there, but I promise to follow up. I won't let anything happen to your boys."

When he got off the phone, Thorn and Nutsbe were staring at him.

Brian said nothing.

Nutsbe cleared his throat. "All righty then, now that *that* can of worms has been opened and Brian has pledged the safety of two children who are *not* listed on our contract, at least that promise will be short-lived. The judge should rule on the case Monday after next."

"Any chance she'll lose?" Thorn asked.

"We can run it through legal if need be. On the surface, Betty's grabbing at air. I'll bet she's going to make a pre-trial offer for x amount of money to just walk away. Virginia law says that Jane had to live a hundred and twenty hours longer than Matthew to inherit everything. And she definitely did that, so Matthew no longer has an estate. Sophia is being represented by Graham Danforth. A reputable lawyer. He's not going to fall for any shenanigans."

"So this inheritance, it's big enough that Sophia can dig out of her financial crisis?" Thorn asked.

"The house, for sure. That title is clear. Sophia and the boys could continue to live there rent-free. As far as the rest goes, assets have been listed, but they don't have a numeric value, along with a daunting list of liabilities—again, without any particulars. I assume Sophia and her lawyer will present that as evidence when they get to court. Betty's lawyer didn't file for discovery or do any of the things one would expect. Too bad, too. It leaves us in the dark. I bet Sophia'll get out of this with the house and possibly something to pay the lawyer. Maybe make a dent in the debt mountain."

"Hopefully, she can sell the place and move somewhere without that level of insanity," Thorn said.

Nutsbe pulled up a new screen. "You don't think she'd just move on to a new catastrophe? She's kind of a modern-day Calamity Jane."

"Except that Calamity Jane got her nickname because she was riding with her troop when their leader was shot, turned her horse around, rode up and caught the guy as he was falling from his saddle. She pulled him onto her horse and galloped his ass back to the fort, saving his life," Thorn said.

"Yeah—definitely not Calamity Jane." Nutsbe turned to Brian. "Who am I thinking of?"

"I don't know, Typhoid Mary, maybe?"

The computer pinged, and Nutsbe opened the new file. "It's from research." He took a moment to read. "I sent them Pierre and Marla Richards's names to see if they could get anything on that looney tune."

Brian moved to read over Nutsbe's shoulder. "They have Pierre Richards, but no Marla Richards associated. Too many Marla Richards's in her age bracket in their database. None in the Northern Virginia area. More information is required to process."

"We need her wallet," Thorn said.

"She'll be easy to find. I put a GPS tracker on her car so the computer would alert me when she was near Sophia." Brian pulled his phone from his pocket and checked the app. "She's at home right now."

"I'll follow up," Nutsbe said. "I'm starting to get middle-aged spread from sitting behind this damned desk." He tapped the alert button on his computer. "Sophia's landline has an incoming Syrian phone call."

20

BRIAN
Friday p.m.

"Sophia, we're onsite." The heavily accented voice was breathless and jubilant. "You wouldn't believe what we have here. I'd say this area dates back to the Bronze Age, through maybe the classical period."

"How much damage would you estimate? I'm pulling up your coordinates now."

"Surface to air missile batteries. There are three armored vehicles dug in. We've uncovered an ammunition bunker, but it doesn't look like looters have been given this area yet. We could try to excavate the site ourselves." It was a male voice, struggling for air as if he were climbing and talking simultaneously. "But to be honest, we may be targets for US bombs if we do. With this military apparatus around, they might mistake us for an active enemy."

"Why do you think ISIS dug in there and left?"

The three Iniquus liaisons watched Sophia on Nutsbe's screen.

"It is a legitimate military position. Many of our finest archaeological sites are also valuable strategically. Civilizations at war have always sought the high ground. These archaeological tells are prime real estate for ISIS."

"I saw military movement in that area a while back. Did they abandon their equipment, do you think?"

"Surely not. This puts us in limbo. Do I tell the forces who are fighting ISIS this equipment is here? Do I allow ISIS apparatus to remain, with the slim hope they will leave the tells and the relics alone? If I report it, there is a good likelihood the rebels will bomb the site. The artifacts would be at risk. I don't know where to turn, what to do. You have the best access to satellite imagery, far better than what I have. What do you advise me to do, my friend?"

"It will take me a minute to get to the right images. As I do that, I can tell you that on the ground, tanks were attacking Qalaat al-Madiq on Wednesday. The Syrian Observation Group for Human Rights said that twenty-one people died, four of them civilians. They've been shelling in Hama Province for seventeen days now. I'm guessing they're trying to root out the rebels."

"What's happening now?"

"Hang on." Sophia put the handset down and pushed the button for the speaker. "Okay, it looks like the Syrian army's been busy digging tanks into the top of Tell Kifa. The citadel would be a good vantage point to shoot at the lower town. Have you heard an update from Krak des Chevaliers?"

"It is taking repeated air attacks. There is not much hope left for that area."

"I am so sorry. It's a loss for all of us. I'm scanning over the images, and I'm not seeing much in the way of military activity in your immediate area. I think the plan right now should be to watch and wait. Let's see if ISIS is going to come back to this tell. If you can keep me updated with specifics, I have contacts who can get the information to the military. Whether they'll pay attention or not, I can't promise. But if you start trying to excavate the tell, surely someone's going to say something to someone else, and you'll make ISIS think you're stealing from them. I don't want anything bad to happen to the villagers or our friends." She reached over and picked up the receiver again, pulling her foot under her thigh and leaning her weight onto her elbows. "I'm sending the 3-D cameras that we spoke about soon. I've approved them. We have financing in place. The AACP is going to airship them as quickly and quietly as possible. Jael will make sure that your group has what you need. As far as the artifacts on your tell go, we'll need to be satisfied with the documentation for now."

"Yes, yes. We can do that. Thank you so much for everything. I pray every day for you and Nadia. That you will continue to be able to help our efforts. Thank you."

"It's my pleasure," Sophia said, and the call ended.

Nutsbe blew out a breath as the team watched Sophia hang up the phone and walk out of her office. "When she says 'my pleasure' in that bedroom voice of hers, all kinds of pictures pop into my brain."

Brian sent daggers his way. "Lips and dick zipped."

"We're not going to be on this assignment forever, man." He smacked Brian's chest with a grin. "Too bad she'll probably be in supermax when we're done."

"Let's get our notes together for Finley and Andersson." Thorn shifted papers out of the way. "In my mind, there was debt hanging out there on Sophia's end. It was the perfect reason for Sophia to make a choice to do a deal with the devil. This lawsuit may take some pressure off. On a personal note, I hope that's true. Another piece to that is, if she *is* guilty, I'd still like to press the FBI to turn her, keep her out of jail in return for her cooperation. If she's not helping ISIS for ideological reasons, that is. Her knowledge and contacts are unique and listening to her on that call, I'm convinced she'd be a good person for Iniquus to partner with. Add in her language skills, her knowledge of the area, and prison would be a huge waste of her talents. Any thinking person could see that. She could still present in court as if she'd been functioning as an informant all along."

Brian was right on board with that line of thought.

Nutsbe was bending a paper clip back and forth until it broke. "There's always the possibility that the perp isn't motivated by money. You mentioned being ideologically aligned with ISIS. Do we know anything about Sophia or Nadia's religious views? This new player on the scene, Jael of the effing Rex Deus, that's got me stymied."

"If we're stretching the envelope to see how wide we can make it," Thorn said, "why couldn't the perp be aligned with the Museum of the Holy Bible or be madly in love with one of the Gilchrest clan? Maybe even *be* a member of the Gilchrest clan."

"All right, stop." Nutsbe shifted in his seat. "I can take a look at those things, but in the meantime, there's one of those cloak and dagger phone calls to Sophia that you two need to hear." Nutsbe pulled up a video of Sophia at her desk with the sound on mute. Then he tapped to play the audio file that would include both callers' voices.

"Did you get my message?" Sophia asked.

"We did. Well done." It was a man's voice this time. *"This is exactly the opportunity we've been looking for. We passed the*

information through the channels, and an arrangement was agreed to."

"Where did you find this package?" Sophia asked, rolling her chair over to enter the coordinates as they were readout. *"Got it. I don't want any mistakes. It's imperative that it is that particular piece and no other."*

"Understood. It's in our possession."

"Is it en route? How is it getting to the US?"

"The courier will hand-deliver the item."

"Okay, good. And the money?"

"It will be transferred as we hand the piece to its owner on Monday."

Nutsbe grunted. "I do believe that Sophia has stuck her foot in the FBI web and is about to get stung. The coordinates on her computer are for the site listed for the tablet. It sounds like she's sent her people to pick up the artifact the FBI is tracking. And it's headed for the US on Monday. The same day, by the way, their buddy with the Rex Deus tattoo is headed to town." He lifted his brows. "An interesting coincidence, don't you think?"

Thorn and Brian left Nutsbe to his searches and headed to the cafeteria for some grub.

"You've got your heart on your sleeve, man," Thorn said quietly as they moved down the hall. "Titus put you in one hell of a fix by asking you to go after Sophia when he knew you had a previous relationship."

"We had a conversation, not a relationship," Brian countered.

Thorn put his hand on Brian's shoulder, moving him toward an empty office and shutting the door.

"We're all brothers on Panther Force. I'm doing a gut check. This isn't looking good for Sophia. Even you have to admit that.

I like Sophia, I really do. I wish to hell that her life was easier and this wasn't happening. I'm hoping we can find a way to dig her out. But you've got to be prepared for what's coming. You have to know, I'm going to hate putting those cuffs on her wrists. But if she's guilty of providing information to fund terror—"

"Then, she needs to be punished. Agreed." Brian was short-circuiting. The mental image of Sophia on the ground with her hands cuffed behind her and some asshole's knee in the small of her back messed with him in ways he'd never experienced before. He needed to forgo his dinner and hit the gym hard. Burn through the chemicals that made his brain crazy. He needed to be the steady, clearheaded force that figured this out and wrangled the best possible outcome. At least Sophia had Lana to keep her kids when the shit hit the fan. *If* the shit hit the fan. "Let's not get tunnel vision. There are a ton of moving parts on this one."

"Means, motive, opportunity, bro."

"Got it." Brian moved to the door. "Now we need to find the evidence."

21

Sophia
 Saturday a.m.

"Here it is," Nadia said from under the pool umbrella. She held up a plastic dolphin and made her way back to Sophia and Lana. The kids were splashing around in the kiddie pool while the women dangled their feet in the cold water.

"They aren't going to last long. Their lips are already turning blue," Lana said. "It'll be a few weeks yet until the water really warms up."

"Gorgeous day, though." Nadia pulled her sunglasses from her hair and put them in place, turning her face toward the sky.

Lana handed the dolphin over to Chance. "Hey, guys, let's keep the splashing down, okay?" She pulled out her phone and flipped through it. "I saw something on TV last night. This guy looked like he was kin to Brian. Hang on. Yeah, Brian's definitely got a Stephen Amell vibe going for him."

Nadia pulled her phone from her beach bag. "Stephen who? Spell the last name."

"A-M-E-L-L. A Canadian actor. He played—"

"Hmm. Maybe. Brian's got a better jawline. And better shoulders. But I guess I get what you're saying. It's those amazing blue eyes. Like Zac Efron."

"Not Efron. He's too unapproachable. Shiny. Like he's trying too hard. Brainiack is a good combination of a stud muffin and a man willing to take out the garbage."

Sophia glanced their way, then put her focus back on the boys. "Lana, you're married."

"You and Nadia aren't."

"Nadia and I aren't in the market."

Nadia leaned sideways until she and Sophia were shoulder to shoulder. "Look at this, Sophia." She pulled back. "No, wait. It says he has a brother—oh wow, yes, Robbie, that dark hair... Yeah, Brian could fit right into the Amell clan." She leaned back over so Sophia could see as she flipped through the pictures. Sophia glanced down for a second, then back up to take a head-count of their kids. The pool was filling up as people made their way in for the opening day party.

"I bet you anything Brainiack was raised with a houseful of sisters. Maybe even by a single mom. You can tell how much he respects women. His smile just says nice."

"Wrong. He grew up on a farm in Idaho with nine siblings. At least seven of them were boys because he's the seventh son of a seventh son."

"That's supposed to be something, isn't it?" Lana glanced her way with a grin and a flick of her brow. "Does it give him magical powers or something?"

Nadia kicked Sophia's leg. "Do tell. What are Brian's magical powers? Does he sparkle when he's excited?"

"Shut up." Sophia looked up just as Marla, Penny, and Kay walked through the gate with their kids. *Shit.*

"Brainiack is a terrible nickname. Why do they call him that?" Lana asked as she stowed her phone in Nadia's bag. "It reminds me of those horrible songs mom used to make us listen to in the car. Remember, Nadia?"

"That was the Animaniacs," Nadia said, bumping Sophia and lifting her chin to make sure Sophia realized Marla was there. "Yeah, I hated them too."

"Brainiack comes from his full name. Brian Ackerman—the Iniquus operatives all go by their radio handles from the military."

Nadia tossed a loose ball back over to the kids. "How do you know that?"

"He told me."

The ball sailed back over their heads, and Nadia caught it with her fingertips. "Huh, I should ask Thorn how he got his name. What else did Brian tell you?"

"Nothing. Though you should know, I asked him about learning more self-defense. I want him to teach us how to shoot a gun and beat someone up." Sophia hid the fact that her gaze was tracking Marla with the mirrored lenses of her sunglasses. It meant keeping her head forward while her eyes strained to the left in order to keep Marla in her peripheral vision. It was giving her a headache as she slid her attention from the boys to Marla— back and forth.

Nadia showed her a photo of Brian in his Iniquus uniform, standing outside on Sophia's sidewalk. "Come on, Sophia, you have to admit Brian has some serious hunk power in that uniform."

Sophia turned her head. She didn't want to encourage this conversation any longer. She had another problem to deal with.

She'd deal with her Brian issues a different day. "I see Brian as a teammate. A professional. I don't need to be comparing him to Hollywood hunks, getting my panties in a bunch."

"But you asked him to teach you how to wrestle." Lana laughed. "If I had a man like that holding me down… Whew!" She fanned her face.

"I was thinking more of kicking someone in the nuts to give myself enough time to put a bullet in their head. The last time we were in the field, things didn't go very well." Sophia turned to catch Nadia's eye, remembering the sheer terror of the experience. Lana had never been interested in archaeology. She spent her summers in the US with her mom. She'd been safe at home when Sophia and Nadia were kidnapped and their dads held at gunpoint. They'd never told anyone except for Lana about the "incident." Their dads made them promise. It was safer to keep their mouths shut.

It had been bad advice. Sophia's therapist said that stuffing those emotions at the beginning of her long road had complicated her recovery, leading to her problems with post-traumatic stress and NEAD. To be honest, since the kidnapping, her life had been a series of traumatic events. That's why she disagreed with the "post" part of the diagnosis.

"Mommy, I have to pee." Turner stood beside her, pinching himself through his swim trunks.

"Bathroom run," Sophia called. "Chance, Joshua, Francis, Jake, come on, guys." Lana's boys helped Chance get over to her, and they all clambered out and made their way to the bathroom.

Sophia stood at the sink, lifting one little boy at a time up onto her elevated knee to help them wash their hands. Joshua and Turner were already playing under the hand dryer, so Sophia missed Marla sneaking up behind her.

"Shhhhhhhhhh." Marla hissed like a Dementor come to suck all the happy from the environment. She stood so close that her warm breath tickled the tiny cilia in Sophia's ear. So close that Sophia could feel Marla's body heat. Sophia's skin iced.

"I'm going to get you," she whispered. Her spittle flecked Sophia's cheek and throat. And then she moved off, heading back outside before Sophia could react.

"Ouch, Aunt Sophia, you're squishing me!" Francis wriggled on her knee.

Sophia set the child down. Fear was a throbbing pain behind Sophia's eyes that clouded her vision. She could no longer feel her feet against the cement, her legs bearing her weight. The sounds of the hand dryer and the boys' giggles hung in a cloud over her head. Her breath stopped. Held. A push sent her reeling into the sink. Snapped her back into her body.

"Sorry, Mommy." Little black eyes looked up at her.

"It's okay, baby, let's wash your hands."

Sophia shook herself to get rid of the veil of anxiety that Marla had left behind. She forced herself to smile at Jake. "You're up next, buddy." The boys were oblivious, but Sophia knew that she had been slipping into a seizure. The second one this week. If she told her doctor…if anyone knew, she could lose her driver's license for a year. She reflected on how hard things had been when she wasn't allowed to drive. Back then, she was living on the bus line with a student pass. Now, she'd have to pay for Lyfts. Wait for them to show up. Transfer the car seats. The hassle would be enormous. It also would put her and the kids at risk by not being able to jump into a car and go. Right there and then, she decided to hide this from Lana and Nadia. No one could know she was having problems again.

She moved back toward the kiddie area. The five boys tucked their hands into their armpits, quacking as they waddled after her. Lana was grinning at the kids. "Come on, little duckies, it's time to eat."

Nadia's face was painted with worry. "What happened?"

Sophia blinked innocently. "What do you mean?" Nadia wasn't buying her act. She sent Sophia a worried look as she bent down and took two little hands in hers and moved toward the parking lot where grills were being manned by dads in "King of the Coals" and "In Dog Beers, I'm Two" aprons.

Sophia could smell the meat cooking, and it turned her stomach. Lana held the hands of two more boys, and Sophia scooped Chance into her arms. "Where are your flip-flops, sweetie?"

A dimpled hand pointed to the corner of the children's area. Sophia moved to get them—she wouldn't be able to balance their plates and Chance at the same time, and the pavement would be blistering hot in this sun. She bent to pick them up, and as she righted herself, she realized that she had been cornered. Wedged into the corner with fencing to her right and left, Marla stood behind her, hissing like a snake. Sophia searched her brain for a quip or a something. Her muscles held her frozen like a mouse between the paws of a cat.

"Mommy, down!" Chance wriggled himself out of her arms and down her leg.

"Sophia!" Nadia's stern voice yelled from behind her. "Come on."

Sophia was freed. She pushed to the side to follow Chance as he ran toward Nadia and his brother.

"I'm going to get you," Marla whispered.

Sophia fell in line with Nadia. "What the hell was going on?"

"Marla's nuts. We all know that. Don't respond. Any reaction is a victory."

"I don't think that strategy is working. Look, you've got goosebumps. What did she say?"

"Nothing worth repeating," Sophia said, waving at one of the lifeguards who always smiled at her kids. "Let's get the little ones fed."

Lunch did not go well. As Sophia stood in line, Marla stood inches behind her, so close, her breath shifted the hairs on the back of Sophia's neck. Her heart was pounding as she warned herself to ignore the woman. Pleaded with herself not to react. But her mouth took control, and Sophia turned. "Get away from me, you psycho." The moment she said it, she regretted it. Marla's eyes lit with triumph. She had given this woman proof that she was getting under her skin.

Lana and Nadia were flanking her in a moment. They walked together back to the pool and to the privacy of their umbrella-covered table. Lana and Nadia took control of the kids and let Sophia sit with her back to the rest of the pool, looking out over the lawn to the trees beyond. Repeating the mantra her meditation teacher had given her, trying to keep her sanity intact and her outward composure calm, Sophia knew she would need a new strategy to handle Marla. Maybe Brian would know what to do.

Pierre Richards had brought one of his kids in to play in the kiddie pool. He waved to the women then moved over to chat. Pierre had an easy-going disposition, a wiry, runner's body, and a persistent Quebecois accent. "Are you ladies having a fun time at the pool?"

"No. Not particularly." Sophia stood and moved to talk with him.

"No?" he asked, seeming a bit mystified that his banal greeting didn't get the usual "Great! How about you?"

"Marla is a certifiable nut job. Your wife has been following me around all day hissing in my ear and telling me she's going to get me." Sophia's anger felt good. She liked the power it gave her and wanted to keep that sensation brewing.

"Wait. Marla's not my wife. We're just…she just decided… *Hissing*?" Pierre drew his brows together. His gaze sought over the area, trying to locate Marla.

"Slithering up behind me, leaning up against me, *hissing* in my ear," Sophia repeated.

Marla barreled in their direction.

The lifeguard was blaring her whistle. "No running in the pool area, even if you're an adult."

Marla slammed to a halt next to Pierre.

Sophia planted her hands on her hips to make herself look bigger like Brian had when Marla tried to run them off the road.

"What are you telling Pierre? What poison are you pouring into his ears?"

Nadia stood up. "Why would you be so freaked out, Marla, if you hadn't done something crazy in the first place? Why wouldn't you assume they're talking about the kids and vacation plans?"

Marla hadn't moved her eyes from Sophia. "Don't you dare lie about me. Don't you *dare* spread your vile filth." And then she hissed. Spittle dancing over her tongue as air streamed between her lips and teeth.

Pierre's eyes widened; confusion painted across his face. "What the…" He moved to get his body between Sophia's and Marla's. He fixed his hands on Marla's shoulders and gave her a shake. "What is wrong with you?" He pointed toward a lounge chair. "Get your things. We're going home."

Marla didn't move.

"Get. Your. Things. We're going home."

Marla tried to send Sophia a hate-filled glare around Pierre's shoulder, but he leaned to the side to block her.

Marla stomped away.

Pierre turned toward Sophia. "I thought you were kidding. If I hadn't seen that—I'm so sorry. I'm at a loss. Here, here, you're trembling." He put his hands on Sophia's arms. They felt warm and supportive. His eyes were pleading with her, but Sophia didn't understand why. "You'll feel better when she's home behind closed doors. I'll get her out of here."

"She was hissing at you again?" Lana was now standing by her side as they watched the Richards crew scrambling out the gate. Marla turned and flipped Sophia the bird, but Pierre grabbed hold of her arm and wrenched it until she stopped.

"I have to get out of that house. I've got to get my boys somewhere safe. I have no idea what that woman is capable of." She turned frightened eyes toward her friends. "Now that I've outed her to Pierre, she's going to come after me with a vengeance." She put her hands on her head. "What did I do?"

BRIAN

Saturday a.m.

Nutsbe sat back in his chair, tossing a crumpled up ball of paper into the trash like it was a game-winning basket. "Thorn asked me to do a background check on Nadia's foreign family connections since her Dad is Palestinian," he told Brian, who was getting settled in front of a file. "There's nothing in her call history or her passport history that would suggest that she has any family interaction. I shook her family tree to see if there was any fruit. Nadia's grandparents are in Gaza. Her father's brother and two sisters, their families—in-laws and cousins. I looked back at the phone records from the parents to see if there was a connection there. I took the search back to the point where Nadia's dad had his stroke and couldn't speak coherently. There's no communication from that direction. The parents live in upstate New York, and Nadia talks to her American-born mother every Sunday."

"We have two clients on this case, remember." Brian put his finger on the file in front of him. "The AACP thinks we're putting together a team for them down in Peru. Human Resources gave me some people we've worked with in South America, their expertise, and availability."

"You don't think it's a waste of time?"

"I think that if we're taking a paycheck from them, we should be fulfilling our obligations. Even if AACP sends other archaeologists in to do the core samples, the teams will still be in place. We'll need to be able to adapt to new circumstances."

"Sophia's back home," Nutsbe said. "She's kissing the boys goodbye. Huh." He leaned forward and messed with the controls. "Something's not right."

Brian moved around the desk to check the monitor. "The look on her face—"

"Shell-shocked. I've seen that one before." Nutsbe looked over his shoulder at Brian. "I thought you said she was going to the community pool for a potluck and to spend some time with her kids."

"That was the plan."

"You think the psycho stalker nut job might have been there giving her grief?"

Brian pulled out his phone and scrolled through the apps. "Marla's at home. Wanna look back at her history and see if she was up at the Community Center?"

Nutsbe pulled up a split-screen. While he typed the information in, Brian watched Sophia fling herself onto the couch. Tears flowed down her cheeks, but her gaze was straightforward.

"Marla's van was at the pool," Nutsbe said. "She got there a half-hour after Sophia left the house in Lana's van. She got home about twenty minutes before Sophia did. No way to tell if that's what upset her. What's on the wall she's staring at?"

"A picture of her sons."

A knock sounded at the war room door, then Lynx stuck her head in. "Nutsbe, hate to bother you, but I'm checking to see if you heard from Honey today? He's supposed to pass on a message from our contact."

"He hasn't called in yet. Communications in his area are kind of squirrely. I'll give you a call when I hear if you'd like."

"Yeah, that would be great."

"Hey, Lynx, can you come here for a second and look at this?" Brian asked.

Lynx moved up behind the men, leaning between their heads to see the screen. Brian got up and offered her his chair, moving to grab another one for himself.

"Wow, what happened?" Lynx asked.

Nutsbe had honed the camera in on Sophia's face. "We have no idea."

Suddenly, Sophia jumped up and screamed.

Brian's body jolted with adrenaline.

"What the heck are you doing here in my house?" a man yelled.

"Nutsbe, flip to camera E. That sounds like it's coming from upstairs," Brian said.

With a few taps, the image shifted to a split-screen to include an image of Sophia's stairs. They could see two scrawny bare legs at the top.

Sophia pressed a fist to her chest. "Mr. Rochester, you scared me to death."

"Who are you? Why are you in my house?" The elderly man stomped down the stairs, making himself as large as his emaciated body could look. He was wearing blue boxers that hung open, revealing gray hair and soft flesh. "Answer me! Who the heck are you?"

"How'd he get in? I didn't get a warning beep," Brian wondered, pulling his phone from his pocket.

Sophia stood, wide-eyed, shaking her head. Her hands stretched out as if to ward off blows. The other side of the screen showed Mr. Rochester storming his way toward her, grabbing Sophia and throwing her down. He gripped her swim cover-up and shook her until her head bounced on the floor.

"Holy shit," Nutsbe said under his breath.

Brian reached into his pocket for his keys. "I'm heading over."

Lynx put her hand out. "Give her a second. Let's see if she can't talk her way out of this. You barrel in there now, and she's going to wonder how you knew to show up."

Sophia crab-crawled backward. "Mr. Rochester. I'm Sophia. Please don't hurt me. I'm Joe's friend."

"How'd you get in my house? What are you trying to steal?" Rochester yelled.

Sophia had worked her way over to the side chair and used it to pull herself up and hide behind. "Mr. Rochester, Joe, sent me to get you. He fell and hurt himself. He wants you to put on the bandage."

"Liar!" Rochester's fists were up. "You came to steal from me. What did you take?"

Sophia inched her way from one chair to the next.

"Mr. Rochester, Joe needs you. Let's go find Joe. Your son? Joe?" Her voice was shaky and pleading.

Rochester sprang toward Sophia. Sophia ducked and wove, grabbing the front doorknob, yanking the door open until it hit the wall and bounced back in place. But Sophia was already down the front steps, running for her neighbor's house.

Rochester locked the door behind her.

"She's coming back. That must be Joe," Lynx said.

A younger man tried the door, then rang the bell. "Dad, open up. Dad!" He rang again. When the door popped open, there was Rochester with his blue boxers askew, his junk dangling out. Joe turned toward Sophia. "I'm sorry. I am so embarrassed." The younger man's face was red. "This has gotten out of hand. *Obviously.*" He looked back at Sophia. "I'll make sure this doesn't happen again. This has," he bent his head, "clearly surpassed my ability to deal with."

Mr. Rochester had gone back in the house to sit on Sophia's couch.

Joe caught Sophia's eye. "Would you mind stepping out of sight for a second? I'll get Dad home. I promise this won't happen again. I'll find some way…" he trailed off softly.

Sophia moved behind a tree. And Joe very quietly encouraged his father to head home.

After the men had left her property, Sophia went inside, shut the door, locked it, and leaned her back against it. Her breathing was ragged. Loud. She labored to get air into her lungs.

"Do you know what that was about?" Lynx asked.

"One of her neighborhood stressors. The old guy lives next door. Alzheimer's. He gets confused," Nutsbe replied.

Lynx shifted toward Brian. "A lot?"

"Almost daily, it seems."

She flicked a worried glance toward Brian. "Does she normally leave her door unlocked?"

Brian had his focus on Sophia as she moved around her house, checking the doors. "I don't think so. Nutsbe, let's go back and review the tapes."

"Brian, she's not okay," Lynx pointed out. "Look at her coloring. Her eyes. She's visibly shaking. She's like a hurt animal trying to find somewhere to hide and lick her wounds."

"I'm heading over. I just need to know how the guy got in, so I can fix the glitch in the monitoring system." Brian said.

"Here we go." Nutsbe stopped the fast reverse on the video. "Look, Lana pulls up. She goes to the door and rings the bell. Sophia gets the door. She goes in. There's the neighbor. He walked from his yard to Sophia's while the van was in front of the sensor."

"Yeah, I monitored that this morning. I didn't pan out for the whole yard." Brian said.

"Sophia comes out with the boys and is getting them into the van, moves around to the passenger seat, and buckles up. Lana comes out. She didn't check the door. I'm guessing Lana didn't lock it behind her. Scrolling forward... Here we go. Van's gone, old man in blue boxers goes right in the front door."

"Switch to the interior. What does he do next?" Lynx asked.

"Locks the door, goes up the stairs," Nutsbe narrated. "We don't have warrants for visuals of any space but the office and exterior. We were allowed audio in her bedroom, but other than that, we can't tell what's happening upstairs. Luckily, her open floor plan means that, with the right placement, we have a pretty good view of everything on the first floor."

"I'm taking a few more cameras with me today. I need one pointing at the Florida room, and I want one over in that corner between the office and the living room. There's a blind spot Rochester slid into that didn't make me happy."

"Incoming." Nutsbe pointed at the red light flashing at the bottom corner of his screen. He tapped it and watched as Sophia moved hesitantly toward the house phone on her desk. She put her hand on the receiver. Paused. It rang again, and her whole body jerked. She lifted the receiver slowly to her ear. They all listened as five staccato beeps sounded, then the line went dead.

Brian could feel his heartbeat at his temples and the side of his neck. His body sensed a threat and ramped up to meet it with violent force. He held his breath. Was Sophia about to give information to the caller that would further compromise her? Put her at risk for being labeled a traitor? A terrorist? An ISIS sympathizer? It would ruin not only her life but her kids' lives. People's memories were long with crimes like this.

Sophia's cell rang. And rang. And rang. She stood with it in her hand. It stopped, and she put it down on the desk. She grabbed at her hair and pulled.

"What is that, Lynx? Is that part of a seizure?"

"Why did I do it? Why?" Sophia screeched at the ceiling camera as if she knew it was there. "Why can't you just leave me alone? Why?" She reached over to her desk, picking up a file and flinging it across the room, making papers flutter across the floor. She turned to her bookcase and pulled textbook after textbook off the shelf, throwing them with all her might, strewing them around the room. She was crying. Screaming.

"Not a seizure. She's melting down. We need to get over there." Lynx stood and put her hand on Brian's shoulder. "I'm coming with you."

They raced for the deck and Brian's car. His tires squealed around the turns as Lynx pulled her seatbelt across her lap. Brian's foot was lead on the gas pedal as he raced toward the highway ramp.

Lynx's phone buzzed.

"Nutsbe here. Sophia's on the move."

"What? Okay. I'm putting you on speaker. Can you give us a direction?"

"She's heading out of her neighborhood now. She was looking pretty effing determined as she headed out the door, right on Pemberley. I'm guessing she's headed for the highway. I have you up on the screen. If she keeps calm enough to stay at the speed limit, and you guys keep up your present speed, my computer says you'll catch her in less than ten minutes."

"Copy that." Brian checked his speedometer to make sure he wasn't going to get pulled over and arrested for reckless driving. He'd be no help to Sophia in a jail cell. "What happened? Any clue where she's headed?"

"She finished throwing all the books on that shelf. She was standing in the middle of the room yelling shit in a foreign language—Turkish, I'm guessing. Then she grabbed her purse and ran out the door. She only stopped to make sure the door locked behind her. Other than that, she's in tornado mode. Ruh-roh. Marla's on the move."

"Is she chasing Sophia?" Lynx asked.

"Wait for it… Nope. She turned left on Pemberley. Hang in there. You're making progress. She's on the southern entrance ramp. I'm not sure how you're going to explain how you happened to show up at wherever you're heading. But Lynx's presence can be a good cover. You're driving your friend to X Y or Z…"

"Nutsbe? What are you seeing?" Lynx held her phone between Brian and her.

"She's on Route 1. I was looking at what's up the road to see where she might be going. Keep on moving…"

The air crackled in Brian's car. Both operatives were silent as Brian wove through traffic, trying to make better time.

"Okay, she's pulled into a parking lot and parked. I'm texting you the address, Lynx."

"What is it?" Brian asked. "Please tell me it's her therapist's office."

"Nope. It's a gun shop."

23

SOPHIA

Saturday p.m.

Sophia sat in her minivan, giving herself as much time as she needed to compose herself. She wasn't sure this was going to work. She knew from watching the news that there were some restrictions on gun ownership. You couldn't have been found guilty of a federal crime, and you weren't supposed to have a mental health condition. But Sophia thought that her case probably hadn't been reported. She'd never done harm to herself or others. She'd never been institutionalized. She'd never been deemed a risk by the courts. So if she didn't walk in acting like a maniac, there shouldn't be any reason she wouldn't pass a background check and that she couldn't buy a gun today.

Sophia pulled down her visor and looked in the mirror. She pulled her purse over and dug out a brush. She had yanked her hair earlier, and now she looked half-crazed. She smoothed the long strands into a quick ponytail. She was just an easygoing girl who'd heard too many stories on the news and wanted to protect herself. Gun people liked that, didn't they? They thought everyone should be armed and ready. She pulled out a lipstick, colored in her full lips, and inspected her handiwork. She rubbed a little lipstick onto her finger and then onto her cheeks.

Gathering her purse, she exited, smoothing her clothes into place. Would they care that she was in a swimsuit cover-up and flip-flops? Would she stand out? Did she look out of place? She watched as another woman, similarly clad, pulled the heavy door open and walked into the shop. *Okay, good.* Sophia gave herself a shake, squared her shoulders, and made her way up to the counter.

"Hello." A man with a wooly beard and a prominent limp made his way over to her. "What can I do for you?"

There was a constant *pop-pop-pop* coming from somewhere in the back. Sophia sent a worried glance in that direction.

"We have a practice range behind the shop." The man leaned an elbow on the counter and waited.

"Do you offer classes here too?"

"Whatcha lookin' for?" he asked in return.

"I'm a single mom, and I don't live in the best of neighborhoods. I want to buy a gun to protect my kids and me. And I want to know how to keep my kids from getting hurt by getting hold of it. I also need to learn how to shoot it and hit my target. Do I need a license for that?"

"Concealed carry class will give you a lot of what you need. A gun basics class would be good too. We teach those here." He pushed a brochure her way. "As far as the gun goes, first, we need to talk firepower. How many bullets do you want to shoot to take someone down?"

"One won't do it?" Sophia asked, a tremor in her voice. She cleared her throat, hoping that would take care of it. But truth be told, she was terrified about what she was doing. About the ramifications.

"With a .45 caliber, hollowpoint bullet, it's a one and done. 'Course, you've got to get that bullet where it belongs."

"Hollowpoint?"

He pulled a small cardboard box from a shelf and fished out a bullet. "Round tip," he said. "It goes in the front, out the back, and keeps flying. Could go through your wall, through your neighbor's wall. Through someone on the other side. It's fine for range shooting. It ain't the best for home security."

"Oh, no. I can't have bullets flying about!" Sophia sent him a horrified glance.

He fished in the box again and pulled out a bullet that had a hole in the top. "Hollowpoint. When it goes into something—a wall, a body, what have you—it expands out. It mushrooms." He pulled out a blob of metal and put it in her hand. "Like this. More impact on a body. It causes an internal concussive force that can kill someone even with a shot to the leg. It would be rare. But it could happen. But what you really want to know here is that once it goes in something, it's no longer flying around, pinging off things in the environment and hurting you or your kids with a ricochet."

The shop bells jangled behind Sophia.

The man at the counter glanced that way. "I'll be right with you, ma'am." He fished in his box again. "This is a 9mm. This is a .40, and this is a .45."

Sophia picked up the .45. "This is much bigger than the others."

"Sophia?"

A familiar voice had Sophia spinning around. It took her a minute to remember the woman's face, but when the woman lay her hand on Sophia's arm, the effervescent warmth radiating across her skin told Sophia that this was Lynx, the woman who had helped her when she'd had her seizure on the side of the road.

Lynx knew Sophia had PTSD. Would she tell the gun guy? Sophia smiled over her shoulder at the man behind the counter. "I'll be right back." Catching Lynx under the arm, she moved off toward the shelves displaying concealed carry purses. "Small world," Sophia said.

"Yeah, Brian's here with me." Lynx glanced out the picture window, then back at Sophia. "He's getting something out of the car. We're here a lot, seeing what's new, adding to our collections. Kind of goes with the job." She smiled. "Do you shoot? What brings you here?"

Sophia felt her artificial smile slide off her face before she pasted it back in place. "You and Brian?" she asked sweetly. "I didn't realize you were a couple."

The bell rang, and Brian walked through the door. "Hey, Sophia." He made his way over to the women. "You mentioned you were interested in getting a gun. Is that why you're here? I'm sorry. I didn't realize you meant so soon. I would have come with you to help."

"I was asking questions about their shooting range. I think I have to take a class to carry a gun." She held up the brochure. She felt panicked that Brian had found her there, and she couldn't figure out why. She looked between Lynx and Brian, imagining them together. They did look like they were a good fit. That they belonged together. With that thought, Sophia looked around, confused. What the heck was she doing? Sophia couldn't remember the thought process that landed her in a gun shop, other than that she had to protect her boys. She had to save them. She tried to remember leaving her house. Driving.

The walls closed in around Sophia. Her fingers tingled, and she couldn't hold her face in a polite expression. She felt as if she were softening, dissolving like one of the melting clocks in a Salvador Dali painting. She reached out and squeezed Lynx's arm. "It was nice seeing you." Her voice slurred like she'd been drinking.

Sophia had to concentrate very hard on getting her feet to propel her forward. It was as if she had been sitting on them long enough that now she was numb and uncoordinated. She made it to the door, pushing it open with the weight of her hip and body. Her arms had lost their strength.

She didn't know that Lynx was beside her, and Brian just behind, in case she should start to fall. She didn't hear either of them talking to her. She was laser-focused on getting to her van and privacy. She should be out of the gun dealer's line of sight by now. *Another step, Sophia, come on. Move your feet.*

She didn't hear Brian's frustration. She didn't feel him sweep her up into his arms. Her torso was painfully rigid. Her brain screamed for air. Her lids slid down over her eyes. She was in the dark. And now she was without sensation. She wondered if the nothingness meant she was dead.

There. She sensed something. Warmth. It radiated over her back, releasing her frozen lungs. Sophia felt like she had dived off a cliff, and her velocity pushed her farther than she thought possible under the water. But now, finally, she broke free. Her face above the surface, she gulped at the air. Her body was elec-trified as consciousness flooded back. The sensation burned under the surface of her skin, and Sophia cried out in pain.

Strong arms wrapped around her, held her, rocked her.

Brian's voice was in her ear, telling her that she was going to be okay. To hang on. Breathe.

She was too exhausted to do anything but collapse against him. Her head lolled to the side, and he lifted it back into place against his shoulder, cradling it there. Stroking his hand through her hair. Murmuring, "I'm here. I won't let anything bad happen to you. You're safe. Just relax. Everything's going to be fine. You're going to be fine."

Sophia knew in every cell of her body that she wasn't safe. That he couldn't protect her from the bad things that happened to her. And no, everything *wouldn't* be fine. She sniffed and tried to sit up, quickly realizing she wasn't up to it yet. She needed more time.

Sophia hoped Lynx wouldn't feel jealous that she was in Brian's arms. Sophia was glad that Brian was here with Lynx. Since he was assigned to her, she had been so afraid that if he became emotionally invested in her, he'd get sucked into her vortex of destruction. That was her good angel's fear. Her bad angel wanted to stay in Brian's arms, to have him in her life to comfort and support her, maybe even to love her. But Sophia wasn't selfish enough to allow it. Though it was like handing back a full plate while she starved, Sophia swallowed and pushed herself to a sitting position. Her time for comfort was up. She realized she was on Brian's lap and had drooled a big wet spot onto his chest.

"Slowly," Lynx said. She was crouched on the pavement beside Sophia's van. Lynx looked up at Brian. "We should get her home. I'll follow in your car."

Sophia listened to Lynx say "we" and felt reassured. Brian belonged to someone else. He was safe.

Brian hugged her close as he moved from sitting in the van to standing in the parking lot. He set her effortlessly back in the seat, pressed a button to lean her back a little, and adjusted the seat belt around her. Sophia's arms dangled lifelessly in her lap.

It was a quiet drive home. Brian didn't say a word to her. She didn't have the wherewithal to coordinate her lips and tongue for speech. Hopefully, Brian would get her to her couch and leave her to sleep. Alone.

24

SOPHIA

Saturday p.m.

"You're still here," Sophia said, looking over at Lynx and Brian sitting on her couch, each with a computer in their lap. She sniffed; something was cooking.

"You thought we'd leave you alone?" Brian asked.

"I hope you don't mind. I started dinner," Lynx said. "Can I make you a cup of tea? I'd like you to take it easy as you come out of your sleep."

Sophia looked out the window. It was almost dark. She had been out cold for hours.

Sophia hadn't said yes to tea, but Lynx bustled around the kitchen, getting a pot together—like they were old friends, and she knew where everything was stored. She came back in with a tray. "I used one of your ready meals, and I have to say you are an absolute genius for doing that." She smiled and poured the tea. "Brian says you take your tea without milk or sugar?"

Sophia nodded. Brian had only seen her drink tea one time. That was observant of him.

"Is there a story behind your ready-made food supply?" Lynx asked conversationally like they hadn't just scraped her off the sidewalk at a gun shop.

Sophia cleared her throat and reached for the cup and saucer, gratified that they only rattled a little as she moved the saucer to her lap. "When I was little, and Dad and I went on digs together, my mother would make ready meals for us in plastic bags and sent them on with us. All we needed was water and our solar cooker. It was handy and tasted good. When my mother-in-law was injured in the car accident and my children and I moved in with her, I simply didn't have the luxury of leaving the house except for a quick trip to take the boys to and from daycare. So I did what my mom had done. I bought a bunch of freeze-dried ingredients from the prepper store, then I sat down for a few hours one Sunday afternoon and made up enough meals for four months. Breakfast, lunch, and dinner, each has its own shelf. It saves me enormous amounts of time and takes a big chunk of mommy guilt out of the equation, knowing that, if nothing else, my kids are eating nutritiously." Sophia pushed her hair out of her eyes. Somehow, between the gun shop and now, she'd lost her elastic band. "After she died—Jane, my mother-in-law—well, I never got my act together. I seem to fly from one fire to another, putting them out, so…" She lifted a hand and let it drop. "It is what it is. My sons can see what fruit and vegetables look like fresh from the store over at Lana's house."

"Wow," Lynx said. "With all you're going through, you are still such a great mom. I'm so impressed with everything I know about you."

Sophia lowered her lashes. That compliment squeezed her heart. The voice in her head was unforgiving when it came to her failures concerning her sons. It berated her for the hell that was sure to be visited on them because of her. She sniffed and shook her head; she was grateful that the conversation sank into silence. Sophia drank her tea and watched through the window as the first star blinked into view.

After a while, Lynx got up to ladle stew into bowls. Brian had gone out front to check on things. They all gathered and ate in the family room with Sophia tucked under her blankets like an invalid.

Lynx sent a questioning look Brian's way. Sophia thought they must have been a couple for a long time; they seemed to be able to communicate with a mere glance. Lynx would send him a look, and he'd act on it, and vice versa. Like this had all been choreographed in advance.

"Your neighbors across the way are having a party." Brian's voice was a sudden splash of color against the silence.

"That's Kay's house. If you follow the local gossip, she makes killer margaritas that make you want to shed your inhibitions and act like a fool." Sophia stirred her stew without any desire to eat.

"Your other neighbor, Will Sheppard, looks none too pleased. He's watching from his usual spot, standing in his window. What's his story? Do you know him?"

Sophia shrugged. "He's quiet. Nice. He helped me out this morning, for which I am very appreciative."

"Yeah? What did he do?" Brian asked.

"My car wasn't working. I was out of gas, and my lights were left on, so I ran the battery down. He came over with a gas tank, and he gave my battery a charge."

Brian sent her a quizzical look. "In your driveway?"

"I was parked in the cul-de-sac last night. That was a little piece of luck."

"Sophia, your gas tank was full when I drove you home Wednesday. Have you been driving a lot?"

"I haven't been driving much at all. The boys were with Lana." Sophia stared at her lap. "Someone sabotaged my car, didn't they? I found the metal and prevented the flat tire, so they moved on, just like you said they would."

"We can't jump to conclusions." Brian probably meant to sound reassuring, but he was doing a lousy job of it. Concern rippled out with his words. "Would you please park your car where I asked you to? That way, if someone wants to do something to your car, they'd have to expose themselves under the security light. I'm thinking your neighbor is vigilant enough that he'd see something if it were to happen."

"So how did it come about that he helped you this morning?" Lynx asked.

"His wife was having coffee on her front porch, and she must have seen me in the street. She went in, and a few moments later, Will drove over to help. He had a couple of gallons of gas for his lawnmower that he lent me, and he had jumper cables. I went up to the station, filled up my tank, replaced Will's gas, and got some chai. It wasn't nearly as bad as dealing with a flat tire, believe me. That was easy." Sophia smiled. She took a bite of stew because Brian was giving her a funny look, and she was afraid he wouldn't leave if he thought she hadn't physically recovered.

"That whole story's odd." Lynx's eyes were thoughtful. "I have to tell you, I had someone stalking me once. I may not understand your exact situation, but I understand some of the thoughts and stresses involved. It's crazy-making."

Sophia gave her a tight-lipped smile, then forced another bite into her mouth.

"I called Nadia while you were sleeping," Brian said.

Sophia's eyes widened. *Shit.* "What did you say?" she whispered.

"I wasn't ratting you out if that's what you're thinking. Is that how you'd perceive it if I told her you were having a seizure?"

"Yes, actually." Sophia's voice was defiant, just this side of furious. Brian had no idea what the ramifications might be if people knew.

"Well, I didn't tell her anything. I asked what her schedule was like this week. You said you wanted self-defense classes, and given your situation now, and in the field, I believe it's a good idea. I think we need to start as soon as possible."

Sophia let go of some of her tension. She nodded.

"I asked how her day was going. She told me about Marla threatening you at the pool. I think we need to have a serious talk about this."

"Marla doesn't concern you," Sophia said.

"*You* concern me. A lot." There was an intensity about the way Brian said the words that made Sophia turn her head and stare out the window. There was an emotion there that she couldn't examine too closely.

"Sophia, turn around. This is serious." He waited for Sophia to face him again.

She took her time making eye contact, placing her bowl of stew on the coffee table. She couldn't fake eating it any longer. The smell was nauseating.

"Tell me how you're feeling right now," Lynx asked gently. "Do you feel like you're back in your body?"

Sophia turned to Lynx. "Yes. Though I'm still tired." She used her fingers to comb her hair out of her face, twisting it into a rope and letting it drape over her shoulder. "But I'm always tired. I guess I feel like I normally do." Back in her body? That was an excellent way to describe the experience of a seizure like she'd floated off and needed to gather herself back together and anchor in.

Lynx sent Brian a look, then took over the conversation. "I know that the decisions you're making every day are difficult. You've been following your therapist's suggestions and doing everything you can to contain the situation, but today changed things. Would you agree with that?"

"Yes." Sophia wondered what that would mean. She wished she'd been able to get her hands on a gun today.

"Marla has power in the neighborhood because everyone fears her. You can expect your neighbors, except the Sheppards, who seem to be her victims as well, to turn on you. Things might feel like they're getting more difficult."

Sophia filled her lungs with air, then exhaled forcefully.

Lynx scooted to the edge of her chair and leaned forward to touch Sophia's leg. "It's best to have a safety net in place." She paused, letting that sentence sink in. "The police can't act as things stand now. We need to give the police the authority to help you." She paused again. She was speaking slowly, enunciating clearly. That helped the words to make their way into Sophia's consciousness. "We would like you to come with us to the police department and talk to a magistrate."

Sophia didn't know what Lynx meant. She dipped her head to the side.

"The magistrate can issue a temporary restraining order. An Iniquus lawyer will meet us at the police station. All you need to do is walk in with us and answer any questions the magistrate might have."

Sophia shook her head. "That sounds like throwing gasoline on a fire."

"It does. I agree," Lynx said.

The phone rang at Sophia's desk. Her muscles tightened, and she scrunched her shoulders toward her ears, like a child afraid of a thunderstorm.

"Do you want me to get that?" Brian asked.

"No, thank you."

After the last ring, Lynx said, "We absolutely believe Marla will retaliate. But—and this is an important but—she's going to anyway, whether you go to the magistrate or not. You exposed her to her husband. There's been a fight over at their house. I can almost guarantee you. If you leave things the way they are now, you have little recourse. If you have a restraining order in place, officers can arrest Marla for coming near you, your boys, or your property. Give the police the tool they need to help you. Yes?"

"They won't believe me. Why would they believe me?"

"You have witnesses. Brian was driving when Marla tried to run you off the road. He was also at the restaurant when she was spit-balling you. If need be, we can get Lana and Nadia in to tell the magistrate about what they saw at the pool. Getting a temporary restraining order isn't going to be a problem."

Sophia rubbed her fingers over her gold bracelet, staring into her lap, wishing for inspiration.

"You need this. It's going to mean being brave. But you're not talking to Marla. You're talking to the magistrate. The magistrate will listen and file some paperwork. The sheriff will drive over to Marla's house and serve the papers. You won't have to see Marla. Though you should know that won't be the last step. This order would only be temporary, then you'll have to go to court to see a judge and explain why the restraining order should be kept in place. But we'll be with you. As many operatives as you want will be with you. We'll all go and make sure that you feel safe at the courthouse." Lynx stood up. "Come on, let's get this done so that Marla's sober when she gets the restraining order in her hands. If she gets drunk and forgets it exists, it loses some of its power."

Sophia decided not to think more about it. Lynx and Brian did this for a living. They probably knew what was best. "I should probably have something else on besides a bikini and flip flops when I go. Let me change." Sophia moved up the stairs with the distinct feeling that this was the beginning of the end. Not in the happily-ever-after ending kind of way, more like the holy shit, I never saw that coming ending. But maybe this would give her some much-needed respite, letting her stand, even if for a brief moment, in the calm eye of her hurricane.

25

*B*RIAN

Saturday p.m.

"When Lynx left, she took your car." Sophia pointed out the obvious as she unlocked her house. She had her paperwork from the magistrate held tightly in her hand.

Brian was glad that hadn't been as painful as Sophia had expected. Having talked to the police about the situation before and not gotten any kind of support, she hadn't expected to be successful. But true to their word, an Iniquus lawyer had shown up to assist them. Brian had flashed his credentials and explained what he'd witnessed. The magistrate didn't blink an eye as she filled out the requisite form and gave the information to the sheriff's office.

"Lynx is picking up one of her team members, Deep Del Toro, and they'll drop my car off. They should be back soon." Brian scanned the yard, then pushed the door wide, flicked on the lights, and pulled her inside. "Wait here, please." He slid the bolt into place then moved on silent feet through the downstairs —opening closets, looking behind furniture. He took the stairs with his shoulder pressed to the wall.

"All clear," he called as he jogged down the stairs.

She turned from her place at the window and watched as he moved to stand behind her. He rested his hands on her shoulders, easily able to see over her head. Sophia stiffened, but he didn't move his hands. He was standing close enough that he could see around the curtain she had shifted out of place.

"There are blue lights up at Marla's house. Do you think that's the sheriff, serving her notice?" she asked.

"We'll know in a minute. I gave them Kay's address as an alternative. Yep, looks like they're headed this way. That's a sheriff's car, not the police, so now we just need to see if Marla's at the party." Across the street, Brian spotted the odd angle of the Sheppards's curtain. "Looks like someone over at the Sheppards's is interested in what's going on too."

Sophia followed his finger to the upstairs window.

Brian laid his hand back on her shoulder. "You're shivering."

"I'm scared." Sophia's admission seemed to encompass more than this particular situation; it seemed to define her lot in life.

The sheriff climbed slowly out of his car, taking a moment to assess the situation. He reached up to put his hat on. Standing at the end of Kay's driveway, clipboard in hand, he turned and looked directly toward where Brian and Sophia huddled. He turned his focus to the window of the Sheppards's. Brian would bet this guy had combat experience. The sheriff could feel and find the eyes on him. The man had a good handle on the situation. Though Brian was ready, if need be, to head over and give the guy a hand.

The sheriff rang the bell, and there was a decided increase in noise as the front door swung open and women with margarita glasses in their hands swelled out of the door and onto the porch. The sheriff called out directives.

"It's like herding cats," Brian said.

Finally, the sheriff got his finger in Marla's face and directed her away from the rest. He turned to the others and must have ordered them into the house because they gathered in a swarm and headed back into the hive. They moved to the front window, and like Sophia and him, watched what happened next. And it was something to watch. Like a fireworks display, Marla went off. Brian saw the sheriff tapping the radio strapped to his shoulder; he must be calling for backup.

Marla was stomping away from the sheriff and toward Sophia's house when the phone in Sophia's office rang. Brian hated what came out of his mouth next. "You'd better go get that. Someone's been trying to reach you all day."

He didn't watch Sophia as she moved away from the window. He needed to keep his eyes on Marla and her craziness. He hated it, though, that Sophia picked the receiver up and put it down without a word. He hated that his job was to take Sophia down if she was culpable. That was a pretty big *if*. Brian wasn't convinced she was a bad guy. Too much circumstance, not enough cold hard fact.

Brian knew that Thorn and Nutsbe were in the war room right this minute, culling through the data, and putting together a timeline for the FBI. There could be a reasonable explanation for what Sophia was doing and saying, though none of them had been able to fathom what it might be. He knew that Monday the FBI would be at the airport ready to gather the last of the evidence to put the icing on the cake, the lid on the box, to hammer this one home.

Sophia went upstairs to the hall bathroom. She shut the door, and Brian could hear the lock click, the faucet flowing, then the ringing of her cell. Her voice washed down the drain with the water.

Brian watched out the window as backup came into view. Someone must have called Pierre Richards because here he came through the trees and over the lawn toward Marla. Interestingly, Richards stood next to the sheriff, not next to Marla. He knew the sheriff wouldn't like that much. And sure enough, Richards was sent to sit on the steps, but that told Brian that this guy wasn't feeling very protective of his wife. Two sets of car head-lights lit up the window. Brian watched Lynx get out of his car. She saw him in the window and signaled him out.

Brian jogged up the drive.

"Brian." Lynx leaned against his car and looked up at the sky, indecision on her face. She shook her head. "I'm just going to say it. You do with it what you will," she said. "This is between you and me and *not* to go beyond us." She lifted her brows and waited for his nod of agreement. "I have a strong sixth sense. Knowings, I call them." She looked over to the house and back at him. "When I was in Sophia's house, I realized there's some-thing wrong there. I mean scary wrong. And it's angry."

"Someone?" Brian tried.

"Some*thing*. Otherworldly. Evil intent is what I'd call it."

Brian gave a short shake of his head. He wasn't following.

"I think Sophia has a strong sixth-sense too—I imagine she's empathic, that she can pick up energy signatures. It's not an unusual trait for people who have gone through trauma. It's a survival instinct that's magnified, much like our hearing acuity increases when we're stuck in the dark."

Brian crossed his arms over his chest and leaned his hips back against his car.

"Science shows that sociopaths tend to target empaths because they don't have to say or do anything to make someone who is empathic a victim. Sociopaths have an instinct for finding and singling out empaths. Empaths can feel the sociopath's viciousness and threat in the air and over great distances. An empath doesn't need to be in the same area as a sociopath to be victimized."

"Go back to this angry energy. Is it Marla?" This was a conversation he never thought he'd have. Brian had experienced some inexplicable things on his own out in the Middle East. Things he had no context for. And he truly believed he had survived over there because of his own sixth-sense. His ability to pull his foot back just before he stepped on the mine or snagged the tripwire. He was open to the idea that Sophie could sense such things as a survival technique. Her life was filled with trauma after trauma, after all.

"No, it's bigger than Marla. Marla is a sociopath, but this energy is pure evil. Keep a close eye on her. If I'm right about all of this, it makes her even more vulnerable." Lynx reached out and gripped Brian's arm. "She's in serious danger." And with that, Lynx walked over to Deep's car and climbed in.

Brian scrubbed a hand over his head and blew out some of the stress that had filled his lungs. He walked back to Sophia's living room and sat down. He put the conversation in a box. He'd have to look at it later when he could focus on what that all meant.

"You should go."

Brian turned to see Sophia standing at the bottom of the stairs with a frown pulling down the corners of her mouth. He'd never seen her look so sad. Terrified, frustrated, exhausted, yes. But this was deep down grief.

He stood and ran his hands down the thighs of his pants. "What happened?" He took a step toward her. "Are you okay?"

"No. Not really. Look, it's late. Marla has been served her papers." She gestured toward the door. "If I have any trouble, I'll call the police."

"I'm not leaving you here alone tonight." Brian's voice was flatly adamant.

"Lynx is on her way home. She'll be waiting for you. Go, spend some time with her. She's been so incredibly kind and generous to have let you stay here this week. Would you please tell her thank you for me?"

Well, that was unexpected. "Sophia, do you think that Lynx and I are a couple?"

She didn't answer, just made her way into the living room and sat on the sofa in front of her boys' picture.

"What happened on the phone call? Did you get some bad news?" He moved to sit in the chair opposite her.

Sophia did what Sophia always did when she didn't want to answer. She played with her gold bracelet and didn't make eye contact. Well, he'd find out soon enough, by listening to the recording back in the war room—no need to press. "You look exhausted. Go take a sleeping pill. Get some sleep."

She sat there and said nothing. He wanted Lynx's question out of Sophia's thoughts. He needed to make a case for staying there. His gut told him to hang on tight; things were about to spin out of control.

"You mentioned my colleague, Lynx. I didn't do a good job of introducing her before. Lynx Sobado is an intelligence operative who works on another Iniquus team called Strike Force. Their commander is Striker Rheas, and he's Lynx's fiancé. All of us operatives work hand in hand. We often rely on each other to stay alive in some very bad situations here and overseas. You probably thought we were together because you were picking up on that closeness. I'm her brother in arms. I'd do anything for her, and she for me. But we don't have feelings for each other. I don't feel anything for Lynx, not like—" Brian slammed the door on that thought.

He certainly couldn't say "what I feel for you," though that's what he wanted to say. There was so much he wanted to say to her. Like, it tore at his heart that she was in so much pain. Like, he would crawl through fire for one of her smiles—to hear her laugh. Like, though he'd barely met her boys, he'd seen so much of her in their eyes that he couldn't help but fall in love with them. Just as he'd fallen for Sophia the moment she'd walked into the bar. He'd looked up, and he knew that there she was, the woman he had been made to love.

"It must be weird for you," Sophia said, her finger sliding in and out of the bracelet's clasp. "You probably thought I was a completely different person last fall. I bet you had no idea that I was such a mess. Thank you for keeping me company on my birthday. Thank you for making my birthday memorable."

Brian pushed back in the chair and crossed his arms over his chest. Where the heck was she going with this? "Yes, I thought it was memorable too."

"I want to make sure, though, that we understand each other. I consider that night to be an aberration from who and what I ordinarily am. Normally I don't have sex outside of a committed relationship."

"I understood that night that sleeping with strangers wasn't your deal." He watched her face flame red. Brian kept his expression unaffected. He thought maybe she was trying to bait him. No. That didn't seem right.

"I want to make sure you understand that I don't date. It's nothing personal." She glanced up at him briefly, then lowered her lashes again. "It's simply practical. I don't know if you thought that it might be a possibility, and maybe that's why you're going out of your way for me." She cleared her throat, then muttered, "God, that sounded egotistical." She gathered her hair over her shoulder and twisted it around her hand.

Lynx had told Brian that it was a self-soothing gesture. But Brian didn't need to know that to understand Sophia was stressed.

"Please don't go out of your way for me. I'm not interested in a relationship of any kind. Not emotional, not intimate." She swallowed audibly, then fixed her gaze on him steadily. "I'm saying this for your own safety—you need to keep your distance from me. You need to stay uninvolved except within the scope of your contract with my company."

Brian leaned forward and put his elbows on his knees. "I'm caught on the 'for your safety' part of that sentence. Would you care to elaborate?"

"No. I would not. Just take it at face value."

"You want me to act within the scope of my job and not consider you romantically because doing so would put me at some sort of risk. Emotional risk?" He canted his head. "Physical risk?"

"Stop pushing me."

"I just want more information."

"I'm done with this conversation." She stood. "I was clear. There can be no misunderstanding about our association." She tilted her head back as if she was talking to someone hovering above them. She raised her voice, but not at him. "We have a professional relationship contracted through my employer."

Brian looked around to see who she was communicating to. This last part was obviously not meant for him but for someone else. He wondered if someone might be listening in on comms. He'd definitely do a sweep next time she was out of the house. Brian felt a cold prickle start at his hairline and crackle its way down his body. He felt spooked. He had never been spooked before. It was an eerie, otherworldly sensation that made him think of the broken goblet and the story about the Ouija board.

"Sophia, things have been going badly for you for so long you can't tell up from down. You have to lean on people you trust." And as he said it, he realized that his name was going on the long list of people who were taking her down. Though he would do everything in his power to make the landing as soft as possible. Maybe if she approached the FBI before the FBI caught her, if she showed good faith, things might be all right. She'd have to trust him, though. And he didn't have much time to make his case. It was Saturday night, and Jael was flying in on Monday.

Sophia shook her head. "I don't want to become dependent on anyone. If I use a crutch, how am I going to be strong?"

Brian stayed seated so that she would feel like she had control. "Sophia, are you hearing yourself? Tell me one physical problem that requires a crutch that doesn't help you get stronger quicker for using it? What if you had a strain, or a break, or a twist in your ankle? Would you be better or worse for the crutch?"

"Better." She pouted.

"What are you trying to prove to yourself?"

"It's not what I'm trying to prove to myself. It's what's already been proven to me. I can't depend on anyone. Not my parents. Not my husband. Not my children's grandparents. Not through their own fault, but that's how the stars lined themselves up. When I lean on a wall, the wall topples. It's better to build up my own muscles and not lean because when the wall goes, I go with it. I can't play the trust game and lean on any more walls. I don't think I can survive it."

"That's a metaphor that I can understand better. It's rational from where you're standing. I get it. I've never lived through what you have. But if you changed 'person' to 'team,' I think you might change your mind. There are people who want to play on your team. Nadia, Lana, me, Lynx, Thorn, Nutsbe. If you have more players on a team, then if someone fumbles—and they will —the others can step up and help you move the ball to the end zone."

"Are you really talking *sports* with me?"

"You're trying to deflect. In this metaphor, the ball is your boys. You have to be happy and healthy for your boys. If you stand alone, and God forbid something were to happen to you, it's not the wall that comes tumbling down. It's their whole world. If you're their everything, and fate steps in, then they have nothing. Build a team for their sake."

Sophia's gaze was on the photo of her children. Maybe he'd pushed too far. Her eyes were glassy with unshed tears. He held very still. If she said yes to help, he could make a case with Iniquus to bring in the FBI and create a new plan, one where she wasn't in prison, away from her kids.

"I'd like to have some time to myself, to sing in the shower without you hearing me." She smiled vacantly. She stood and headed for the stairs. "Feel free to check and make sure everything is locked up, so you feel comfortable about leaving. I'm going to go wash away this day and go to bed."

"You had another seizure." Brian couldn't hide his frustration.

She kept walking slowly up the stairs like she was carrying the weight of the world. "And it's over," she called over her shoulder. "Really." She stopped with her hand on the newel post. "I want you to go home, Brian."

Brian was standing at the bottom of the stairs looking up at her.

"I'm not asking you to leave."

Relief flooded through Brian.

"I'm telling you to."

26

*B*RIAN
Sunday a.m.

"How'd the thing go yesterday?" Brian asked as he moved to Nutsbe's work station and looked at what he had going on. "Do we have everything ready for Finley and Andersson?"

"We're still dotting our i's and crossing a few t's," Nutsbe said. "I did background checks on Will and Janice Sheppard. He's an accountant at an insurance company. He's been there for fifteen years. Been in their house for twelve. Nothing on his record, not even a traffic ticket. Janice hasn't paid taxes in two years. It looks like she's a stay-at-home wife. Her record is clean too. Nothing sticks out on that end. Have you met them?"

"I've seen them. There's something a little off about them, I think. They always seem to be looking out their windows. Sophia says they're paranoid because the neighborhood women keep ringing their bell and throwing rocks at their windows. To be honest, if I lived in that neighborhood, I'd be a little paranoid too."

"Or it's another family with deep-seated psychological problems. I wouldn't drink the water in that neighborhood. Just sayin', man." Nutsbe raised his eyebrows for emphasis. "I ran them through the system because Lynx popped in to tell us about your adventure at the gun shop. She suggested I give the Sheppards a quick look-see."

"I'm mostly interested in last night's cellphone conversation with the mystery contact."

"Yeah, you're going to want to hear this." Nutsbe pulled up a file.

"777RFT6Y6." Sophia's voice warbled. "This has got to stop. I can't handle any more."

"We're almost to the finish line. You can't stop now. Everything you've been working for is right within reach."

"I'm serious. I can't."

"Before you say any more, you should know that Aml Al Ahr has been captured."

There was a long pause with the sound of tap water running in the background.

"Is he dead?" Sophia whispered.

"I hope so, for his sake," came the woman's reply.

"Red, please hear me. I don't want to be involved anymore."

"You're being weak. And this is not a time for weakness. We are *too* close to the finish line. I need to know. Did you talk to Nadia about the tablet?"

"No, the information came to my attention by mistake. I thought the obvious—that they'd realized the truth. I informed you, and that's the scope of my interaction. There would be no reason to talk to Nadia about it."

"We've picked up on some chatter that makes us concerned about the transaction. You have a security group, Iniquus, working with you. Did you mention this to them?"

"How do you know about Iniquus? Of course, I didn't mention it to them or anyone else—only you. Iniquus was assigned as protection for Peru. They have no interest in anything other than securing the site at the boiling waters and protecting Nadia and me on our travels."

"That's what I needed to know."

The line went dead.

Thorn had joined them while the brief recording played. "Nutsbe and I did some digging last night. Aml Al Ahr was an academic who worked with a different consortium along the same lines as AACP. They work to save artifacts in Middle Eastern war zones. He was traveling to a planning meeting in Turkey when he was captured. He's been gone for about forty-eight hours. How did Sophia act after that phone call?"

"Like she'd taken a blow to the ribs. She was a mess yesterday."

"She's not great this morning either. She's been crying almost since she woke up." Nutsbe checked his watch. "About an hour and a half ago." He dragged the small window he had up into the center of the monitor and expanded it.

Sophia sat on the couch, wrapped in a blanket, with a box of tissues in her lap, sniffing and wiping her nose.

Thorn shook his head at the visual. His voice was defeated when he said, "So our takeaway is that Sophia kept the information from Nadia as she was told to do."

"Nadia didn't bite at her hook?" Brian asked.

"Not as far as we can tell. We haven't picked up on anything that looks like Nadia's trying to broker a deal or that she paid any attention to the information after it was sent out. Her only calls went out to her mom, her sister, some friends. She doesn't go much of anywhere. She looks clean as a whistle."

"Sophia was talking to a woman named Red. That's a new piece." Thorn folded his hands behind his head. "Whatever is in play is about to be over with. Luckily, it's the FBI who has to connect the dots. Solving the puzzle isn't part of our contract, just gathering the surveillance. Good damned thing too. I want as little to do with that takedown as possible."

"I hear you, brother," Nutsbe said. "If that tablet makes its way to the US, and the FBI tracks it to its new home, there's definitely a case to be made that puts Sophia in the driver's seat."

They all sat quietly for a long moment.

"Good, then we all agree that sometimes our job fucking sucks." Nutsbe scratched his thumb between his brows and looked over at Brian. "Talking about things that suck, yesterday, after you and Lynx took off after Sophia, I went to find that stalker-chick, Marla. She was grocery shopping and walked away from her purse for a moment. I took her wallet out to my car, photographed it, and put the wallet back, all without her being any wiser. Surprising that someone so trusting could be such a shit."

"Sociopaths hit high on the narcissism scale," Thorn said. "I'm assuming she thinks she's so in control that no one would dare do anything to her. Her guard is always down."

"Good that you have that info now." Brian lifted his chin toward Nutsbe. "The magistrate was asking for defining information, social security number, date of birth, and all we had was a physical description, name, and address."

"You didn't have her name. Her ID doesn't say Marla Richards. She's Mary Johnson from Texas. I checked her driver's license, and it was issued a year ago before she moved to Virginia. I sent everything, including her wallet photos, to the research techs to see what they could come up with. My services included ingratiating myself to the research hounds by bringing pastries from La Bouche. They said they'd put me at the head of the queue."

"Above and beyond, thanks." Brian gave Nutsbe a fist bump. "What time are Andersson and Finley getting here?"

"Noon. It's hard to ask them to get up too early on a Sunday morning. Most folks call this a day of rest, you know."

Thorn gave a one-sided smile. "Rest is for wimps."

"Sophia's on the move." Nutsbe flipped the camera and watched her gather her purse and keys and head out the door. He panned out. "What's wrong with this picture?"

Thorn and Brian both looked at Sophia standing on her driveway. Even from the side view, they could see she had a perplexed look on her face.

"Check the van. Is there something wrong with the van?" Thorn asked.

"I had the alarm set to high last night. Nothing passed the infrared line."

"She's in her car now. Let's see where she's headed. Five bucks says it's chai." Nutsbe pulled up a split-screen that put the van on a GPS map. Out of the neighborhood. A U-turn. Back into the neighborhood, back into her driveway. Now she was jumping out of her van, slamming the door shut, her face red with anger. She had her phone in her hand.

"Who's she calling?" Brian asked.

"That's the non-emergency police number," Nutsbe replied, tapping his computer to turn up the volume.

"What is the nature of your call?"

"My name is Sophia Abadi. I recently had a restraining order taken out against my neighbor. This morning I woke up and my garden is missing. My flowers are all gone. I was driving out of my neighborhood, and I saw that all my flowers are now planted over at Marla Richards's house. She obviously has to have broken the restraining order for her to have been on my property destroying my garden."

"I'll send a police officer to your address to take a statement. Please stay at your home and wait until they get there. Do not confront the neighbor on your own. We'll handle this."

"What the heck?" Thorn swatted Nutsbe's arm.

Nutsbe moved to a different camera to bring more of the property into view. "I've got no visual."

Brian thought about the beautiful garden of perennials that Sophia said had been planted to keep her mother-in-law calm after her son's brain injury. He imagined vast stretches of dirt and holes that looked like a prairie dog colony lived there. "Have we got anything on camera to take to the police?"

Nutsbe began scrolling through what he had. "I didn't get any flags…"

"The flowers were there when I left last night. They aren't there now. Unless a ghost reached down and yanked them up by the roots, something went wrong with the perimeter," Brian said.

Nutsbe finished his task. "I've got nothing."

"Okay, here's part of the problem. Stop on that image." Brian put his finger on a bush at the top of Joe's property. "That's where I have a sensor. The other one is way back here. There was nowhere to put it until this tree. That angle protects the driveway and sidewalk but cuts off the whole garden. Someone in this area, here," Brian pointed to the spot, "wouldn't have been picked up."

Nutsbe turned toward Brian. "But you installed night-vision cameras. They would have recorded the heat signature of someone or something in the garden."

"Some*thing*?" Brian asked.

"Not as in ghost activity," Nutsbe clarified, "as in animal."

"Not here in the front," Brian countered. "Her property dips down a hill. In order to get the cameras to read what was next to the house, I had to angle them in such a way that the top third of her property was cut off. Getting a camera into range, I'd have to set it on her chimney. There were always too many eyes to make that a smart move."

"And the lights were angled up after her disco show pissed the neighbors off," Nutsbe said. "If they figured that out through trial and error, they'd know they were safe as long as they were crawling on all fours."

"Well, we know where the flowers went. So maybe Marla-Mary-what's-her-name will be headed for jail." Thorn didn't sound very hopeful.

"You know that's not going to happen." Nutsbe clicked back on the screen, and they could see an officer standing in the driveway next to Sophia, listening to her tale.

She held out the paperwork the magistrate had given her the day before. He looked it over and handed it back.

Thorn sat forward. "I wish we could hear what they're saying,"

"Yeah, check out the look on the guy's face. What's he going to do? It's not like the flowers have serial numbers on them. Sophia can't prove they're hers."

"He can go over and ask Marla some questions, scare her a bit. See if he can't trick her into admitting something. He's telling Sophia to go inside. He's probably afraid she'll go storming over to confront Marla, and he'll have to dive into a catfight." Nutsbe shook his head. "I'd rather fight a man any day. Women? *Woof.* Once you've got them riled enough to fight, they're all kinds of vicious. They don't have boundaries. Anything they can grab, claw, or bite is fair game. I can't blame the guy for wanting to avoid that. It's just too early in the day."

Nutsbe switched the camera back to the interior of the house and turned up the audio. The doorbell rang. Sophia opened it to a woman in a swimsuit and a pair of shorts.

"Who's that?"

Thorn and Brian shook their heads.

"Sophia, why is that police officer here? He's walking over to Marla's."

"Marla's a nut case," Sophia answered. She stood holding the door mostly shut. She hadn't invited the woman into her house.

"It wasn't enough that the sheriff crashed my party last night and put everyone in a bad mood? Now you have to ruin her pool party too?"

"Is that where you're going?"

"Not until I know what the police are doing there. My whole family's dressed and ready to head over. What did you do now?"

"Did you notice my yard?"

The woman turned and then looked back at Sophia. "You're blaming her for that?"

"Well, *someone* moved my flowers from my yard to hers. It wasn't the Easter Bunny."

Nutsbe smacked Thorn with the back of his hand and grinned. "Feisty."

"You do know, don't you, that her husband has his office over for brunch by the pool? His boss. His boss's boss. That officer just went over there in front of everyone. Marla isn't going to take that well. I guess we'll hang out and wait for things to calm down before we go over. Girl, I wouldn't want to be in your shoes right now."

The woman moved out of the camera's view, and Sophia slammed the door shut.

"She's right," Brian said. "I'm going to head over to Sophia's."

"You'd better cook up a good excuse for showing up this morning. Last night's recording sounded crystal clear, bro. She doesn't want you there," Thorn said.

"Yeah? Well, if she was just some woman I knew, I'd respect that. But my job is to protect her. My excuse is that I'm taking over some automatic locks with keypads." He turned to Thorn. "Lana was over at Sophia's house while we were getting the restraining order, wasn't she?"

"Yeah." Nutsbe shook his head. "She forgot to lock the door again. Wasn't ten minutes later that Rochester went in and tried to make himself a sandwich. Too bad Sophia doesn't believe in keeping non-dehydrated food in the house. That was entertaining to watch, though. That man cusses like a Marine."

Thorn pointed at Brian. "While you're there, go talk to Joe Rochester about getting a tracker on his dad, so he gets pinged when Pops steps out of the house. Lucky for everyone, this guy doesn't wander far."

"Not lucky for Sophia." Brian stood and pulled his keys from his pocket. "All right, I'm heading out."

"I'll keep a close eye while you drive and buzz you if you need to stomp on the gas," Nutsbe said. "And hey, while you're over there, try to find out what time her buddy Jael's coming in tomorrow and if she plans to meet his plane."

27

BRIAN

Sunday a.m.

Brian drove slowly into the neighborhood. A steaming cup of coffee and a cup of chai were snugged in the beverage carrier on his passenger seat next to a bag with some breakfast sandwiches. Sophia needed protein to help her body deal with all the stress. He hoped like hell that she wouldn't have another seizure. Nutsbe said he'd call if Brian needed to intervene quickly. So far, so good.

He pulled up in front of what had once been a beautiful garden, like a treasure chest brimming with jewels that had adorned the top of the hill. He hadn't thought much about it until that moment. Gardens didn't happen for free. Even if these were perennials, they took tending to look nice. In the great big mess of Sophia's life, she took the time to make it look beautiful. He wondered what the impetus was. Was she keeping nervous hands busy while her boys played out front? Did she think of it as a tribute to her deceased husband and his parents? For whatever reason, she had been meticulous. Now, it looked like a roadside bomb had gone off in her yard. He felt the atmospheric change. This was a war zone now.

Brian scanned down the road. It seemed like the guests at Marla's poolside brunch had cleared out when the police did. There wasn't an extra car in sight. There was no happy laughter floating in the warm air, no squeals from kids splashing in the water. The neighborhood was eerily silent. Without shifting his head, Brian let his peripheral vision scope out the windows on the Sheppards' house. Sure enough, someone was at the upstairs window, tracking him. He bet it was weird for Sophia to know she was under the Sheppard microscope, always being watched. But what did he know? Maybe it was reassuring to her.

With any luck, Brian could get Joe Rochester to get his dad under control, get the locks changed out so Lana couldn't keep leaving the door unlocked, and get Marla arrested for ignoring the restraining order.

But Brian couldn't forget that tomorrow was Monday.

Anything he did to scrape those monkeys off Sophia's back today would be meaningless if that tablet came into the US and the FBI walked their intended path.

This case was FUBAR from the minute he took the assignment.

His phone buzzed, and he dragged it from his thigh pocket. "Brainiack here."

"You aren't gonna believe this shit." Nutsbe was laughing. "This is like a damned rollercoaster ride from hell, dude."

Brian rubbed a hand over his tightly cropped hair to stop his scalp from prickling.

"Research earned their pastries this morning. They found Marla-Mary-what's-her-face through a picture of her kids. I kept a gift card from The Morning Grind when I was scanning her wallet, and the techs ran fingerprints. Boom. They've got a match."

"Tell me there's an arrest warrant out for her."

"Better. We've got both kids listed with the FBI as kidnapped by their mother. Are you ready for this? Betty Greer, from Pennsylvania. The dad was given full custody of the children, and Mom was remanded to the state mental hospital for evaluation. The children are listed in grave danger. And guess what Betty's maiden name is?"

"Are you freaking kidding me right now? It can't be."

"Yup. *Betty Ann Campbell*—hubby's half-sister who's suing for a stake in the Campbell inheritance. Hang on. Andersson and Finley are walking into the war room. I'm putting you on speakerphone."

Brian leaned against the back of his Range Rover, thinking this would be an appropriate time for a cigarette, though he didn't smoke. He popped the hatch to look busy while he listened in to the information Nutsbe had on the kidnapped children, who had disappeared the year before. It included photo recognition of the mother and both children and fingerprints from mom and the daughter, Raina.

"Brian, what are the kids' names?"

"I can ask Sophia."

"Hold off. They're contacting Aiden O'Connor in missing persons for the next step. We don't want to get anyone's antennae up."

Brian could hear several conversations going at once.

"Are you there in the neighborhood?"

"Affirmative."

"The Richards's still having their party?"

"Negative. I think the police showing up, and the ensuing

screamfest was probably a buzzkill. No one's outside but me. The Sheppards are doing their surveillance duty. Other than that, things are quiet."

"Hang on… Okay. They're sending the photo I snagged of Marla Richards and her kids in front of the house to the biological father for confirmation. We need you to be eyes and ears until further notice."

"Wilco. Out." Brian stared at his phone. *Huh.*

Brian moved to the barren flower garden and looked around to see if he spotted something the cop had missed. A footprint. Something that might have fallen from a pocket. Anything to identify who had done this. There was always the off chance that it wasn't the psycho up the street but someone else who wanted them to think it was. *Now wouldn't* that *be bat-shit crazy?* In any other scenario, Brian would consider and reject the possibility. But here? In this neighborhood? There were no holds barred on the improbable.

He stooped as he checked Sophia's tires for any new hazards. There, under the car, by the right front tire, he saw a trowel. It must have slid down the drive last night. Whoever had lost it knew they couldn't retrieve it; the lights would flash on this far from the road.

Brian went to his cargo bin and pulled out an evidence bag. Making sure he angled himself so that any watchful eyes wouldn't know he'd found it and packaged it up. He put the bag on the floor of his car. He'd take it to forensics to see if they couldn't pull anything interesting from it.

He glanced up as Sophia came out to stand on her porch. Her arms crossed over her chest, and wearing the most unwelcoming face he'd ever seen on her. Even from here, he could see the red splotches around her eyes from crying. His heart stuttered. How the heck was he supposed to deal with this? All he wanted was to warn Sophia and whisk her away to somewhere safe. It was a fantasy that formed and blew up at the same moment. He wouldn't do that. She wouldn't do that. They'd both have to keep themselves belly to the table until their hands had been dealt, and they knew what cards they were playing.

"You've got one hell of a vole problem," he said and felt like an idiot. He moved to the passenger's door and retrieved his duffel and breakfast. He held up the drink carrier, then sauntered down the sidewalk toward her. Before she could reject him, he sat down on the stairs and said, "I brought breakfast."

She didn't move.

Brian tore the bag open, using it as a make-shift placemat, laid a sandwich out for her, moved the chai over next to it, and then unwrapped his food. "I also brought you a possible solution to a problem." He took a bite and chewed slowly, giving Sophia a chance to make up her mind.

Finally, she sat down beside him and picked up the chai. Her thank-you sounded suspicious.

He pulled the duffle over. "Locks," he said. "They throw the bolt automatically when the door is shut. I have one for each of your doors. It'll help keep Mr. Rochester out."

"That's too dangerous. What if I were outside and didn't have my keys? My boys could be locked away from me."

"It opens with a code. Actually, you can have seven different codes. You give each person their own. For example, Lana and Nadia would each have their own personal PIN. The computer saves that information. You can check your phone and see who's been at your house while you were gone. One of the codes is a designated service code. You give that to people who might come to check your dishwasher or what-have-you. You schedule the time it can be used, and that's the only time they can come in. It even has a face capture camera, so anyone who steps onto your porch gets a mugshot and a timestamp coming and going, whether the door opens or not. It's an effective system." He handed one of the boxes to Sophia.

"That's kind of cool," she said, looking it over. "You know what? You might be right. This might stop Mr. Rochester from getting in. I can't figure out how he's doing it now. I'm so careful about locking up. But if nothing else, I guess I'd have a warning that he was in my house before I got home, right? You said it tells a computer."

"It goes to a phone app. I'll make sure it's all hooked up and working for you."

Sophia handed the box back to him, and Brian was gratified to see her pick up her sandwich and take a bite. Besides adding another layer of security for Sophia, working on the lock project would give him a good excuse to hang around, keeping track of the comings and goings in the neighborhood while the FBI put a plan in place.

His phone buzzed. "Sophia, I think you should go in the house and shut the door."

She looked over at him with confusion.

"Marla and her kids are heading into the cul-de-sac. I'll stay out here."

Sophia didn't need to be told twice. She gathered her food and cup and, without further conversation, went inside.

Brian swiped his phone. "Brainiack here."

"You're on speakerphone. Thorn, Finley, and Andersson are in the war room with me. We've got ID confirmation from the dad. FBI SWAT mobilized the second Finley made the phone call."

"She's walking up the road now. She's got both kids with her. Pierre Richards isn't in the picture. She's looking rabid, so I'd say things didn't go well at her house after hubby's office peeps got front row seats on the crazy train."

"Finley here. Tell us when she gets where she's going. Our team is suiting up at the cars and will be moving in."

"They went up to Kay's. She opened the door, and they're going inside. Nutsbe, you have the address?"

"Roger that."

"SWAT is moving through the trees at the top of the road. They're watching Marla's house. Turn them around." Brian could see one of the men clearly. Dressed head to toe in black, with a balaclava hiding his face, he had an automatic rifle slung from his shoulder and plenty of cartridges held at the ready in his vest loops.

Brian edged over to Sophia's door and cracked it open. "Sophia, come here," he used the combat whisper that he hoped would carry to her ears only.

"What are you doing?" she asked as she tried to jerk the door open.

Brian had a solid hold on the handle to stop just that from happening. "Sophia, get down here and listen to me."

Thankfully, she crouched, putting her ear to the crack.

"Do you have a basement, somewhere below ground?"

"No. Why?"

"Sophia, I need you to trust me. Please. And do what I say. Go upstairs to the kids' bathroom, shut the door, get into the tub, and lay down."

"What? No. Why in the world—"

"Sophia, the tub is metal. It's going to be the safest place to be for the next little bit. Do it now." Even though he was whispering, he used his voice as a weapon. The timbre made even non-English speakers do what he wanted them to do when he wanted them to do it. It was the voice that said, do as I say, or you're going to be in for a world of hurt.

The door shut, and Brian could hear Sophia running up the stairs and a door slamming shut.

"She secured?" That was Andersson.

"Affirmative."

"We've let the team leader know you're on site. You are not to engage. They've got this." It was Finley this time.

"Roger. Wilco." Yeah, he'd wait and see.

"Good morning!"

Brian turned his head to see Joe heading across the side yard with his arm raised in a wave. He stopped when he was standing on the driveway. He stared at the empty garden space. Brian turned back to see SWAT stacking up at Kay's front door with a breacher in front. Second one in was a guy looking through the window of his ballistics shield with a can in his hand. Brian was assuming it was smoke and not flashbang since there were kids in the house.

Brian made his way calmly toward Joe and put his hand on his shoulder. "Go home."

"I'm so sorry to bother you. Have you seen my dad?"

"Go home." Brian turned Joe and gave him a push in the right direction.

Joe turned back, his brow scrunched together in confusion. "I know we've been a pain. But I can't find my dad. I put him to bed last night after you guys brought him back. I went to find out why he was sleeping so late and—"

There was a bang as the breacher crashed his tactical ram into the door, breaking the lock's hold, splintering the wood.

Yelling filled the air as the SWAT team shouted their orders. It was always hard to listen to terrified children shrieking, "Mommy!" Brian hated the fear in the kids' voices, no matter what language they were screaming. Brian twisted Joe's wrist, locking his elbow out, forcing him to the ground behind Sophia's van. He flopped on the ground beside Joe, hoping Sophia had followed his instructions and was keeping her head down. "FBI SWAT is across the street. We're going to stay down in case anyone feels like being stupid and starts firing a weapon."

Joe nodded his head to show agreement.

28

SOPHIA

Sunday a.m.

Sophia was in the fetal position with her cheek pressed against the cold surface of the bathtub. She didn't know what was going on, but the screaming and yelling outside had finally stopped. Still, she wasn't sure if it was safe to get up.

"Sophia, I'm coming up the stairs." It was Brian's voice.

The door to the bathroom opened, and there he was, reaching down his hand, pulling her up.

"Sorry about that. It was just a precaution. I was worried about stray bullets."

"Bullets?" Sophia held her arms against her chest, protectively. She reached for the ring on her bracelet and twirled it around as she searched Brian's face for more answers.

"The FBI was apprehending Marla Richards. They had an outstanding warrant for her arrest." Brian put strong hands on her arms and helped her step out of the tub. He had a worried expression, and Sophia thought that look probably wasn't about Marla but more about if he'd have to contend with another one of her seizures. She was wrong.

"Have you seen Mr. Rochester since we took him home last night?"

She tilted her head back, so she could see his eyes. "No. Do you think he's in my house?"

"I already looked. Joe said his dad was missing from his bed this morning when he went to check on him. Since this is where he usually shows up, it's kind of weird that he'd wander farther away."

"The doors were locked last night. Maybe when he couldn't get in…"

"Has she seen him?" Joe called from downstairs, and Sophia made her way down to talk to him.

She found Joe standing by her living room couch, where the dirt from his father's shoes had left streaks on the arms as Mr. Rochester had made himself at home the night before. "I'm calling the furniture cleaners Monday, first thing," he said, his face a strange collage of frustration and chagrin.

Brian put his hand on Joe's shoulder. "You need to call 9-1-1 and ask for a search and rescue team." He used the commanding voice he put on from time to time. It left no wiggle room, no opportunity for dissent.

Joe pulled out his phone and dialed as he walked out the door with his free hand raised in a thank you and goodbye.

Sophia stood in the middle of the room, feeling mildly responsible. There were actions that needed taking, but she had no idea what they were.

"There's going to be a lot of activity around here soon," Brian said. "Let's finish our breakfast and wait to answer questions from the police. They'll want you to give the searchers permission to be in your yard. When that gets going, we can go somewhere that's quiet. Maybe to Lana's house, so you can see the kids." Brian seemed to understand her confusion and helped her regain some semblance of order by handing her a plan.

Sophia pinched the ring on her bracelet. "Why do they need permission to search my property? Surely they can see he's not in the yard."

"They'll have people come out who can look at shoe prints and follow the tracks to get a direction. They'll have K-9 units out, air sniffers, and ground sniffers. It's possible the dogs can pick up a trail as long as he's alive. They won't bring out human remains search dogs for a few days. Those teams of dogs have different jobs and capabilities."

"They said that on the radio. There was a woman whose dog brought home human bones from the woods last Monday. They had search dogs looking for the rest of the body. The dogs found an undisturbed area where the searchers dug and found it was a recent grave. It didn't belong to the leg bones the dog recovered. They found that grave, too, later in the day. It's pretty amazing what a dog can smell." Sophia shifted on her feet. "You think Mr. Rochester might have passed away?"

"He's pretty old and pretty frail. The temperatures were down in the sixties last night. I think it's a possibility they'll consider, depending on what they find when they start looking." Brian put his hand on her back and steered her toward the kitchen. "Let's eat before they get here." He flicked his finger toward where she had put her sandwich and chai, then pulled her chair out. "That's an unusual ring you're using as a clasp for your bracelet. Does it have a story?"

Sophia wasn't the least bit hungry, but sometimes going along was easier. So she plopped down at the table in front of her now-cold sandwich.

Brian sat down next to her, looking expectant.

Sophia unclasped the bracelet and laid it on the table. "This ring is from the Ugarit and dates back to around 1300 BCE. I stole it from Syria," she said. "Well, it wasn't my intention to steal it. I just haven't found a way to get it back to where it belongs."

The ring was stylized. The top was a flat teardrop-shaped piece of gold where a face and breasts could be made out. Below the indentation that could be a navel were dots that might be a pubis but were formed to look like a root system for the tree that grew onto the torso.

"This is a Near Eastern Tree of Life. This design was specific to Ashtart, a virgin warrior-goddess. Have you ever heard of her?"

Brian shook his head.

"Legends that we've found on tablets and scrolls say that in the 14th century BCE, on the coast of Syria, a young god named Ba'al wanted to overthrow the river god, Yam. Ba'al took Yam captive and killed him. Ashtart rebuked Ba'al and protected the river, and thus the people survived because of the river's water. Ashtart protected their 'tree of life.' To honor her for this protection, there was a tradition of virgins keeping a temple for the goddess. These women were considered magically powerful. Leaders from around the Middle East sought their counsel, much like those who went to the oracles at the Temple of Apollo at Delphi. This ring was worn by one of the priestesses."

"Did you find it on a dig?" Brian asked.

Sophia pushed her hair out of her face, tucking it behind her ears. "One day, when we were in Syria, my dad and I went to see a professor friend of his, Dr. Omar. The night before, Dr. Omar had found a package at his door that he wanted my father see. It contained a tablet and a letter. The letter said, 'I am so sorry I disturbed your grave, Ashtart, forgive me. Release me from your curse.' Another piece of paper said, 'Please return this to her grave.' This ring was in that envelope. My father and Dr. Omar recognized the design and were very excited. They got to work translating the tablet. While I was listening, without thinking, I picked up the ring and slipped it on my finger."

"What did the tablet say?"

"It was basically an ancient curse. You know, the stuff of legends like King Tut's tomb or Pele's wrath if you take anything from a volcano in Hawaii. It was a warning that was very much in keeping with the region and the time period. Nothing extraordinary. While Dad and I were at Dr. Omar's, a haboob descended on us. I'd read about those massive dust storms, but I'd never been in one before. Even inside the house with the windows covered, we had to put blankets over our heads, so we didn't suffocate by breathing in the dirt. It was terrifying. The sound—it was like the whole house was being crushed in the fist of the devil. When the storm moved on, there was a great deal of destruction in the village. My father and I left so as not to impose on our host."

"And you were still wearing the ring."

"I had forgotten all about it. As a matter of fact, I didn't realize I had it on for quite a while. Dad and I traveled back to Israel that day. My dad was in a terrible mood. He was very angry with Nadia's father, for some reason. Dr. Omar had told my dad something about Nadia's dad. Dad sent Nadia and me out to get dinner so the men could talk. We never made it to the restaurant. We were kidnapped by our taxi driver. It wasn't until we were saved and on our way to Turkey, I saw the ring on my hand. Dad said to keep it on so it wouldn't be stolen or misplaced and that he'd send it to a friend of his at the museum as soon as we were back in a village with mail service. But ever since I put that ring on my finger, life has been turmoil."

"You decided not to send it back?"

"My dad got sick, and we had to fly home. At that point, I didn't know who to send it to, and really it was such a low priority. Things seemed to be happening very fast. Life…" She sighed with her gaze on the ring. "When I got back to university, I worked on thoughts—the tablet translating the tablet myself. I had pictures of it. We had left the tablet with Dr. Omar, of course. I have to admit, the letter it came with had planted a very bad seed in my head." She stopped to smile. "Crazy. Absurd. Thoroughly unscientific said what they typically say, that bad stuff wouldn't stop until the stolen item was returned. I've kept the ring on me because…" Sophia's attention drifted to the window where she could see Joe out looking between the storage pods lining her backyard.

Brian sat silently. He obviously wanted the end of the story.

She turned back and cleared her throat. "I swore a holy oath to Ashtart, on the day Chance was born, that if she spared my sons, I would keep the ring with me as a penance, to remember all those I loved who have fallen to the curse, and I would find a way to return this to her."

"You didn't send it back to Dr. Omar?"

"He died when a wall, damaged in the haboob, fell on him the day after the storm." Sophia's laugh was paper-thin. "Who said archaeology was for the faint of heart? It's a story right out of *Raiders of the Lost Ark*."

She expected Brian to laugh with her. Expected him to say something like, "You're a scientist, surely you don't believe that hooey written on a clay slab." Or any of the other million arguments she had made in her head. "Have you ever heard of apophenia?" she asked.

Brian canted his head. "That's when people find the face of Jesus on their breakfast toast."

"Ha! Yes, that's true. Apophenia happens when the brain makes leaps of perceptions, connections, and causations, giving meaning to unrelated phenomena. What statisticians would call a type one error, a false positive. The story in my head that describes my life—since the time I slipped the ring on my finger up until this very moment—is absurd. It only sounds more ridiculous for saying it out loud. I worked very hard on being rational until the completely irrational happened."

"Would you tell me about that? What happened?"

"It was a stormy night when things were going very badly last fall. Lana, Nadia, and I decided to chat with my grand-mothers about it. What an eye-opening conversation that was." Sophia looked toward her curio cabinet and decided not to tell him she'd been playing with an Ouija board. She'd probably said too much as it was. "I had a lovely goblet that was an heirloom. It broke during the last thunderstorm when you were over. I know it sounds silly, but that was a real loss. The glass had come over with my ancestors when they moved from Ireland to the United States. Something about the continuity of handing it down from generation to generation felt important."

Brian ran his finger over the design on the ring. "Did you find where this belongs? Do you know the exact location of the grave?"

"Yes, I found it while I was working on my Ph.D."

"Give me those coordinates." Though his voice was its typical soft timbre, he used his commander tone—here's an order, act on it.

So she did. She knew those numbers by heart, but they were well within the lines of ISIS-held territory, and there was no way for her to get the ring back. Only terrorists were in that area, and of course, she had no contacts among them.

Sophia took a bite of her egg sandwich. It was hard to swallow. She was sitting next to Brian as he, in all earnestness, was on the phone with Iniquus, giving them the location of the Syrian cave and asking them to do a search of all available resources in that area to make a delivery. Inside, Sophia felt completely, sickeningly out of control.

When the bell rang, Brian, with the phone still pressed to his ear, followed Sophia to the door. She opened it to the police.

The neighborhood was bedlam. Local TV vans crowded in with the FBI, who were interested in Marla, and the police, who were focused on finding Mr. Rochester. Thorn said the Search and Rescue team was setting up their trailer at the community pool parking lot, and cars were pouring in, filled with volunteers. Thorn had needed to pay someone who lived in a neighborhood on the other side of the subdivision to let him park in their driveway. The police were trying to dissuade the looky-loos by posting "no street parking" signs and writing tickets. Thorn had hiked his way to her house.

Another knock sounded at her door, and another set of people were there to write down the timeline and ask questions.

"Yes, last time I saw Mr. Rochester, he was dressed in street clothes, a pair of khakis and a green polo."

"Yes, he had shoes on. No, I didn't notice what kind beyond brown."

"Yes, the trackers can come in and look at the mud he left on my couch to try to get a shoe print to follow, not a problem."

"Yes, it was hard on Joe."

"Yes, Joe was distraught. But no, I have absolutely zero reasons to think Joe did anything to hurt his father."

She shut the door and turned to Thorn, "Some days, I wish I drank or at least kept an emergency bottle of liquor on hand."

She left the men in her living room as she moved to her office to catch the phone call coming in. Sophia picked up the receiver, listened, and set it back down. She moved into the kitchen and turned the fan on her stove on as she pulled her keys from her pocket and read the alphanumeric code into her cell. "All good?"

"Everything is going accordingly. We received your provenance and have included it with the shipment. Jael has new information for you, but a small window. Can you meet him at Dulles at three p.m. your time?"

"Yes, Nadia and I can do that, no problem. Where should we meet?"

"The private jet terminal. Ask the concierge for the diplomatic flight out of Turkey."

After Red hung up, Sophia called Nadia to tell her when Jael was coming in, then took a moment to catch her up on the craziness happening in her neighborhood. "I need to call Lana and have her keep the boys a little longer. It's mayhem here, and I can't see this letting up for a while. The dogs are super cute, but they're working. Keeping the boys away from them would be a fight."

"Do you want to spend the night here with me?" Nadia asked.

"I feel like I need to be with the computers overnight. Right now, I think I'm going to go to the nursery and buy some new flowers. Once everyone's done trouncing over my lawn, I can get them in the ground."

"Now, why would you do that?"

"Court is coming up, and one way or the other, I'm getting the heck out of here. As soon as the judge makes his decision, I'm putting a for sale sign in the yard. It can't look like it does now. The curb appeal says, 'stay the heck away, this place is hell.'"

"Planting pretty flowers might be construed as false advertising."

"Absolutely. But I'm not planning on leaving a forwarding address. They'll never find me to press charges. I may just go live on some desolate island somewhere where my only human contact is the boys and the internet."

"Hard to get cable service on those uninhabited islands."

"True. I may have to reconsider that plan. Right now, though, doesn't it sound like Nirvana?"

"Speaking of which, we have our Boiling River dates. We need to leave on July 3rd. I've already talked to Lana, and she's ready to keep the boys for you."

"Your sister is a saint and my savior."

"Yeah, she likes to polish up her halo. She thinks it's a good look on her."

29

BRIAN
Monday a.m.

"Well, I'll be damned," Nutsbe said, checking his computer screen.

Brain and Thorn were settling into their seats with coffee. Today was the day. No one was happy.

"What've you got going on?" Thorn asked.

"The forensics report on the trowel Brainiack brought in last night. It's the same fingerprints as the bolts that popped Sophia's tires."

Brian canted his head. "I thought you said those prints didn't ping the computer. Marla's prints—well, Betty Campbell's—were in the FBI database."

"And we would have gotten a hit if these were Betty's, but they're not. I'm doing a side by side right now, and they're not even close. That means that while Betty was hissing in Sophia's ear, threatening her, and trying to run her off the road, she was not popping her tires, and didn't dig up her garden and move it to her own house."

Thorn leaned forward. "Sophia has two people stalking her? Could it be Mr. Rochester? Or Pierre Richards?"

Nutsbe brought up more files. "No to Mr. Rochester. Checking Richards…and that would also be a no. Any other ideas?"

"Sophia's life is kept deliberately small. Her kids. Lana. Nadia. And we can account for Nadia's whereabouts, and for the most part Lana's as well," Thorn said. "Of course, a lot of times a stalker picks up on a victim for random reasons. Though Sophia eats dehydrated food and avoids being seen in public. That leaves her chai shop, her daycare, and her colleagues whom she accesses online—none of whom are close enough to have done this."

"The whole thing is damned improbable." Brian stared at the floor between his boots, searching who and what he knew of Sophia's life. "I would have bet good money on Betty being culpable for it all. I guess we could have her minions trying to ingratiate themselves. There are two who are frequent fliers in the Marla/Betty crazy-club, Penny and Kay. I've met Kay. I've never seen Penny. And then there's the Sheppards across the street. But Sophia says they try to keep their heads down just like she does. She doesn't see Janice at all, except in the window or sometimes on the porch for coffee."

"It's off the charts, I'll give you that. But it's not going to matter for much longer." Thorn scowled. "What's the newest on the FBI playbook, Nutsbe? Have they said what they want to do? Are they going for headlines or the long game and turning Sophia?"

"They said they're going to see how she behaves. If she's forthcoming and helpful, they might be able to work a deal. If she lawyers up and won't answer their questions, they'll go for the jugular. They'll have folks in the airport in time for the Turkish jet. They're hoping Jael isn't flying in on diplomatic credentials. They'd like to pick him up for questioning. They're going to be moving on him as delicately as they can. US relations are already stressed with Turkey and Israel. No one wants to start an international brouhaha."

Brian crossed his arms over his chest, trying hard to keep the scowl off his face. "What's the plan once they're in custody?"

"The FBI is bringing them here. Titus and the three of us will be in the peanut gallery. We'll be doing the videography and feeding information into Finley's and Andersson's ears so they can ask the right questions, in case we know something that one of the suspects is dithering over."

"Who's on the arrest warrants?" Thorn asked.

"Sophia, Nadia, and Jael. The goal is to keep Sophia in their pocket. Nadia and Jael are there to give information and to have on hand just in case we missed something big. The special agents will be following the tablet on its route to the buyer. Interestingly, Gilchrest's jet happens to have a Dulles landing scheduled for this afternoon. The FBI is assuming the Gilchrest's are the ones making the buy. After the transfer of the tablet, the FBI will scoop up the archaeology department and also the folks on the Gilchrest plane. I've been assured there is no chance the FBI will be turning assets from anyone in that family. The best they'll be able to do is score a lesser sentence based on useful intelligence."

"That's where the FBI plans to make their splash to warn other investors off buying relics and funding ISIS," Thorn said. "They won't need Nadia or Sophia for their anti-terror propaganda campaign."

That gave Brian little peace. "All right." He stood. "I'm off to Sophia's to make sure the stalker doesn't do something today that would stop Sophia from getting to her date with destiny on time. I'll keep you guys in the loop. Let me know if anything comes up."

Brian drove slowly into the neighborhood. He'd taken a tour to figure out who was on hand. The TV vans had lost interest after the eleven o'clock news when they reported that the FBI had saved the two children, and their mother was on her way to a Pennsylvania mental hospital. The kids were taken to the precinct where their dad met them to take them home. The disappearance of an Alzheimer's patient was the icing on the cake, but this morning that story was stale.

It was a little after zero-nine-hundred hours. A group of searchers with their backpacks and orange shirts huddled under the tents in the pool parking lot. It looked like they were getting briefed on their search areas for the day. Brian headed over to Sophia's house. He found her in shorts and rubber boots in her garden. Her car was pulled next to the house, and the driveway was lined with the flats of flowers they had bought the night before. He took a moment to appreciate the view as she crawled on all fours to her next row.

Brian was glad as hell that he wasn't going to be on hand when the FBI took her down. *Coward.* Brian had started many a morning knowing that people he cared about were going to get hurt, maybe not even survive the day. He'd jumped onto the backs of trucks, fully aware that all hell was about to break loose. Orders were orders. Fate was fate. Shit was shit. This felt different. This felt like someone was carving his heart out of his chest with a dull blade. He knew he had to keep it together, watch for every opportunity to help Sophia, and at the same time make sure he was true to his mission.

He popped the car door open.

"Good morning." Sophia's smile was radiant. She had color in her cheeks. Her eyes sparkled.

"You look happy," he said, his voice caught in his throat.

"It's going to be a fabulous day. I'm so excited. Beautiful flowers, warm sun, Marla out of my life, Jael coming into town, and the culmination of a project that I've been working on for a very long time." She stood up and brushed the dirt from her knees. "I feel like I can breathe for the first time in years."

Her dark brown eyes were velvety soft, and he thought, as he often did, of a beautiful doe with long lashes and a gentle heart. He was seeing Sophie, the woman who'd walked into that bar, and not Sophia with her ties to ISIS. He was seeing a woman that he wanted to gather into his arms and hold, not the woman who was about to be shackled. Standing there framed in sunlight, she took his breath away.

A dog, barking off in the distance, broke the spell.

Brian pulled a padded envelope from his pocket and walked over to her. "Iniquus has a route for the bracelet. It needs to go out today before noon. It should be at the cave in the next twenty-four hours."

Sophia blinked. "What? Are you *serious*?" She unhooked the clasp of the bracelet with shaking fingers.

"Are you ready to let it go?"

Sophia kissed it. "I'm sending you home. You're going home, just like I promised. Now you hold up your end of the bargain," she whispered to the ring. She held out the bracelet and dropped it into the envelope. Tears slid out from behind her tightly closed eyes. She was shaking, her breath coming in gulps.

"Whew!" She fanned her face. "That was an unexpected reaction."

Brian quietly sealed the envelope and put it back in his pocket. If he could do nothing else for her, he could at the very least free her from the idea that she'd been cursed. Maybe with a new mindset—a new perspective—she could make new choices for herself and her kids. He was just grateful he had the resources to get this done.

Sophia took a step toward him, and putting her hands on his arm for balance, rose on her toes and kissed his cheek. "Thank you," she said, settling back on her feet and looking up through her lashes at him. "While you're giving me a miracle this morning, all I can give you in return is coffee and a breakfast strudel."

"Coffee?"

"I picked some up when I went to give the boys a kiss at their daycare and got myself some chai. It's on the kitchen counter for you."

"You knew I'd be here this morning?"

"Lucky guess." She smiled at him. Her armor was falling away. Brian wasn't sure that was such a great thing. She'd probably need it today.

30

SOPHIA

Monday a.m.

The bracelet was off her wrist, packaged up, and headed for Syria. This was a day of miracles. Brian had done so much for her in such a short time. Her luck was changing. Her life was turning around. Marla was gone. No more flat tires. No more fear of being out in

time Sophia had public. She would be able to take her boys up to the park to play. She'd be able to browse the grocery aisles and decide what fresh, lovely things they could eat that night.

Jael was coming in with the tablet. The last seen Jael was when he'd saved them from the kidnappers and taken them on the back of his motorcycle to the US embassy. She had kept her promise and never told anyone she knew who he was. The tablet was the end of a long road they'd traveled together. Today, they'd get their well-earned prize. Today felt like a success. The flowers she was planting were celebrating with her. She looked down the hill to where Brian was drinking his coffee on her steps and smiled.

She lugged a flat closer to her and picked up the next pot. Turning it upside-down, she carefully removed the plant. She held it in her left hand as she reached out to make a new hole.

Sophia's trowel caught with the next plunge. She tried again, then scraped the dirt away from the roots that stopped her progress. She looked in the hole. *I don't remember there being irises here.* Sophia reached down to pull them up. Holding the root in her hand, her brain stalled. Still not fully comprehending, a scream shrilled from her throat, filled the neighborhood as it echoed off the houses and swelled into the trees.

Something tangled around her, gripped, and pulled her. When the scream ran out of fuel, she sucked a deep breath into her deflated lungs.

"Sophia, what is it? What's wrong?"

Her brain rubbed against the words as if they were braille. She could feel the texture of concern but couldn't make out how the raised dots formed sentences or thoughts. The one thing she could make out was that it was Brian's voice. He shook her. Made her head bobble about.

"Look at me. Look in my eyes. *What* is going on?"

Sophia got it. She knew what he was asking. Okay, now it was her turn. She fought for some words but ended up pointing her finger at the iris roots in the hole she was digging.

He pushed her down until she was sitting on the curb, then pressed her head between her knees. "Stay there," he commanded, quickly followed by a "Holy shit."

Sophia's hands were on the road. She pressed her knees against her head and stayed in the position Brian had folded her.

He was standing next to her with a hand on her shoulder. "This is Brian Ackerman. I believe we've found Mr. Rochester, the missing Alzheimer's patient." There was a long pause as he listened. "No, ma'am, he's deceased."

Brian sat down behind her, wrapped his body around her, and held her physically together while they waited for the police to arrive.

Thorn was sitting in her living room with the detectives, taking notes about what was being asked and answered. She was wrapped in a blanket but still shook like a leaf. Brian sat shoulder to shoulder with her. It kept her in her body and kept her upright.

Their other liaison, Nutsbe, had swung by and picked up the package heading to Syria. How Brian had remembered that with all this going on was a miracle. But Brian had promised it would get to Iniquus in time for its journey home.

"Sir," Thorn said. "Sophia was having trouble with someone puncturing her tires. We were able to get several samples of fingerprints from construction materials. After her flowers were stolen, Brainiack sent a trowel found on the scene to our forensics lab. Sophia Abadi's fingerprints were not on it. There was no sign that the tool was wiped, and fingerprints that match the construction materials were found. That evidence is available at Iniquus. We can't identify the prints. They aren't in our databases."

Joe Rochester came back into the room. He was holding himself together pretty well for a guy whose dad had just turned up, buried in a shallow grave in front of her house. The detective sent a speculative glance his way.

"I have a forensics app. If you'd like, we can rule Joe's fingerprints out right away," Thorn said.

"What?" Joe asked. "Yeah, let's rule me out. I didn't kill my dad and plant him in Sophia's garden."

Thorn swiped at his phone and brought up a fingerprint screen.

Sophia looked at the clock. "Am I under arrest?" she asked the detective.

"No, ma'am," he replied. He'd been going over and over her story since this morning.

They'd had a break for the pizzas that Nutsbe had brought in. But time was ticking by. "I have to get ready for a meeting. A colleague is flying in from Turkey, and I'm supposed to meet him at Dulles. Excuse me." She pushed the blanket from her shoulder and stood up. She turned toward Brian when she felt his eyes on her. The look she found was impossible to interpret, but something was there. Something that made a shiver crawl up her back. *A scalding hot shower is what I need.* She wanted to wash this mess away—all of it.

31

Sophia

Monday Afternoon

"You know, I'm an extremely brave person to be in the same car with you," Nadia said as she wove over to the ramp that would funnel them to Dulles.

"Brave enough to have me in your car, not brave enough for me to do the driving."

"I don't see any reason to tempt fate. You're like Sisyphus, only in your case, you push your boulders up the hill, then you roll down to find another one waiting for you."

"Mr. Rochester died and was buried before I handed over the ring to Brian. He said it would be back in the cave in less than twenty-four hours. I only have to hang on for twenty-one more hours and counting."

"That mindset is nuts."

"I can't say I disagree. But by tomorrow, things in my life should improve—with or without the curse lifting."

"Do you want to elaborate on that?" Nadia flicked a glance Sophia's way.

"No. Not really. Look, there's a spot right by the door. See? Already my luck is changing."

Nadia glided smoothly into the spot and put the car in park. "That's apophenia in reverse."

"Ha! Who knew apophenia could go in reverse? Now, let's go find Jael."

There was no one in the well-appointed private hangar when they walked in. They milled around for a minute before a man in a blue uniform with a gold-winged pin and a name tag approached them and gave them directions to the meeting room where they could wait for the diplomatic envoy. The plane had landed ahead of schedule and was already on the runway.

"See? Good fortune," Sophia said. They walked into a room that held a beautiful cherry table and well-padded armchairs. To the side, there was a table laden with snacks, a bowl of fresh fruit, and a beverage station if one wanted a cup of coffee or some tea. Sophia was buzzing in happy anticipation.

"Nadia, after Jael takes off again, we need to go back to my house. I need to move the computers to your place for now. Get our equipment set up over there. I'll pack some bags for me and the boys. I'm not staying at that house anymore."

"But I thought the lawyer said you had to stay there until the trial."

"She did, but that was before there was a dead body in my yard. I mean, it was crazy before, but this is getting into Twilight Zone territory. I won't be staying there until the killer is found."

"He could have died of natural causes, and then someone just buried him. Like a dog who finds a bone."

"Nadia, that is all kinds of messed up. Seriously." Sophia felt the floor shift, and the room start to oscillate. She'd managed to avoid a seizure through all of this, and she couldn't handle one now, just as Jael was arriving. Nadia's hug stopped the spinning and allowed her to focus on the concern in her friend's eyes. Sophia fastened her consciousness onto the pressure of her friend's hands, the smell of flowers in her hair. She worked to find things around her that her senses perceived in the here and now could help keep her from slipping away. It was the technique she'd worked on in therapy. It had kept her seizure-free for over a year. In this last week, things had spiraled too fast, too frequently. She hadn't had a chance to ground herself in the moment. Her brain had slipped into its defensive posture and held her there.

Nadia reached out and arranged Sophia's hair. "You can bunk with me until we find you a suitable place, but I don't have room for you and the boys. You know that."

"No, I'd never impose. I'm planning to get a motel room somewhere at least for the next few days—the trial is in one week. Then I'll have more options."

The door swung open, and there stood Jael with a grin across his face, and his arms spread wide. Nadia was up and launching herself toward him. He lifted her off the ground and spun in circles with his head thrown back, laughing. He set Nadia back on her feet. She was flushed, and happiness lit her eyes. Jael kept her tucked in his arms as he met Sophia's gaze and winked.

"We did it." He raised his arm, and Sophia high-fived him then laced her fingers with his.

"Thank you. This means everything to me."

Nadia pulled back and turned from Jael to Sophia. "What does?"

"Oh, seeing Jael looking so well," Sophia told Nadia, then turned her attention to Jael. "How was the trip?"

"Good. Too short. They're refueling, changing pilots, and we're heading right back to where we started from. Good thing the seats are comfortable enough for sleeping." He peeked at the food table. "They didn't feed us very well. Nadia, could I impose on you to make me a cup of tea? Perhaps a plate of something to eat?"

Nadia sent him a confused glance then went over to the snack station.

Jael leaned closer to Sophia's ear. "The transfer of property has been made. I met Josh Gilchrest himself out on the tarmac. I watched them load it onto his corporate jet. I'm assuming they're taking it to Tulsa."

"It went through customs okay?"

"Not a hitch. Your provenance was perfection."

"Do you want cream and sugar in your tea?" Nadia called over.

"Yes, please," Jael said with a smile.

"The monies were transferred?"

Jael pulled out his phone and scrolled forward to the forms that Gilchrest had signed. He swiped his finger and showed the bank deposit in the offshore account.

"So it's done."

"It's in the bag." Jael put his hand on her shoulder with a grin.

The door popped open, and FBI SWAT stormed into the room. Jael pushed Sophia behind him as he took in the scene. The room swarmed with men in black battledress with automatic pistols in their hands. Jael, Sophia, and Nadia were grabbed and forced to the ground where they were frisked. Sophia's arms were wrenched behind her back. Cuffs were snapped into place.

All she could think was that the police had decided she was guilty of killing Mr. Rochester. But why would they be arresting Jael and Nadia?

They were hauled out of the airport and each placed in a separate black SUV. Sophia had trouble negotiating the step up with her hands behind her back. The FBI guy helped get her in. As soon as she was in place, he held her securely against the seat with his forearm across her chest while a guy on the other side crawled in to shackle her ankles and attach the chain to a bar on the floor. Her arms behind her back were cramping at her shoulders due to their unnatural position. The man who had helped her in the car pulled the seatbelt into place and cinched it down tightly before he drew the balaclava off his head. He looked like just an average guy without it. Someone who picked up his kids at daycare just like she did. Her boys were at the forefront of her thoughts. She'd promised to pick them up at daycare tonight. She'd have to find a way to get in touch with Lana.

Now that the door had been slammed into place, all Sophia could think was that if there were an accident and the engine caught on fire, she would be left to burn alive. She couldn't imagine how excruciating it would be to burn to death.

Time seemed to blur. She had been hyperventilating in the airport parking lot, and now they were pulling up in front of the Iniquus compound. They stopped and showed their ID at the guard tower. The gates opened, and they powered in. Sophia turned to see the other vehicles following suit. She was thoroughly confused. At least Brian and their other Panther Force liaisons would be here. They'd help figure this mess out. But why come here to Iniquus and not the police station or FBI headquarters? Maybe this wasn't about Mr. Rochester—that was a police matter. Maybe this had to do with Marla; she had been arrested by the FBI.

Sophia was hustled into the building and moved into a room. There were mirrors lined along parallel walls, and Sophia thought, having watched her fair share of cop shows, that there were likely people watching her from the other side. The room was white. There was no other color except the silver of her handcuffs, which were laced through a hook on the table. It was freezing cold. The goose flesh on her bare arms was as much about the overabundance of air conditioning as it was about fear.

A woman and a man walked into the room. They moved to the other side of her table and sat in the two empty white seats waiting for them. Sophia noted that they were both dressed warmly for the nearly ninety-degree day. They must have known it was going to be a refrigerator in here. This must be a tactic.

"My name is Special Agent Alandria Andersson. I work for the FBI in their Arts division. This is my colleague, Special Agent Steve Finley with Terror."

Sophia nodded. It made sense that they'd want to talk to her since she had expertise in both. The cuffs still didn't make a lot of sense, though.

"We'd like to talk to you about a tablet that was delivered to Joshua Gilchrest, CEO of Crafts&More."

"All right," Sophia said.

"Do you recognize the provenance that was attached to the customs forms?" Alandria laid the paper in front of Sophia.

Sophia's scanned down the paper to her signature. She swallowed and looked up. "Yes. I wrote this."

"It's illegal to bring antiquities from their country of origin into the United States, but you already know this, given your job," Special Agent Finley said.

"That's true. But it's not illegal to bring in *copies* of antiquities, and you will see that I very plainly described the piece as such. Since I'm handcuffed and here against my will, I'm assuming I'm under arrest. I think it would be best if I had a lawyer here representing my interests. If you would please get in touch with my employer, AACP, they can arrange for someone to come."

"You misunderstand your standing in this meeting, Dr. Abadi," the female special agent said. "You are being investigated as a terrorist. As such, we will not be calling a lawyer for you. A different set of rules applies."

32

BRIAN

Monday p.m.

Brian shut his eyes and willed Sophia to be cooperative. To bend and fold. To do whatever she had to do to save herself. He imagined her at intake with a prison jumpsuit and shower shoes, shuffling to her cell with her month's supply of toilet tissue and toothpaste. His stomach churned. He tried to play this calm, but he noticed Nutsbe and Thorn were riled too. The only one who was cool about this was Titus Kane. He sat with his hands folded on his stomach, his customary scowl across his face.

There was a knock at the door, and Lynx poked her head in.

Titus nodded in her direction.

She gave the team a finger wave as she made her way in and took her place in one of the captain's chairs that lined the small room facing the two-way mirror. "Titus asked me to be here to give my opinion on Sophia's body language. He also wants a heads up if I think she's starting a seizure. None of us wants that."

Brian agreed with that. Sophia needed her wits about her, and getting her brain scrambled with a seizure would be problematic on several fronts. She'd need a good rest afterward to get her wiring back in place, for one. Brian wondered what would happen if Sophia short-circuited and the FBI kept pressing her. The thought tightened his jaw. Lynx caught his eye and read him like a book. She sent him a warning look then turned her attention to what was happening in the interrogation room.

"Fine. What do you need to know?" Sophia asked. To his eye, she looked calm for someone who was being accused of terrorist acts. Aside from her shaking with cold.

"Titus, did the special agents require Sophia to be put on ice?" Lynx asked.

"Standard operating procedure," Titus said.

"It seems to me that putting her in a physical and mental state of discomfort, while normally effective, might be counterproductive in this situation. Would you please bring the temperature up to something that would be comfortably cool for her?"

Thank you, Lynx. Brian sent the message mentally but refused to catch her eye.

Alandria Andersson moved to the door and brought in a trolley with a tablet resting on it. She placed the trolley next to Sophia. "Tell me what you know about this piece."

Sophia licked her lips and turned her head toward the stone. "Sure. This is about a point-one-eight square meter marble slab that weighs approximately fifty-three kilograms. It is inscribed with a script called Samaritan, which was an early form of Hebrew. It is believed that the original slab adorned a Samaritan synagogue or perhaps a private home in Jabneel, Palestine. That area is now called Yavneh in modern Israel. The original tablet would be significant to the Jewish, Christian, and Islamic faiths, in that it lists nine of the Ten Commandments from the Book of Exodus."

"Why not ten?" Andersson asked.

"There are ten listed on the tablet in total, but only nine that are familiar. My professional guess would be that they wanted to keep the number at ten, so they omitted one and replaced it with another. This tablet does not say, 'You shall not take the Lord's name in vain.' Instead, it commands people to worship on Mount Gerizim, which is in the West Bank."

"Tell me more about the slab," Andersson pushed.

"It was uncovered in 1913 during excavation for a Yavneh railroad station in Israel. It is believed to be the only tablet version of the Ten Commandments to have survived intact into the modern age. The workers who dug it up had no idea what they'd found. They sold it to an Arab man who used it to form the threshold that led to his inner courtyard. When the man placed the stone, he did so with the inscription facing up. That's why the letters of the central part of the inscription are all but obliterated. They can be made out under the right lighting, and with the right technology."

Finley stood and moved over to the stone. "This is smooth because some guy let people trod on the oldest known version of the Ten Commandments?"

"This, no," Sophia said. "This is a copy of the original."

"Made at a later date?" Andersson asked. "How old is the original?"

"The Samaritan Decalogue is one of five Roman-Byzantine era stone inscriptions that we know about. The dates for the piece are thought to be between 300 and 640 CE—around the time of the seventh century CE Muslim invasion. A man named Kaplan bought the original in 1943. He was a municipal archaeologist at the time. Kaplan and Ben-Ziv wrote papers on it and worked to develop a provenance."

"And so what date would you assign to *this* artifact?" Finley asked.

Sophia shot him a strange look. "I don't know, sometime in the last year, maybe?"

Andersson rolled her eyes. "It says on the provenance that you sent along with the piece that it is a copy of the original."

"That's right."

Lynx moved to the edge of her seat.

The air in the observation room shifted perceptibly. Everyone was feeling the strain of the unfolding drama.

Finley handed her a photograph. "We have Jael Cohen's computer. He showed you a bank statement for eight-hundred-and-fifty-thousand American dollars that was transferred from one offshore account to another."

"Yes," Sophia said.

"That money came from…"

"My understanding is that it came from the Gilchrest family."

"And the other bank account belongs to you," Finley said with authority.

Sophia swung her head toward Finley. "How…" She didn't finish her sentence, just looked down at her hands, her body going still. Even from this angle, the team could see the thoughts racing through her mind.

Brian's phone vibrated against his thigh. He checked the app that monitored Sophia's place, thinking the police were knocking on her door again. But it was Lana tapping in her new code and going into the house. "Have any of you noticed that Lana likes to go over to Sophia's house when she's not there?"

Nutsbe turned his way. "What's she doing?" He leaned over to look at the screen.

"Looks like she's sending a text again."

"Why'd she walk over there to send it?" Lynx asked, leaning in from the other side.

"The hall light shines down on that spot, and you can read the screen without turning on the living room or office lights. She's normally at Sophia's to pick up something for Sophia's boys. Toys, clothes, what have you." Brian flipped to his newly placed camera, the one that captured that corner of the room. "Son of a bitch." He tapped the phone to take a picture. He used his fingers to make the image large enough to read the nine-digit alphanumeric code on the screen. "You guys got this?"

He pointed to Sophia. "I'm going to her house to see what the mice are doing when the cats away."

"I'll head back to the war room." Nutsbe stood. "See if I can figure out a correlation between Miss Lana's visits and anything interesting."

Brian made the twenty-minute drive in fifteen minutes flat. Still, he missed Lana.

Mr. Rochester's body had been removed from Sophia's gardens. The police must have finished up their crime scene investigation. The yellow tape was gone. So were the patrol cars. They'd left a pile of dirt sitting to one side. Brian would try to shovel it back in place, maybe put the rest of the flowers in before Sophia came home. A cold buzz crawled over his scalp as he realized that very probably wouldn't be happening. It didn't

290 | FIONA QUINN

feel to him like Sophia was forthcoming and compliant with the FBI. It seemed to him she was too measured and calculating about her word choices. He could see in the special agents' body posture that they were making up their minds about her future— and it was looking bleak.

Brian had put his own code into the security system during the installation. It allowed him to disengage everything from his phone. That way, if he ever needed to sneak into her house, there would be no alarm or image of him being telegraphed to Sophia or the computer. He tapped the button, waited for the lights on the lock to turn green, then went up the steps and into the house.

His first stop was the curio cabinet. He'd already given it a quick shake. Time to be more thorough. He pulled up the picture of Lana and positioned himself precisely as he had seen her, then lowered himself from his six foot two height to her diminutive five feet. He squatted until his head was exactly in line with where her head appeared in the image and looked in the direction she looked when texting. A beam of light hit his phone screen at exactly this spot, making it much easier to text. Also true, when he was at this angle, he could see a slot that held the PIN code developer. He took pictures of what he saw.

He moved to Sophia's desk, facing the coder, and slid down in the chair until he had a good visual. This would be about Sophia and Nadia's height when seated. They were both about five foot five. They could turn, read it, and enter it into the computer without moving it from its hiding spot. He waited for the code to change and then typed it into the computer. Bam, he was in.

He pulled his phone out and dialed Nutsbe. "The code's for the computer, not a phone code like Sophia was using."

"Yeah, I came to that conclusion too. I wish we had Lana's phone bill. I'd like to see where the codes went. I'm looking at her on video. She texts, waits, texts again. Seems like the calls Sophia was getting on her house phone. A check to see that she was there, then a follow-up call. Could be Lana texted to get someone's attention, waited for the number to change, and typed it in quick. They only have forty-five seconds to make that turn around once the coder puts up the new number."

"With the spyware we installed, can we check the computer for other malware? Something that would let someone in behind a blank screen?"

"No can do until we get a warrant and get the hard drive into forensics. I'm sure I can get Finley to hand me one before you leave, so you can pack everything up and bring it in with you." Nutsbe's voice had the hollow sound of someone on speaker-phone. "But I can tell you this, looking at the texting times that we have on video, and comparing it to the computer history, there's a direct pattern of log-ons. And I can also tell you that, off the top of my head, I know some of these were times when Nadia and Sophia were with either you or Thorn. I'm not sure how this information is going to pop Sophia out of the trap she's in, though. Short of chewing off her own foot, I think she's been bagged." There was a pause before he added, "Sorry, man."

The phone rang at Sophia's desk. Brian picked up the receiver and listened as the beeps sounded once, twice, three times. "Sophia Abadi is in FBI custody at Iniquus Headquarters in Washington D.C. She is being interrogated as I speak."

There was a pause and then, "Do you know the names of the special agents conducting the interrogation?" It was the same woman's voice that Panther Force had picked up over surveillance.

"Steve Finley and Alandria Andersson."

"I'll take care of it." The woman hung up.

"Dude, what did you just do? We don't know who that

woman is, and we certainly don't know what she means by *taking care of it*." The incredulity in Nutsbe's voice coming over the speaker on Brian's cellphone perfectly matched Brian's disbelief.

What the heck had he just done?

33

Sophia

Monday Afternoon

Finley's cellphone rang, and he ignored it. Andersson's phone rang, and she ignored it. Both phones rang simultaneously, and they moved out of the room. Sophia assumed that they were finally taking the calls.

Sophia was glad that her hands were cuffed in front of her rather than behind. She was glad that someone had adjusted the temperature of the room, and her nose wasn't running anymore. And she sent up a prayer of absolute thanksgiving for Lana. No matter what happened to her, no matter how long she would be away, Sophia knew her boys were safe. Okay, that wasn't a good path for her thoughts to wander down. The metal cage around her ribs tightened. Her breathing came in short little puffs. Sophia blinked her eyes as the white walls began to oscillate in and out, each time pushing a little closer, boxing her in. There was no sound. Nothing to focus on. Nothing to distract her brain from its downward slide.

The door behind her slammed open, and a sharp, "Sophia," echoed somewhere behind her. Sophia couldn't turn her head. Her muscles were locked.

A voice murmured beside her. A fairy godmother voice that spun magic in pink swirls around her. Sophia felt warmth on her back. It crackled through her icy cocoon.

"Sophia, stay with me," the fairy queen whispered in her ear.

Like a spell, the voice whirled through her consciousness, pulling the gray mist away and flicking it to the side. Warmth pulsed over her back, up and down, side to side. "This is my hand on you, Sophia. Focus. Can you feel my hand on your back?"

Sophia could feel the heaviness of her lids as they stayed open, and tears slid down her cheeks. They were gently wiped away. Sophia could feel the texture of the tissue. She could see the red fingernail polish on a distinctly feminine hand. After a long moment, she could shift her head and see Lynx sitting beside her.

"That wasn't bad," Lynx said. "You were gone less than a minute. Come on. You need to be completely settled in your body. Rub your feet on the floor." Lynx tilted her head up and spoke to the air. "Let's dim the lights a bit to lower the glare, please. And can someone bring in some color and texture for her to focus on?"

Surprisingly, or maybe not so surprisingly, the lights immediately dimmed, and the shiny white lost its overpowering glow. The door opened, and Thorn came in. He had a large potted plant in one hand and a red mug in the other. He set them on the table in front of her. It was jarring to have this sudden influx of color. It was just what she needed.

Thorn must have been on the other side of the mirrors for him to have reacted so quickly. He must have grabbed the first things he saw. Sophia tried to send him a look of gratitude but had a sudden thought. Thorn was in on this? Did that mean Brian was too?

"You were supposed to protect me." Sophia's words had a weird ringing to them.

Thorn focused on Lynx. "What else?"

"How about a cup of tea? Something with a lot of taste. And a pillow."

Thorn left. Sophia wasn't trusting herself or the environment. She'd been told no lawyers. That meant she needed to wait for someone to figure out that something was wrong. Nadia had been taken. Jael had been taken. Red? No. Lana? Yes. Lana would freak out when neither she nor her sister checked in. She'd start making calls. She'd probably start with Thorn and Brian. Would they tell her the truth? Would Lana think to call AACP so they could get them some help? Maybe. Her brain was foggy, and her thoughts came mostly as animated pictures and not words.

Sophia drank the tea Thorn set in front of her. She rested her head on the pillow he provided. Lynx, who had kept her hands on her the whole time with that magical touch of hers, encouraged her to close her eyes and rest. It was a cramped kind of nap with her arms and hands forced into an odd configuration by the handcuffs holding her to the table. But it felt good to shut her eyes. Sleep stole over her.

When she woke up, Lynx was still by her side, murmuring, "Sophia, you need to wake up now. Slowly. Slowly."

Sophia realized that Lynx was not the only one in the room. The Special Agents were there too. She sat up, and Lynx reached over to brush her hair back into place and pull down her blouse.

She pulled the throw pillow from the table and tossed it into the corner. "How about a glass of water?" Lynx asked as she moved a cup in front of Sophia. It had a lid and straw that would make drinking easier while handcuffed.

She was cuffed.

Under arrest.

Nadia. Jael. He had missed his plane. Since he had to travel on diplomatic flights, Sophia wondered if he'd be stuck here in the US for a while. Well, they might be accusing him of something to do with terror too. He may not ever get home.

"Stay present time," Lynx said.

That was a good reminder. Sophia leaned forward and focused on the straw's slick plastic, the sensation of sucking, and the cool water as it filled her mouth. Survival techniques taught to her on the therapist's couch. She wasn't sure they were strong enough to combat today's events, though. Sophia found herself wishing for Brian. Where was he?

The door opened again. Sophia saw that more chairs had been added to the table since she'd gone to sleep.

A man stepped forward and shook hands with Andersson and Finley. "Good to see you again," he said without an ounce of warmth. Everything about this man seemed distant and cold. "Thank you for waiting. It will be just another moment." The door opened to the sound of sniffling. "Ah, here we are."

A man in a dark suit led Lana into the room. Her hands were handcuffed as well.

Sophia felt the blood drain from her face, her neck, her torso. There wasn't enough blood for her heart to pump, and the room began to spin.

Lynx leaned in. "Stay present. Touch your thumb to your pinky." She waited for Sophia to comply. "Now your index finger. Now your ring finger."

The simple physical task was a puzzle her brain had to work through. By the time Lynx said to touch her middle finger, Sophia's blood rushed to her face and made it blaze with heat. Sophia had no idea what was going on, but Lana was her safety net. If Lana was here, who had her boys? Sophia reached out to touch the ring and remind Ashtart of their agreement, but of course, the ring was gone.

Sophia turned when the door opened. Titus was standing just behind her with his shoulder pressed into the wall.

Brian walked in with Thorn. They pulled their chairs around to face her. This only added to her conflicting emotions. She wished he wasn't here, seeing her like this, and yet she was so glad he was nearby.

The newcomer turned to Sophia. "I'm John Black with the CIA."

"Oh, thank God," Sophia said, clasping her hands together.

Black continued as if she had said nothing. "I was sent by CIA Officer Johnna Red to intervene on the part of our asset, Dr. Abadi. It seems the FBI has entangled itself in our intelligence operation."

"Or the CIA has stuck its foot in an FBI sting," Finley countered. There was an underlying current brewing between the two that wasn't hard to miss.

Titus came into her line of sight and leaned his back on the wall. He crossed his arms over his chest, making his arm muscles bulge. He was obviously asserting himself as alpha supreme in this room brimming with alphas. "Iniquus has a long history of working with both the CIA and the FBI. We know, as does everyone in this room, that communication is often a challenge. We are all working to keep America safe. It doesn't surprise me that both the FBI and the CIA would be highly interested in Dr. Dajani and Dr. Abadi. They have unique skill sets that set them apart from most. From what Mr. Black has explained to me, Dr. Abadi has an ongoing relationship assisting the CIA and has recently come under the FBI's scrutiny. Can we all agree that it would be the best plan of action to try to lay out a timeline and figure out what's going on?"

"I'll begin," Black said. "We became aware that Dr. Farid Dajani was involved with Hamas several years ago. The Israeli government offered assistance in tracking Farid Dajani through Jael Cohen, an Israeli special operative. Cohen had contact with the Dajani family since his youth, and his presence would raise no one's suspicions. I believe the FBI is also holding Mr. Cohen?" Black sent a scathing look toward the FBI agents but didn't wait for a reply. "Sophia and Nadia, at the time both university students, were kidnapped by Hamas, and Jael found them and effected their escape. While being held, our operative spoke with Sophia, explaining that Hamas was trying to extort information from the archaeological team, raising money for terrorist activities and that we at the CIA would like to have an ongoing relationship with her to thwart the pillaging of ancient artifacts."

"Sophia, not Nadia?" Thorn asked.

"Nadia didn't have the same force of character as Sophia. We had been watching the girls closely. We believed that Nadia would have told her father and thus informed Hamas that we were on their trail. It had to be Sophia. She was younger but mentally stronger."

Sophia thought she was being talked about like a horse for sale. Next thing they'd do was check her teeth. And why was Lana here? That question had been looping through her mind. Sophia tried to listen and puzzle through this situation. She wished her brain was clearer.

"With Sophia Abadi's assistance, we've been following the black market monies for years. We had certain members of the Gilchrest family in Tulsa, Oklahoma, in our sights. We wanted to show how they were funding ISIS by purchasing antiquities for a museum they're constructing. Sophia found the perfect means to our end. It came to her attention that a fake tablet was 'found' in Syria. She could provide the paperwork, and it could be brought to America. Once the Gilchrests—thinking it was an authentic artifact being brought to them disguised as a reproduction—paid the money, and it was tracked to an ISIS affiliate. We could work through our channels to freeze the accounts and starve ISIS of their funding."

"Sophia, how did you know that piece was a fake?" Brian asked.

"There are only five examples of that kind of tablet known to exist. That particular tablet was worn in the center, as it was used as a threshold. It would be inconceivable that another example would have the same tread marks. Also, it would be odd for another tablet to have changed one of the commandments the way this one had."

"Where is the original for this piece now?" Finley asked, shooting a look at Andersson.

"The Torah Museum in Brooklyn."

"Brooklyn?" Finley shook his head. "So you established this was a fake. Then, when you were told the information had been sent to you erroneously, you acted on it."

"I told my handler, yes."

"You told no one else?" Andersson pushed.

"The tablet data was on my computer. I researched the piece and took notes. I plotted it on the grid. All of that was information I called in to Red."

"Lana, would you like to tell us how you found that information on the AACP computer?"

"I didn't." Lana's left shoulder jerked, and a nervous tic had started on the left side of her lip.

Brian leaned in. "Of course, you didn't," he said softly. "You have no idea what is on that computer. But you gave access information to someone who could look at it. Didn't you?"

Lana's head drooped. "I had to."

"Tell us about why you *had* to." Brian's voice was like a silk ribbon that wanted to wrap around the truth and draw it out. Sophia almost wished she had something to confess to, so she could answer Brian's request. What a strange thought. Sophia wished, again, that her brain was functioning properly.

"My family in Gaza was being threatened. My grandparents, aunts and uncles, my cousins. Dad had been giving Hamas information to protect our family, but he had a stroke, and they needed another way to get information. At first, I took it from Nadia's computer. But after Sophia began working with AACP, I used her computer instead. Sophia didn't have familial connections to Palestinians and Hamas, so I thought it would be safer for everyone." She peeked up at Sophia. "I'm so sorry."

"That confirms what Nadia said in interrogation. Hamas approached her after her father's health crisis. She said that she wouldn't help, thinking it was probably a bluff. When she didn't hear anything further, she decided that she was right. It seems they just moved on and tapped Lana instead."

"The tablet is a fake," Brian said.

"We get that now," Finley replied.

"It's not illegal to bring a copy of an artifact into the US." Brian's gaze held Finley's. "Especially when the provenance that traveled with that piece indicated exactly that."

Finley nodded.

"I think you should uncuff Dr. Abadi and release Nadia and Jael. Unless you have other charges to level?"

Finley pulled a key from his pocket. "My apologies, Dr. Abadi."

"The goal was to catch the Gilchrests." Sophia rubbed her wrists, where they were red and raw. She cast a frightened gaze toward Black. "The FBI can't arrest them for having a fake tablet, but I was promised that America would get them. That they would pay." The fear that they had failed in their mission slipped away as anger took its place. "The Gilchrests are the reason that Nadia and I were kidnapped. They're the reason why we went through that hell. They're why I've been tormented with seizures and PTSD. I want them to pay for what they did to us. To *me*." Sophia was shaking with fury. She had been the good soldier all these years for the best interests of America, of Syria, and the whole damned world. But she'd also done it to make the Gilchrests pay.

"The Gilchrests believed the tablet was an artifact. Our operatives discussed the transaction—how we'd move a relic from Syria to America through customs without it being confiscated at the border. They believed it was the real deal. They conspired to bring in a conflict relic. They paid nearly a million dollars—which would be an absurd amount if they genuinely believed this was a fake. All of that is on video. We have their banking information, and we're set to act on it. As we speak, the American government has frozen just shy of a billion dollars of the Gilchrest family assets contained in off-shore accounts.

"Finley, Andersson, and I have worked together before. I assure you that all our information will be shared. While the CIA does not enforce laws or act on American soil, the FBI can certainly make the case that the Gilchrests knowingly funded ISIS." He sent a look to the Special Agents before turning his attention back to Sophia. "Your services, Dr. Abadi, have been invaluable. We certainly want to continue our relationship. Though I know you had a very specific goal over the last few years, the artifacts, the people in harm's way, terror—they are bigger than the Gilchrest family."

34

*B*RIAN

Monday p.m.

Sophia had rolled her shoulders forward like an armadillo in its protective posture. Lana was taken to another room. After that, everyone but Brian left. Only Lynx said goodbye to Sophia as they exited. She was that unapproachable.

"Lana isn't a threat to America," Brian said. "She was frightened for her family. She isn't in this for ideological reasons. They're going to use her as an asset. She won't be held prisoner. They'll dangle that threat over her head to make her comply with what they want. But she's going to go home to her family. I feel almost a hundred percent sure. She's too valuable to them."

Sophia turned turbulent eyes his way. "Who has my boys?"

"Margot—she's our Panther Force auxiliary. She steps in to make things run smoothly in our operations. She took your boys to her house. I suggest you let them stay with her tonight while you get your feet under you. You've had one hell of a week."

Sophia squinted her eyes.

"We've arranged for a suite at the hotel up the street. We'd like you to stay there until new housing can be arranged for you. Your environment is concerning."

She crossed her arms over her chest. She was as shut off as she could physically make herself.

"AACP gave us permission to bring their computers here to Iniquus. Black and Finley will make a plan for how to address the malware on your computer."

"You know how Lana accessed the information?"

"We have a good guess. We know some of the steps."

"You knew Lana was involved but didn't warn me?"

"We just got that information during your arrest."

"*Abduction*."

Brian thought that one through. Yeah, it must have felt that way to her.

"I'm not legally obligated to do what you say. I don't have to go where you tell me to."

Brian hadn't seen this one coming. He thought for sure Sophia wouldn't want to go home. He pictured the mound of dirt in her front yard. The unplanted flowers wilting on her driveway.

"I want to sleep in my own bed tonight. I'll make other decisions tomorrow. Marla's in custody. It should be safe for me to go home."

"We don't think that Marla had anything to do with the flowers and Mr. Rochester."

"She was a crazy person. Titus Kane said that she was really Betty Campbell, and she was remanded to a mental hospital. She kidnapped her children. She *hissed* at me! Of course, she's responsible. If she's not responsible, how do you explain everything?"

"The fingerprints—" Brian started, but Sophia threw her hand up to stop him.

"I need a ride. Take me home or call me a Lyft."

It was a quiet ride. Sophia kept her gaze out the window the whole way. She held her body tightly together. Unyielding.

They pulled up to her house, and Brian unsnapped his seatbelt.

Sophia's head swung around. "Where do you think you're going?"

"I've been hired by AACP to keep you safe. You signed contracts allowing me to do just that. It includes access to your house. I'm going to go in to make sure that it's clear." Brian made sure his tone was calm and professional, his face neutral. He was just doing his job.

Sophia let him in but left the front door open—the message clear. Get in, get it done, get out.

He searched the house, and it came up clean. The whole time he'd been in soldier-mode. But when he saw Sophia sitting on her couch, staring at the picture of the boys, it was a gut punch. Brian didn't want to go. He'd learned on the battlefield to trust his gut. His survival instincts were engaged. He needed to convince Sophia to leave.

When Sophia turned toward him, he saw the eyes of mothers who faced daily bombings. Grief, hopelessness, pain.

The pain was directed at him. He'd hurt her. She knew he'd had a hand in today's takedown. The trust was gone. "It's killing me the way you're looking at me. It's tearing me to shreds that you're hurt." He took two steps forward, then took a knee, so they were eye to eye. "I was doing my job, Sophia. I had to be neutral. I couldn't go in thinking you were innocent when I didn't know if you were or not. My job was to save the antiquities and help stop ISIS."

She said nothing. Her attention was back on the picture. She reached for the ring on the bracelet that was now somewhere over the ocean, heading to its resting place.

"I'm only in your life because of my job." He moved to sit in front of her, his knees, wrapping his arms, and holding his wrist. He realized this was the way he sat in tribal tents when he was talking to the chieftains, trying to get intel and make agreements. He was negotiating. But for what? Brian pulled the phone from his pocket. With a swipe of his finger and a quick code, he turned off the surveillance equipment. He looked up. Sophia hadn't budged. He doubted she'd even noticed.

"You can't imagine how surprised I was when you came into the Panther Force war room."

She glanced his way.

There was a mild spark of curiosity that Brian decided to pounce on. "I want to tell you what happened last fall. When we met on your birthday, I thought we connected. I thought I'd met 'the one.' I felt absolute comfort. Absolute trust. Like I had known you always. It was shocking to me that I didn't know your name. That I didn't know a single thing about you. Nonetheless, I felt as though you were a haven, and I could lay everything in front of you—the good, the bad, the hideously ugly—and you would look at all of it and accept that that's me."

He tried to push down the chuckle that bubbled up. This was far from amusing. It was nerves. Brian swallowed down some of his anxiety and pushed forward. "For me, that night was the beginning of the rest of our lives together." Brian's lips twitched as he tried to regain an impassive expression. He didn't want to frighten her with the intensity of what he was feeling. "Then I woke up, and you were gone. I realized I didn't have your last name. Your address. Your phone number. No way to contact you. No way to know who you were. You paid in cash. You were so familiar—it never occurred to me that I didn't know anything about you."

Sophia's brows drew together. "You tried to track me?"

"Of course, I did! I went back to that damned bar every night for two months."

"And then you gave up."

"My assignment was over, and I headed back to Washington." He fixed his gaze on her. "I was raised on the power of prayer. And believe me, I prayed. Usually, I asked that you be held in grace and kept well. You were always on my mind. I felt like I was failing you. That there was something that needed doing. One night my prayer changed. I said if I was supposed to be with you, I needed to be put back on your path. Three days later, there you were, standing in the Panther Force war room. Hell of a thing. The woman I fell in love with was finally in front of me, and everyone thought you were a criminal."

"And you thought so too."

"I kept myself neutral about the case. That didn't mean that I didn't feel the connection from our night together. Since the moment I met you, loving you has been a hard fist around my heart. It hurts like hell. *You* hurt like hell, Sophia."

Brian saw anguish fill Sophia's eyes.

"It killed me that you walked away. *Ran* away. It hurt that you were suspected of a crime and that I was the one who needed to find out if you were culpable or not. It hurts to see you struggling so hard to keep your head above water. I'm in awe that you're able to put one foot in front of the other. One thing I realized through all this is that my love for you isn't going away. I could still love you, Sophie, even if you got so desperate that you'd do something like sell artifacts to ISIS. I'd turn you in and help bring you to justice. That's my job. But I'd want to be there to make sure the boys were okay, that you were supported."

She tipped her head back and looked at him with a sardonic twist of her lips. "In prison? You'd come to visit me in prison and talk to me on the phone while we put our hands up on the glass between us? Put some money in my account, so I could buy cigarettes to pay people not to attack me?"

She wanted to goad him into a fight. He worked to keep everything on an even keel. So far, he'd done okay delivering the facts. Telling his story. "If you broke the law, yes."

"And you thought I *could*." Now there was a fire in her gaze as her anger heated up. "How could you? We're talking about people I care deeply about. Friends of mine being tortured and killed. Their heads chopped off for propaganda and stuffed between their feet in the town square. Their *families*. Their homes destroyed." Sophia's hands flung out as she spoke to show the enormity of her anguish. "Syrian children are *starving*. Their hospitals are being bombed." Her hand came to land on her head as she whispered, "My God, what kind of person would facilitate that? How could you think that of me? I spend every day—*every day*—working to stop ISIS." She put her hands on the cushions on either side of her, as if to brace herself upright. "How could anyone who says that they love me think that I helped to fund terror?"

Brian felt his own emotions tipping toward pissed off. Not at Sophia, but at the circumstances. "In a normal life, you'd never consider it. But my god, Sophia, the shit that's been thrown in your direction for years now? It's a miracle you aren't strung out on drugs or in the loony bin."

She suddenly stood. "You know what? Get the hell out of my house." She moved to the door and threw it wide. "Please, I need you to leave."

Brian pushed to standing. "Sophia, that sounds permanent. I don't want to go until you tell me when I can see you again. That, at the very least, we can work together."

"You can't. *We* can't. I need to put a lid on this box and file it in the closet with all the other boxes of crap I've got stacked in there. Tomorrow, I'll request that you not be part of our detail when Nadia and I go to Peru. If I'm very lucky, I'll never see you again."

Silently, Brian moved out the door, and Sophia shut it behind him. She didn't slam it, but there was a finality about it, nonetheless.

35

BRIAN

Monday p.m.

"Brainiack here."

"Fucking hell, man, this is soul-crushing." Nutsbe was calling in from headquarters.

"She still crying?"

"Since you turned the surveillance back on. You want to tell me what the hell you said to upset her like that? 'Cause when you get back here, I'm going to Kick. Your. Ass. It's not enough that she finds a dead body, is arrested, interrogated, and hears her best friend is a Hamas asset all in one day? She held it together like a champ. What the hell did you do to her that turned on the waterworks?"

"I, for sure, didn't make things better."

"You were supposed to go home and tuck her into bed, give her a big-ass dose of sleeping meds, and sing her a lullaby. Seriously, man, what the hell happened?"

"She's unhappy that she trusted me while I distrusted her. She no longer wants me involved in her security." He dragged a hand over his face. "I guess we can put Gage in play. I'll have to talk to Titus when I get in."

"You weren't sleeping with her, were you? We've got rules for a reason."

Brian was surprised that Nutsbe was yelling at him. Nutsbe usually kept a solid emotional distance from their clients. Getting stoked like this was out of character. "No, *Mom*, I didn't touch her," Brian said.

Sophia must have gotten under Nutsbe's skin. Sophia had a way of doing that. She was strong as hell, but it was a translucent strength. Underneath, her vulnerability glowed through. That combination was nose candy to an operative addicted to adrenaline. Someone they respected and wanted to rescue at the same time amped their protective instincts. They'd done a shit job with the rescue. *He* had, Brian qualified. He'd done a shit job protecting Sophia.

"You're going to have to explain the surveillance blackout. That wasn't kosher, dude. I'd get my story together for Titus. In the meantime, I have your location as the Community Center."

"Affirmative. I'll keep watch on my phone apps. What time is Thorn relieving me?"

"Zero two hundred hours. He's in the racks now, getting some Zs. I'll do an on-the-hour check. I guess tomorrow I can get her moved so we can stand down. Is she still talking to me?"

"She's only requesting that I get the boot from her detail. You should be fine."

"Here's to a quiet night then, man."

Brian had gone to the store for provisions before checking in with Nutsbe. Now, he forced himself to eat before he opened the apps. He knew that he wouldn't be able to swallow while watching Sophia cry. And one thing he'd learned as a FAST operator was to eat when you can. Running out of fuel could be deadly.

He ate, drank, and went into the Community Center to use the men's room. Back in his car, he felt like a coward as he looked at his black phone screen. It was time to face up to what he'd had a hand in creating. He opened the app to find Sophia on the couch, crying. As he watched, there was a weird scraping noise in the background—metal against rock—that he couldn't place. Brian drove down the street. Parking at an empty house with a for sale sign, he hiked over to the copse of trees at the top of the cul-de-sac.

Joe was shoveling the dirt from his father's grave into the hole. Brian watched as Joe planted the rest of the flowers, put the plastic holders in the recycling bin, then pulled his hose up the hill to clean off the sidewalk, water the new plants, and wash the extra dirt out of the road and down the culvert. It looked nice when he was done. Brian wondered what was going through the man's mind as he did those tasks. Brian would have been suspicious of Joe's actions, had they not determined earlier in the day that Joe's fingerprints weren't on the trowel or construction materials that had punctured Sophia's tires.

Brian made his way down to talk to Joe, crossing over Kay's yard to stay out of Sophia's view in case she were to glance out the window.

"Joe," Brian said in a tone designed not to startle the guy. Joe came over with his hand extended for a shake.

"Thank you for finding Dad. We can give him a proper burial now."

"How is everything going? What are the police saying?"

"They did an autopsy. They said he didn't aspirate any dirt, so he was dead when he was buried. There were no signs of a fight or external force. He was scraped up from being dragged by his ankles. That happened after he died too. A heart attack did him in. Then someone hauled him to Sophia's house and buried him." Joe rubbed the back of his neck. "I can't figure that one out. That or the other thing."

"What other thing?" Brian asked.

"Someone cut off his left thumb and took it with them. They had a cadaver dog out sniffing around, thinking they might find it." He pointed toward the trees. "I've tried to figure it out. I asked if maybe an animal might have bitten it off while Dad was in the garden. You know, moles are carnivores, and we've got a bunch of them around here."

"What did the medical examiner say?"

"It was cut off with some kind of sharp shears. Someone wanted his thumb. The police called it a trophy. It doesn't make sense to me."

"I'm sorry for your loss." Brian put his hand on the man's shoulder.

Joe blinked. "Yeah, it's a weird set of sensations. I'm sorry he's gone. Relieved though. Part of me is glad he's at peace—things were getting hard there toward the end. And then there's that odd gnawing sensation that I failed—it's sort of like shame. Yeah. I'd call that shame. I'm embarrassed someone got hold of my dad's thumb." Joe looked over at the garden. "Sophia said she's putting her house on the market. I figure that's going to be a good thing for me to do too. I don't think I can drive home every day and look at those flowers." Joe reached out and patted Brian's shoulder. "Thanks again for everything you all did for me and my dad." He gathered the hose, hung it on its hook, and went back inside his house.

Brian pulled his phone from his pocket. *Son of a gun.* "Nutsbe, you're going to want to get a hold of Rochester's medical examiner's report," Brian said as he made his way back to his car.

"Ruh-roh."

"Joe Rochester just told me his dad died of natural causes, got dragged to Sophia's house and buried in her garden, but lost his thumb to a pair of shears. The thumb is MIA."

"That's some serious shit going down in crazy town. If Sophia would stop crying, I'd go over and pry her out of there. Take her to a hotel."

"You saying you're too chicken?"

"I'm good to go toe-to-toe with a wacko who steals thumbs from dead guys. Shoot, give me a room full of 'em. But a woman in tears? Nope, not going near that."

"Stay sharp. I'm out." Brian swiped his phone to end the call and climbed into his car. He drove to the Community Center, parking once again in the shadowy corner of the lot away from the lights that had blinked on now that it was dark. He opened the app to do his penance and watch Sophia cry. He found her pacing and muttering under her breath in a foreign language.

She went to the cupboard and pulled out the PIN creator, and put it in her purse. She stopped and looked around. "Are you watching me?" she asked the ceiling in English.

Brian wasn't sure if she was talking to him or Ashtart or whatever she thought was in the ether.

"Are you listening to me?" she asked, her focus sliding across the room and up into the crown molding.

Brian chewed his upper lip as she wandered from room to room, scanning.

"You are, aren't you? You're watching. How creepy is that?" She was looking over her family room, pulling down the pictures to look behind. The lamps. She got a screwdriver and pulled off the electrical plates—all the places where the TV spies hid their surveillance.

Brian's phone rang.

"Brainiack here."

"You seeing this?"

"Yup. You want to fax me over a copy of the warrants, so I have them in hand when the cops show up?"

"You need to intervene."

"How? She's kicked me off the case."

"Lynx. I'm going to send Lynx over. She's got a soft spot for our girl Sophia."

"Lynx left for Atlanta, remember?"

"Margot and the kids. I could shoot them over there."

"There's a crazy person who took a thumb trophy nearby, and you want to send in Sophia's kids?"

"Shit."

"Yup." Brian tapped off the phone and watched Sophia take apart her eating area, then her kitchen.

"I'm going to find you. I know you've put something here." Her body grew rigid, her eyes wide. "My bedroom?" she whispered. "Were you watching me sleep? Did you watch me get dressed?" she yelled toward the ceiling. "That is so messed up. That is so creepy!"

Brian watched her storm up the stairs and could hear her in her bedroom. It sounded like she was throwing things around, then there was a squeak of springs, and Brian imagined she'd thrown herself across her bed. The sound of muffled sobbing filled his comms, hammering home the fact he was a piece of shit for telling her what he needed to say. Selfish. Self-centered. Just plain dumb.

Time passed, and now there was silence. Brian hoped Sophia had cried herself to sleep.

Brian wiled away the silent hours listening to an audiobook playing low on his CD player. He still had Sophia's house up on his phone. Every five minutes, he'd do a camera check of her interior. He got to the camera that focused up the stairs and wished he had a way to check on her in her room.

Brian remembered the pill bottle on her bedside table, and he thought about the fragility that Lynx had talked them through. He thought about the paper they were handed with the five-hundred and fifty-five plus reasons why she was in health-threatening, if not life-threatening, straights. Phone in hand, he got out of his car to pace. He thought about how he'd noticed when he was down talking to Joe that Sophia's car had been parked too close to the road, which meant that the infrared perimeter alarm wouldn't engage if someone were to come onto her property from the front. He thought about how the person who had dug up Sophia's garden and buried the body knew how to move in her yard without turning on the lights. Had to be a guy—Rochester weighed a good hundred-and-sixty pounds. A hundred-and-sixty pounds of dead weight was hard to drag. Did the guy know about the thermal cameras? Or the new lock system?

Brian looked at his watch, zero dark thirty. Thorn was probably en route. He called Nutsbe. "Brainiack here."

"Copy. What have you got?"

"Night as dark as Satan's heart."

"I hear you. Nothing's happening up at Sophia's house. She was on the rampage, and then all I got was sobbing. There's been nothing for a couple hours. I was about to call you. I looked back at all the interior video from the point you left her place. I've got nothing. Of course, the lights have been off downstairs, and the interior cameras aren't thermal. Kind of feels wrong. My antennae are up—"

"We're on the same wavelength. I'm going up to look around. If Thorn's playing Sleeping Beauty, shake his ass out of bed, would yah?"

"Wilco. Out."

Brian drove to the empty house with his beams off. Turned the dial so he could exit without the interior lighting up. He did a quick weapons check and pulled his tactical gloves on. Yeah, something was making his senses hum. Brian's eyesight grew keener, his ears increased their acuity. He shifted his head left and right, taking in the whole panorama. A car drove up the main road. An owl hooted over to his right. Brian dropped his weight, flexing his thighs, to walk low and slow across the street and silently into the trees. There, he pulled out the black bag that held his phone. He gave the area a quick sweep before he lowered his head, looking into the bag that kept the light from his cell from giving his position away. He checked the cameras on the back and front of the house. He checked the left side then the right. While the view from three of the sides had shown glimmers of color—a dot of yellow from a bird in the tree, a bit of blue, red from the neighbors' windows—the cameras on the north-east side showed complete darkness.

Brian pulled out the case with magnetic comms buds that slipped into his ear canal. He tapped the collar he wore against his vocal cords that translated the movement of air passing up his throat into words and sentences. "Nutsbe, we've got a situation," he mouthed.

"Copy. What's your sitrep?"

"Cameras on the right have been tampered with. I'm showing black."

"Copy. I have the same. And I know why. On my tape, while the police and CSI were on scene, a guy in a suit and tie, looking like a detective, was on the side of the house, shutting a window. That in itself was odd. But then he pulled out a can of silly string and shot crap all over the camera lens. He must like his true crime shows on TV."

"You recognize him?"

"Negative. He kept his head down or a hand over his face the whole time. I'm assuming that Sophia opened the window, and he wanted an entrance point. If she forgot that she'd opened it, she'd forget to go lock it. And this is the one in her guest bathroom. Out of sight, out of mind."

Brian made his way forward. "Her van is parked in front of the alarm. We wouldn't have gotten a ping from that." He pulled out his night vision monocular and scanned the house. "I'm going in."

"Copy. Thorn is four minutes out. I'll send closest available for back up."

"Keep an eye on the interior. Let me know what you get."

"Wilco."

Brian used the phone app to disengage the alarm and unlock the front door. He slid his tools into his pockets. He did another quick weapons check and worked his way up to Sophia's house. If someone was in there, Brian wanted to get the jump on them before they had a chance to panic.

36

Brian was on the stairs, making his way up with his shoulder pushed against the wall, his gun stacked with his flashlight. He hadn't engaged the beam. He preferred to approach in the dark.

He heard a chuckle in Sophia's bedroom. Brian pressed his body against Sophia's half-open door and sidestepped until he got a view of her bed. A man's form, in women's clothes and a cheap blonde wig, hunkered over Sophia. In the dim nightlight, Brian could see the tango lift the hem of Sophia's nighty in his hands and ease it up. Sophia lay flat on her back, not moving.

Brian slapped the door open. It banged into the wall.

The man turned a startled face in his direction.

"You. Hands in the air," Brian commanded, shooting the flashlight's high-lumen beam into the man's eyes.

"Thorn on scene," Nutsbe's voice said softly over his comms.

The man ducked behind the bed.

Brian hadn't seen a weapon on the guy. Even so, he kept his shoulder against the wall and kept a low profile as he edged into the room. As he came parallel to the end of the bed, the tango uncurled, leaping toward Brian. With the angle and the dark, Brian refused to pull the trigger on his gun. There was no way he was going to endanger Sophia. Brian shoved the gun back in his holster as the man brought his weight against Brian, knocking the flashlight from Brian's hand and burying something hot and sharp into his gut. The man scrambled to get past him, but Brian grabbed the guy's dress and rolled him, then slammed his fist into the man's head. The tango lay between Brian's knees, shrieking. Brian pinned him with one hand around the throat, pummeling him with angry punches.

Thorn flipped on the light, disorienting Brian. "Brainiack. Stop. He's out, man. *Stop*." Thorn caught hold of Brian's fist and held it in an iron grip. Brian looked down at where he had crushed the man's orbital socket, making a crater in the guy's skull.

"Is he still alive?" Thorn put two fingers on the man's carotid. "You're bleeding," he said with a lift of his chin toward Brian.

Brian looked down at his grey camo BVDs to find an ever-expanding bloodstain around his waist and down his pants leg. He could feel the warm wetness pooling. Brian pulled the first aid kit from his leg pocket, found his QuikClot combat gauze, and stuffed it into the slash. "Son of bitch." His skin felt cold and clammy. How much damned blood had he lost? He heard sirens outside. Saw the red and blue lights strobing the walls. But what he hadn't seen or heard was Sophie.

Brian woke up from surgery to find Nadia in his room. When he looked her way, her face crumpled as she started crying. *Shit.* He looked up as Nutsbe opened the door. Nutsbe turned Nadia's way, shook his head, and began to retreat.

"Nutsbe, what happened to Sophia?" It took everything in him to get that one sentence out clearly. His body was still under the influence of some heavy drugs.

"She's going to be okay. They found ketamine in a syringe on her bed."

"Is she awake?"

"Sophia's been out since we brought her in. All her vitals are stable. It's a matter of time." Nutsbe sent an uncomfortable glance toward Nadia, who had pulled her heels onto her chair and was hiding her face behind her knees like a child. "You've got twenty new stitches, dude. Not much in the way of bragging rights. You left a good amount of blood on Sophia's carpet. That's gonna cost you." Nutsbe turned to Nadia. "Hey, Nadia, you know what would help? Brian needs some orange juice and a banana. Could you run down to the cafeteria and get that for him? Make him feel better?"

Nadia stood, nodded her head, and slid out of the room.

"You're an ass," Brian told him.

"I'm protecting her." Nutsbe slid into the seat that Nadia had just relinquished. "You want to hear the shit that went down after your delicate princess-self took a swoon?"

Brian propped himself up on his elbows.

"The tango was Will Sheppard dressed up in his wife's clothes."

"That's very Alfred Hitchcock of him."

"Isn't it, though? It gets better. Thorn let the paramedics in, then slipped across the street to shake the house before he identified Will to the police." He gave a theatrical shiver. "This is going to creep me out the rest of my life, and I just saw the pictures. Thorn's gonna need years of therapy."

Nutsbe moved the chair over to Brian's side, his phone in hand. He held up the screen, which showed a picture of a closet with shelves lined with baby food jars.

"What is that?"

"*Thumbs*," Nutsbe said as he swiped his finger to bring up the next photo. "See this? They're in alphabetical order. This one is for the wife, Janice. Sometimes the names are listed by first, sometimes last. She was under J for Janice. Under each one is a series of numbers—GPS coordinates."

"How did you figure that?"

He flipped the picture to the one that said Keith Rochester. "It has Saturday's date, followed by these numbers, that when you put them into the Garmin give you—"

"Sophia's front yard."

"Bingo. They have CSI following up in the other spots. Homicide down in Harrisonburg now has names and dates to go along with those two graves they found down there." He scrolled to another picture. "Look at this." Nutsbe glanced over at him. "Can you see?"

"Barely. I'm still pretty fuzzy from the meds."

"It originally had Marla Richards's name on it, but it was crossed out, and Rochester's name is written beneath. The original GPS coordinates are scratched out too."

"He changed his mind about who to kill?"

"The date changed to one day earlier. He had planned to kill Marla—Betty, really. Ha! That would have messed up his system, but good—on Sunday. But I guess he was out stalking and saw Mr. Rochester go down. Rochester was an R, and that was as just as good. According to the estimated time of death put together by the medical examiner, he'd already done the whole thing with the flowers. So he tucked Rochester in the shallow grave."

"Why do you think Sheppard moved the flowers from Sophia's yard to the Richards's?"

"'Cause he's bat-shit crazy?" Nutsbe tucked his chin as he shook his head. "Ready for the shit?"

"That wasn't enough?"

"Sophia Abadi is on the next jar with the formaldehyde already in it. The date was last night. And the GPS coordinates are for the one that was originally on the Richards/Rochester jar. We've already got word back from PD that there's a four-foot-deep hole in the woods."

Brian's whole body frosted. His stomach flipped over.

"Dude, you're turd-green." Nutsbe pushed a pink plastic container under Brian's chin.

Brian waited for the wave of nausea to lift, then he brushed the pan away. "Anesthesia," he said.

Nutsbe caught his eye. "She's fine. He didn't hurt her before you got there. She was drugged and has no idea what happened."

Nutsbe and Brian turned their attention to the door as it swung open. Titus moved into the room to stand at the end of Brian's bed. "This week, Panther Force captured a dangerous mental patient and returned two kidnapped kids to their father, revealed a Hamas informant, and solved the murders and disappearances of eighteen people, as well as safeguarding what could have been a nineteenth victim. If Brainiack hadn't got that paper cut, we would have come out looking like superheroes." Titus moved closer to extend his hand. "Outstanding effort, gentlemen."

"Thank you, sir," Brian said as they clasped hands.

"Brainiack, there's a lady outside who would like to see you, if you're up to it." He reached out to shake Nutsbe's hand.

"Nutsbe, Nadia told me to tell you the cafeteria is closed, but she's heading to the grocery store to get orange juice and bananas." He shook his head and left.

Nutsbe grinned. "Good luck." And he slipped out too.

Sophia walked into Brian's room wearing a nightgown and robe, with slippers on her feet. She looked too pale. Her eyes were haunted. Her lips trembled at the corners, and Brian was afraid she was about to start crying again. He didn't think he could handle it.

She swallowed hard and got herself under control. "They say you're going to be good as new."

"A little scratch, no big deal."

"This never would have happened if I weren't such an idiot. I should have let you take me to a hotel. Neither of us would be here now."

"I don't blame you a bit."

She came farther into the room and sat on the corner of his bed. For a long time, they looked at each other. To Brian, it felt like a balloon had been stretched to capacity, ready to pop, and now the air was slowly being released. The tension was easing.

"I was so angry with you." Sophia closed her eyes tightly. "I felt so betrayed."

Brian stilled. *Duty first, always.* But could he have fought harder? Done something different? Brian didn't usually second-guess himself. Review and learn was one thing, but this was a different process—more of the blame and shame variety.

"They told me what happened at my house. Why I was in the hospital. I wouldn't be here if it weren't for you. I'd be dead."

They both sat in complete silence. There was no denying that truth. It was stunning. Incomprehensible. But nevertheless, probable.

"I tried to put myself in your place, to imagine what this was like from your perspective. If our roles were reversed, I don't think I'd have been out sitting for hours in a car, keeping watch. I think I would have said, 'To hell with her, I'm heading home.'"

"Sophie," Brian started, but there were no more words. He didn't know what to say.

"If I were objective, I would say that you did the right thing for your job. I understand that. It just feels violating that I was being watched when I didn't know it. It's creepy. And scary. I could have gone to prison, far away from my boys. That scenario feels every bit as terrifying as being stalked by a serial killer." She pushed her hair from her face and cleared her throat. "All I did every single day was try my best. Every day, when I wake up, I say to myself. 'Another step forward. Just keep trying. Just make it through another day.'"

"One foot and then the other."

"Yup. It's all I could ask of myself. And really, it's all I could or should ask of *you*. I mistreated you. Yet I expected you to be loyal to me above all else."

Brian opened his mouth to speak, but Sophia put up her hand to stop him.

"I have a lot to adjust to—a lot to absorb. But I'm done being angry with you. Right now, all I can feel is gratitude and maybe a glimmer of hope."

Brian reached out and laced his fingers with hers. "What are you hoping?" he asked as his phone buzzed on the counter. Sophia gave him a tight-lipped smile, then got up and retrieved it for him.

He swiped to read the text then handed it to her. It was a picture of a US soldier in a sweat-ripened t-shirt, standing in front of the cave with the ring in his hand. The next image was of him placing it as far as his arm could reach into the small opening. The last picture was a thumbs up with a GPS in his hand with the readout of the exact place she needed the relic to go.

"You're free," Brian said.

He waited while emotion swept over Sophia.

She looked around the room, up at the ceiling, as if she were searching out any menace that could be hiding in the corners. She nodded. "It feels that way, doesn't it?" A surprised smile spread across her face. She lifted her arms straight up, like a runner crossing the finish line. "Wow. It's like... Wow." She hugged herself as she caught Brian's gaze. "I'm free!" She threw her head back and laughed. When she sobered, she looked slowly around the room. "No more curse," she whispered.

"Does this mean you don't have to protect me anymore?" He swallowed hard as she focused back on him. "Now that Ashtart is home, does it mean you and I can be together?"

She blinked. "Yeah." Her smile widened. "I think that's what it means." She crawled up onto the bed next to him. Very gently, she curled herself into his arms and released a deep sigh of perfect contentment.

"Yeah," Brian said, planting a kiss in her hair. "I couldn't agree more."

The end

The next book in the Uncommon Enemies Series is,
DEADLOCK.

He'll get her home safe…or he'll die trying…

Readers, I hope you enjoyed getting to know Brian and Sophia. If you had fun reading RELIC, I'd appreciate it if you'd help others enjoy it too.

Recommend it: Just a few words to your friends, your book groups, and your social networks would be wonderful.

Review it: Please tell your fellow readers what you liked about my book by reviewing RELIC on Amazon and Goodreads. If you do write a review, please send me a note at hello@fion-aquinnbooks.com. I'd like to thank you with a personal e-mail. Or stop by my website, FionaQuinnBooks.com, to keep up with my news and chat through my contact form.

Turn the page for The World of Iniquus in chronological order.

THE WORLD of INIQUUS

Chronological Order

Ubicumque, Quoties. Quidquid

Weakest Lynx (Lynx Series)

Missing Lynx (Lynx Series)

Chain Lynx (Lynx Series)

Cuff Lynx (Lynx Series)

WASP (Uncommon Enemies)

In Too DEEP (Strike Force)

Relic (Uncommon Enemies)

Mine (Kate Hamilton Mystery)

Jack Be Quick (Strike Force

Deadlock (Uncommon Enemies)

Instigator (Strike Force)

Yours (Kate Hamilton Mystery)

Gulf Lynx (Lynx Series)

Open Secret (FBI Joint Task Force)

Thorn (Uncommon Enemies)
Ours (Kate Hamilton Mysteries
Cold Red (FBI Joint Task Force)
Even Odds (FBI Joint Task Force)
Survival Instinct - Cerberus Tactical K9
Protective Instinct - Cerberus Tactical K9
Defender's Instinct - Cerberus Tactical K9
Danger Signs - Delta Force Echo
Hyper Lynx - Lynx Series
Danger Zone - Delta Force Echo
Danger Close - Delta Force Echo
Cerberus Tactical K9 Team Bravo
Marriage Lynx - Lynx Series

FOR MORE INFORMATION VISIT
WWW.FIONAQUINNBOOKS.COM

ACKNOWLEDGMENTS

My great appreciation ~

　To my editor, Kathleen Payne

　To my cover artist, Melody Simmons

　To my publicist, Margaret Daly

　To my Beta Force, who are always honest and kind at the same time.

　To my Street Force, who support me and my writing with such enthusiasm. If you're interested in joining this group, please send me an email. FionaQuinnBooks@outlook.com

　Thank you to the real-world military and FBI who serve to protect us.

　To all of the wonderful professionals whom I called on to get the details right. Especially, D. Hall, for her plotting input; Bart Drummond for his rescue input; M. Carlon for her expertise. Please note: this is a work of fiction, and while I always try my best to get all of the details correct, there are times when it serves the story to go slightly to the left or right of perfection. Please understand that any mistakes or discrepancies are my authorial decision making alone and sit squarely on my shoulders.

Thank you to my family.

I send my love to my husband, and my great appreciation. T, thank you.

And of course, thank YOU for reading my stories. I'm smiling joyfully as I type this. I so appreciate you!

ABOUT THE AUTHOR

Fiona Quinn is a six-time USA Today bestselling author, a Kindle Scout winner, and an Amazon All-Star.

Quinn writes action-adventure in her Iniquus World of books, including Lynx, Strike Force, Uncommon Enemies, Kate Hamilton Mysteries, FBI Joint Task Force, Cerberus Tactical K9, and Delta Force Echo series.

She writes urban fantasy as Fiona Angelica Quinn for her Elemental Witches Series.

And, just for fun, she writes the Badge Bunny Booze Mystery Collection with her dear friend, Tina Glasneck.

Quinn is rooted in the Old Dominion, where she lives with her husband. There, she pops chocolates, devours books, and taps continuously on her laptop.

Visit www.FionaQuinnBooks.com

COPYRIGHT

Relic is a work of fiction. Names, characters, places, and incidents either are the product of the author's imagination or are used fictitiously. Any resemblance to actual persons, living or dead, business establishments, events, or locales is entirely coincidental.

Cover Design by Melody Simmons from eBookindlecovers
Fonts with permission from Microsoft
Publisher's Note:

Lightning Source UK Ltd.
Milton Keynes UK
UKHW012100071122
411795UK00003B/340